ESCAPE POD

THE SCIENCE FICTION ANTHOLOGY

ALSO AVAILABLE FROM TITAN BOOKS

Cursed

Dark Cities: All-New Masterpieces of Urban Terror

Dead Letters: An Anthology of the Undelivered, the Missing, the Returned...

Exit Wounds

Hex Life

Infinite Stars

Infinite Stars: Dark Frontiers

Invisible Blood

New Fears: New Horror Stories by Masters of the Genre

New Fears 2: Brand New Horror Stories by Masters of the Macabre

Phantoms: Haunting Tales from the Masters of the Genre

Rogues

Wastelands: Stories of the Apocalypse

Wastelands 2: More Stories of the Apocalypse

Wastelands: The New Apocalypse

Wonderland

ESCAPE POD

THE SCIENCE FICTION ANTHOLOGY

EDITED BY
MUR LAFFERTY & S.B. DIVYA

TITAN BOOKS

Escape Pod: The Science Fiction Anthology
Print edition ISBN: 9781789095012
E-book edition ISBN: 9781789095029

Published by Titan Books
A division of Titan Publishing Group Ltd
144 Southwark Street, London SE1 0UP
www.titanbooks.com

First edition: October 2020
10 9 8 7 6 5 4 3 2 1

This is a work of fiction. All of the characters, organizations, and events portrayed in this novel are either products of the author's imagination or are used fictitiously. Any resemblance to actual persons, living or dead (except for satirical purposes), is entirely coincidental.

Foreword © *Serah Eley 2020*
Citizens of Elsewhen © Kameron Hurley 2018. Originally published on Patreon. Reprinted by permission of the author.
Report of Dr. Hollowmas on the Incident at Jackrabbit Five © T. Kingfisher 2020
A Princess of Nigh-Space © Tim Pratt 2020
An Advanced Reader's Picture Book of Comparative Cognition © Ken Liu 2016. Originally published in *The Paper Menagerie and Other Stories*. Reprinted by permission of the author.
Tiger Lawyer Gets It Right © Sarah Gailey 2020
Fourth Nail © Mur Lafferty 2020
Alien Animal Encounters © John Scalzi 2001. Originally published in *Strange Horizons*. Reprinted by permission of the author.
A Consideration of Trees © Beth Cato 2020
City of Refuge © Maurice Broaddus 2020
Jaiden's Weaver © Mary Robinette Kowal 2009. Originally published in *Diamonds in the Sky: An Original Anthology of Astronomy Science Fiction* edited by Mike Brotherton. Reprinted by permission of the author.
The Machine That Would Rewild Humanity © Tobias Buckell 2020
Clockwork Fagin © Cory Doctorow 2012. Originally published in *Steampunk!* edited by Kelly Link and Gavin J. Grant. Reprinted by permission of the author.
Spaceship October © Greg van Eekhout 2020
Lions and Tigers and Girlfriends © Tina Connolly 2020
Give Me Cornbread or Give Me Death © N.K. Jemisin 2019. Originally published in *A People's Future of the United States*, edited by Victor LaValle and John Joseph Adams. Reprinted by permission of the author.
The authors assert their moral rights to be identified as the author of their work.

No part of this publication may be reproduced, stored in a retrieval system, or transmitted, in any form or by any means without the prior written permission of the publisher, nor be otherwise circulated in any form of binding or cover other than that in which it is published and without a similar condition being imposed on the subsequent purchaser.

A CIP catalogue record for this title is available from the British Library.

Printed and bound in Great Britain by CPI Group (UK) Ltd, Croydon, CR0 4YY

ESCAPE POD

THE SCIENCE FICTION ANTHOLOGY

TO SERAH ELEY AND EVERYONE WHO SUPPORTED *ESCAPE POD*
OVER THE PAST FIFTEEN YEARS. ONE GOT US STARTED,
AND THE OTHERS KEPT US GOING.

CONTENTS

Foreword by Serah Eley

I

CITIZENS OF ELSEWHEN

Kameron Hurley

13

REPORT OF DR. HOLLOWMAS ON THE INCIDENT AT JACKRABBIT FIVE

T. Kingfisher

33

A PRINCESS OF NIGH-SPACE

Tim Pratt

51

AN ADVANCED READER'S PICTURE BOOK OF COMPARATIVE COGNITION

Ken Liu

73

TIGER LAWYER GETS IT RIGHT

Sarah Gailey

91

FOURTH NAIL

Mur Lafferty

111

ALIEN ANIMAL ENCOUNTERS

John Scalzi

133

A CONSIDERATION OF TREES

Beth Cato

143

CITY OF REFUGE

Maurice Broaddus

163

JAIDEN'S WEAVER

Mary Robinette Kowal

187

THE MACHINE THAT WOULD REWILD HUMANITY

Tobias Buckell

207

CLOCKWORK FAGIN
Cory Doctorow
223

SPACESHIP *OCTOBER*
Greg van Eekhout
265

LIONS AND TIGERS AND GIRLFRIENDS
Tina Connolly
281

GIVE ME CORNBREAD OR GIVE ME DEATH
N.K. Jemisin
303

Acknowledgements
313

About the Editors
315

About the Contributors
317

FOREWORD

I have a "thing about" story. Here is a story about that.

In 2005 I was a guy named Steve, living a very different life than I am today. Things were good. I had a wife and an infant son, a house in the suburbs, a dog named after a Final Fantasy character —all the markers of mainstream American success. Of course, I thought I was *weird*. I had weird geeky friends (by my standards of the time) and did weird geeky stuff like role-playing and writing science fiction. I was even romantic in weird geeky ways: when my wife and I went to bed at night, I'd read to her. Neal Stephenson, Vernor Vinge, Terry Pratchett, whatever I thought was fun.

I know, I know. I was young and innocent, okay? Or at least innocent. I was a cis straight white guy who *truly* thought I knew what weird was, because I read science fiction. "Adorable" is the word that comes to mind now, but I was just making the same mistake almost everyone makes: I believed the world of my own experience was a representative sampling.

Early that year, I read on a geek news site about a nascent internet fad called "podcasts." People were making all sorts of audio and pushing it out on blog feeds. I went looking and found *dozens* of these things—and some of them were *good!* One of my favorites was a freewheeling romp of personality called *Geek Fu Action Grip* by Mur Lafferty. She talked about everything: her childhood, her media obsessions, drinks she invented based on her crush on Keanu Reeves… Her openness and wit helped me realize how accessible and how *personal* podcasting could be. I wanted to be like her and the other pioneers I was enjoying. I wanted to *make something.*

I spent a few days pondering fresh ideas. Some were clever, some were quirky, none excited me for long. The top candidate was a political podcast from an AI who was cynical about humans. That might have worked, but I feared becoming even more cynical myself if I succeeded. The obvious truth finally hit me in bed one evening, as I was reading a Harry Potter novel to Anna. I was *already making* audio entertainment—I was doing it right that second! I'd been producing it for an audience of one, but I could expand that with a bit of work.

Podcast fiction was already an established art form; several excellent authors had been narrating their own novels for months. I hadn't heard of anyone reading *other* people's work, though. Short fiction seemed like a practical fit for the medium, and I had friends who'd run science fiction webzines, so that felt like a familiar model. Most of all, I'd been a writer long enough to hold one value sacred: *Writers get paid.*

That was the origin of *Escape Pod.* I hit up friends in my writing group for the first few stories, shoving a contract and

$20 at them whether they wanted it or not. I did the site design myself and commissioned a logo from another friend, Douglas Triggs, for a case of his favorite ginger ale. (The name of the podcast was the only spec I gave him; the gorgeous starscape with the exploding spaceship was all his idea.) I had once been to a Rasputina concert and been blown away by the opening band, a bunch of Alabamans wearing kabuki masks thrashing out monster-movie surf rock. I emailed Daikaiju and explained my project in a few hundred words; they replied with a dozen words of permission to use their music.

I bought the wrong microphone and the wrong amplifier, made other exciting technical mistakes, and spent six weeks recording the first story ("Imperial" by Jonathon Sullivan) over and over, never satisfied with my own delivery. I finally realized that if I demanded perfection before I started, I was never going to have a podcast at all. I put the first episode online the next day, announced it on the Yahoo! email list that was the focal point of 2005's podcast community, and dropped a couple of lines to some SF market listings. Then I got to work on the second episode. I'd bought just over a month's worth of content, so I resolved to try at least that long before deciding if I'd failed. I'd had fun either way, so it wasn't time wasted.

One week later I had just over a hundred downloads, which was a blockbuster success for a new podcast of that era. And a British fellow named Salim Fadhley had already donated $5 from the site's PayPal link. (Sal was a hardcore indie arts advocate who went on to help me in countless ways, and I'm grateful for his friendship.) Story submissions started to trickle in by the second week, and enough were worth buying that I began to think this *might* be sustainable. I started to reach out to other podcasters to narrate stories I didn't think I could read well—especially those with women protagonists—and found out that community collaboration like that was the best possible networking.

The next few years were a gradual ascent towards Real Professional Success that would have terrified me if I'd known any of it at the start. I formed an actual business, Escape Artists Inc., to get all of those donations and story payments out of my personal checkbook. I printed up bookmarks to give out at conventions, sat on panels as a guest, and schmoozed at industry parties. Eventually we hosted some of those parties. We launched a second podcast for horror stories, *PseudoPod*, and later a third for fantasy, *PodCastle*. We bought a fancy machine that burned and printed labels on CDs in bulk and sold podcast collections as gifts. I found out the hard way that my ADHD brain is really *bad* at business, so I roped another podcasting friend, Paul Haring, into taking on the accounting and management. I nearly broke his sanity and am amazed that he still talks to me.

Success was quite fun and interesting, but one of my bad-at-business signs was that the audience numbers and the dollars never felt fully *real* to me. I was aware of them as facts but didn't know what to do with them. People felt real to me, and I shared words with a *lot* of fascinating people—listeners and podcasters and writers. My world grew a little with each new connection. Most of those people gave me at least a few moments of pleasure; some became core to my life; a very few were abhorrent to me. But I never met or heard from a *boring* person. I used to think boring people existed; I don't any more.

Hey! Wake up! This is the *really important* part. The bridge to the chorus. Everything I have said so far is true, but it didn't happen to *me*. Steve Eley of 2005 and Serah Eley of today are not the same person. Yes, sure, I started with his body, but we have completely different *stories*. Telling his *Escape Pod* story in first person has been feeling increasingly awkward, so I'm going to drop the pretense and speak for myself.

Steve was paying lip service to a philosophy of "Story" long before he started his podcast. He had a whole spiel about the human need for mythology, about our rapidly changing society, the role of science fiction as the literature of change, the vitality of *short* fiction as the purest expression of ideas, *et cetera*. Becoming an editor and speaking at cons gave him chances to talk about these ideas, to polish them to a fine gleam, to be a Voice of Authority™. This was both good and bad for him as a person, but he did get good at performing it, and he believed everything he said.

I have a different opinion of his "Story" theories. I think that, for the most part, they're rarefied bullshit of the sort that white men who edit SF have been spouting at least since Campbell, if not earlier. Steve had exactly one principle that delivered real value to the genre through his editing, and he expressed it best in two words at the end of every episode: "Have Fun." He got that totally right. Everything else, he made too complicated.

Story isn't some grand capital-S ideal to be dissected or worshipped. Story is *basic*. It's the essence of all human experience. Our senses take in an overwhelming amount of data, but we only *care* about the parts that we can attach to mental models of causes leading to effects. Those are stories. We all live in the same physical world, but experience it differently depending on the stories we believe. Our own identities are just contiguous chains of memories: a story *about* ourselves that we tell ourselves and others. Steve's self-story started soon after he was born in 1974. Mine started in 2013 (and is spectacular, but *way* beyond the scope of this foreword). That's how I know we're different people.

Every meaningful experience is a story. Every memorable interaction with someone is a story, and often involves the telling of other stories. No story that *means* something to us is ever boring; boredom just means we stopped paying attention. That's why Steve stopped believing in boring people. His philosophy had nothing to do with it; he just found out that he really liked paying attention to people.

True stories and fictional stories work the same way in our minds. There are no fundamental differences; we can only tell them apart by context. That fact has plusses and minuses, some of which have become screamingly relevant in today's world. But one of the plusses is that fiction has as much power to expand our inner worlds as truth. Cataclysmic fiction can teach us things with none of the risk and mess of a real apocalypse. Fantastic fiction can make us feel *way* more interesting than stodgy physical reality wants to allow. And so on. That you're reading a science fiction anthology means I'm preaching to the choir.

"Expanding worlds," though—that's the theme that keeps coming back. When good fiction, direct experience, and other people all have the same effect, something interesting must be happening. Something real. I'm writing this in the summer of

2020: the year of coronavirus; of Black Lives Matter; of rising American fascism. These are revolutionary times. Through my own weirdass transgender lesbian lens, the revolution looks like people with *small* worlds trying desperately to hold fast to their power and relevance, cowering before a tidal wave of larger, more colorful worlds. That sense of revolution is strong in this anthology, too, because Mur and Divya know very well what worlds *they're* living in and what they're doing.

Steve started to feel burnout in 2010. He'd been putting up an episode every week for five years, almost without fail, while working a full-time job and being a family man and having multiple polyamorous relationships. He also went to cons and played games and goofed off a lot. I have no idea how he did it. The funny thing is that he felt unproductive and irresponsible the entire time, and was never fully convinced he was *good* at *Escape Pod*. But he knew he'd made something people cared about, and he was smart enough to leave his company with people who cared about *that*. I honestly believe that Alasdair Stuart is the most clueful man in the industry today, and that Mur and Divya have made Steve's little hobby project into one of the strongest, most diverse, and most important voices in modern science fiction.

This book is an extension of that work. Some of the authors and stories are familiar, but the style of others is often a significant departure, because what works in audio and what's possible in prose aren't always the same. The energy here runs up and down a tension line between *provocative* and *fun*, but there's one common thread in every piece: a yearning, palpable sense of humanity. These are revolutionary times, after all, and Mur and Divya know what they're fighting for.

It's customary here to say a few words on each piece. I'll do my best to avoid spoilers, but if you want a fully clean slate, my feelings won't be hurt if you skip on to the first story.

- Kameron Hurley's "Citizens of Elsewhen" is about midwives, and a poignant morality tale about the balance between present and future.
- T. Kingfisher's "Report of Dr. Hollowmas on the Incident at Jackrabbit Five" is also about midwives, but with a different tone. It's one of the funniest SF midwifery stories I've ever read, and certainly the funniest involving a goat.
- Tim Pratt's "A Princess of Nigh-Space" starts with a familiar fantastic trope, and then doesn't *invert* it so much as overruns it with a flanking maneuver.
- Ken Liu's "An Advanced Reader's Picture Book of Comparative Cognition" is beautiful, grand in scale, and at the same time deeply personal. Some of these alien races are going to haunt me for a while.
- I shouldn't claim favorites, but Sarah Gailey's "Tiger Lawyer Gets It Right" is my favorite. All I can say is that there's a tiger in it. That's enough.
- Mur Lafferty's "Fourth Nail" is full of privilege and intrigue, both of which are inevitable with human cloning. Like many clever hard SF stories, it stands on its own while evoking the sense of a much larger world and story.
- John Scalzi's "Alien Animal Encounters" is a laugh-out-loud

set of vignettes about people who didn't know what they were getting into. There's sex, drugs, and sadness here, all of it ironic.

- Beth Cato's "A Consideration of Trees" is deft science fantasy. The protagonist is a palimpsest of metastory and magic, at home on a space station with familiars and faerie.

- Maurice Broaddus's "City of Refuge" is the most down-to-earth story, focusing on an ex-convict in a world that *barely* feels different from today.

- Mary Robinette Kowal's "Jaiden's Weaver" will draw tears from anyone who's ever deeply loved a childhood pet. Or anyone who was ever a child. And also me. It's beautiful and heartfelt.

- Tobias Buckell's "The Machine That Would Rewild Humanity" is a post-singularity tale with a novel dilemma: if we are replaced by our creations, will they care enough to preserve us? *Should* they?

- Cory Doctorow's "Clockwork Fagin" yanks Dickens into the steampunk age, with lively prose that maximizes revolution *and* fun.

- Greg van Eekhout's "Spaceship *October*" follows with more downtrodden children, on a generation ship harboring injustice and secrets. It's simple and satisfying, unless perhaps you're one of the 1%.

- Tina Connolly's "Lions and Tigers and Girlfriends" is my winner for pure *fun*. There's revolution, but more importantly, there's high school theater. And the cutest of awkward teen romances that set my little gay heart aflutter.

- Finally, N.K. Jemisin's "Give Me Cornbread or Give Me Death" is a brutally clever story of racism and dragons. This is the piece that most enlarged my world. I was cringing or cheering or both with nearly every sentence.

Reading these stories was a pleasure, and writing this foreword has been a privilege. I'm proud of what Mur and Divya have done, and proud of what the entire Escape Artists team has done in the past ten years to bring smart fun short fiction to more and more people. They're making worlds bigger. They're making *the* world, the one we all share, better.

Enough from me. To quote someone whom I love and respect dearly: "Iiiiiiiit's story time…"

SERAH ELEY
July 31, 2020

ESCAPE POD

THE SCIENCE FICTION ANTHOLOGY

Kameron Hurley is not reticent to express her opinions, whether that's in journalism or fiction. Perhaps that's why she's won multiple awards for her writing. Her essay, "We Have Always Fought," explores the history of women warriors, erasure, and the narratives with which we deceive ourselves. When you read a Kameron Hurley story, you know you're going to see your reality through a new lens, and what you see will likely challenge your assumptions. "Citizens of Elsewhen," is no exception. We've published several of Kameron's stories in *Escape Pod*, and we're proud to open our anthology with this feminist time-travel tale.

DIVYA

CITIZENS OF ELSEWHEN
KAMERON HURLEY

"*Soldiers are citizens of death's grey land, drawing no dividend from time's tomorrows.*"—*Dreamers,* Siegfried Sassoon

We drop through the seams between things and onto the next front.

The come down is hard. It's meant to be. The universe doesn't want you to mess with the fabric of time. Our minds are constantly putting down bits of narrative into our brains, a searing record of "now" that gives us the illusion of passing time. In truth, there is only "now," the singular moment. We are all of us grubs hunting mindlessly for food, insects calling incessantly for mates. Nothing came before or after.

But because time is a trick of the mind, it can be hacked. And we have gotten good at it. We had to. It was the only way to secure our future.

"Who's got the football?" Elba says from the darkness beside me. "Lexi?"

"It's en route," Lexi says. "I'm rerouting the coordinates. Coordinates are 17,56-34-12 knot 65,56-22-75. Confirmed placement."

"Recording," Elba says.

And there is light.

Our brains start recording moments again, rebooted from our last jump. I half-hope this is some new scenario, a fresh start, but the chances of that are slim. We do these over and over again until we get them right. Because if we don't get them right... well, shit, then we don't exist.

We only remember our successes, never our failures. This helps with team morale, or so the psychs told us back in the training days, back when everything was burning, the whole world coming apart, and we got tapped to save it.

When they first started sending us back to secure a better future, the teams could remember every failure. It led to weariness and burnout; only the very stubborn or very stupid can stand living with the memory of compounded failure. Teams engaged in Operation Gray could endure more drops if we only remembered the good times. The successes. It kept us pushing forward.

For the failures, we had the logs. Our logs told us how many times we'd dropped in, and what we'd tried before. The trick, for me, was to pretend the log was from some other team. I pretended I was reading a report about somebody else who failed to complete the mission. I told myself my squad was coming in fresh to solve a problem someone else fucked up. Don't think too hard about the fact that you were thinking the same thing every time you failed beforehand, or you'll get stuck thinking about it, round and round, and then you're not good for anything.

Trust me.

The light and shadow transform into our current coordinates in space and time. It's the last month of autumn in the year we call 4600 BU (before us), known locally as the year 1214 *Ab urbe condita*, or 461 CE by some old alternate calendars. We are in the Western Roman Empire in what is known around here as Hispania, which will become Spain, then the European Alliance, then the Russian-US Federation, the Chinese-Russian Protectorate, then Europe again, and eventually, after several more handoffs, the province that in my time we call Malorian. I know this area, its future, because I was born sixteen kilometers north in the city of Madira. I know this coast because I will, more than three thousand years from now, walk upon these same beaches with my mothers, and raise a little orange flag during a parade celebrating the anniversary of Unification. My first visit here was also the first time I'd ever eaten a lemon, and the sharp, bitter taste is tied so closely with my memory of the coast that I taste lemon as we take in the sight of the sea just to our left.

A soft, salty wind blows in from over the Mediterranean. My bare toes sink into the sand. I bowl over and spit a mouthful of vomit. Beside me, Lexi has taken the jump worse. He's lying on his side, frothing and seizing. Elba stumbles over to him and shoots him up with a stabilizing agent.

I pat at myself as the gear bags materialize around us.

"Got the football," I say.

We're nothing without the gear. Without the gear, we have to start the fuck over again. We've stumbled naked into camps before, no plasma, no flesh fixup, no antibacterial mesh, nothing, and for all our knowledge, we're useless without those things. It wasn't being dumb that killed so many of the people we're here to save. It was simply not having access to what we did.

The wind is crisp. I shiver as I tear open the gooey sac protecting our gear. I make a guess at how all the clothes are supposed to go on; my AI still hasn't completed the download for this mission. I lace on boots over sandy toes. The clothes part is always haphazard, never quite right. I don't care what anyone says—it's clear every time we jet into some other time that we're aliens, strangers in a strange land. Go back far enough, you can claim godhood, but fewer people fall for that than the old stories would have you think. Better to say you were sent by a mutual acquaintance, a family friend.

I give another heave, spitting more bile, and blink as my AI completes the mission download. The AI's presence is a warm, comforting one, sitting there in the back of my head, dutifully making connections faster than a non-augmented brain, and storing more information, more quickly, than a civilian. Four hundred years before I was born, AIs were considered separate entities, a different consciousness, like something that lived on its own. They stuck them into people's heads and gave them names. But that drove far too many people mad. They tore off their own faces trying to get the fucker out. It was better if subjects saw the AI as a part of themselves, an enhancement to their own intelligence, instead of a separate entity.

The AI is how I knew this was former Visigoth territory, only recently brought to heel by the Western Roman Empire.

I knew Majoram, the Western Roman Emperor, had been killed in the summer at the ripe old age of forty, and this being early autumn, there was a heated battle for the Emperor's title still raging here in the west, led by Ricimer, the head of the army who'd had Majoram killed.

But the lofty milestones of history don't prepare you much for the sort of work we do. All it does is provide greater context for what we're walking into.

As we suit up, we don't ask dumb questions like, *Where is she? Where are we headed?* The memories are already pouring in. We have other things to talk about.

"Lemon cake," I say, continuing the last conversation we can remember; the one we were having after our last successful extraction, killing time before the next jump.

"Can't talk about food," Lexi says; he gags again.

"I miss cheeseburgers," Elba says. "You remember those cheeseburgers at that diner back in… the woman on all the pills? That green vehicle? AI says the colloquial year was 1955."

"Should have killed us," I say. "You know how they processed meat back then?"

"Still mad they pulled us before I finished," Elba says.

Lexi dry-heaves.

"Sorry," Elba says.

I heft my pack; I'm the muscle on this trip—every trip—but you don't want to carry stuff that looks too much like a weapon. We aren't permitted to kill anyone anyway. You kill someone you aren't supposed to, and you start over.

"We're four to one," Lexi says, knotting the laces of his sandals. He spits again.

I figure he's referring to the fact that the log says our failure last time was because the subject bled out.

"Your mistake last time," I say. "That's four to two."

"Bullshit," he says. "She'd have died of an infection if she hadn't bled out."

"Who dropped the antibiotic mesh?" I say.

We are dressed in linen tunics, knee breeches, and long coats; the clothes aren't well-worn enough to pass muster, even if they are the right cut for whatever class we're supposed to be, and I'm sure they aren't. When I ping the AI about that, I learn that we tried a more patrician style of clothing on our first drop, and got run out of town for it. This one apparently worked to get us past the settlement gatekeepers. I wasn't going to argue with the AI's memory.

"Up the dunes," Elba says. "You can shit on each other and walk at the same time, right?"

"Memory serves, we sure can," I say.

We walk up off the sandy beach. There's not much I can recognize here, except the sea. The sea has washed up all sorts of detritus. There's broken pottery and tiles, rusted bits of metal, tattered riggings, and refuse of all sorts. Far up the beach, I see what must be beach scavengers. They are headed in the other direction; I'm not sure if they witnessed our appearance on the beach.

Here and there are the jutting ruins of more sea trash, old shipwrecks, discarded implements, reminder that though this place is three thousand years before our time, the world here is already ancient. We've been farther back in time, much farther, but had found the results to be less precise. The farther back we go, the more complicated the mathematical models become. Too many variables. Turns out reverse-engineering a future by fiddling with the past can be… complicated. And often terribly messy. Careening through space-time wasn't exactly what I'd had in mind when I signed up to serve and see Unification through. But here we are.

"If it's the bleeding," Lexi says, "I'll prep the line first thing this time."

On the other side of the dunes are a series of caves. The wind changes, and I catch the smell of the fires. Cave dwellers like these tend to choose these areas because they dislike the oppressive reach of the states. It was a wonder they weren't slaves under some Roman landlord, but our records of Roman activity and expansion have never been exhaustive. Everything that is the past is fragmented. Our models do better tracking people through genetics—births and deaths—than across cultures and kingships and writs of sale on clay tablets that wash away over time. We can read the histories of our bodies in our blood—but less so the history of our cultures.

Our presence is noticed immediately by a young girl scouting on the rocks. She runs into the village for the headwoman. The AI tells me they are fisher folk, protected from engulfment by the wider body politic largely by geography. The able-bodied men are either dead or gone trawling, clinging to the edges of the beachhead, no doubt, worrying after fish.

"We've come for Junia Marcus," Lexi says, "to assist in her time. We saw a storm swing low over the bay, and a two-headed gull led us here. I am Silvius Varis Alexander, freedman of Silvius. I knew Junia's mother, Salia Marcus, freedwoman of Silvius. I've been sent here to assist her daughter for the kindness Salia Marcus once did for me."

Since we'd had this conversation before, the language was already in the banks of the AI. By this time, most of Hispania was speaking Latin, though this dialect could better be described as Sergo Vulgaris, or common speech. I had a grim memory of speaking for six hours on a spur of rock outside a remote cabin in Antarctica, well after the Thaw, trying to get a young girl out there to speak to us so we could get some kind of idea how to untangle her language and figure out where the subject was holed up. She was far more delighted to speak to us the same way people had done from time immemorial, using gestures, exaggerated expressions, and sounds of encouragement and disapproval. Children were often much more accepting of strangers than their parents; children still believed in magic.

The headwoman is leery of us, but Lexi has a way of ingratiating himself. It's his talent. And I know things are desperate inside the caves. Lexi is the one with the anthropology background; Elba came through via the medical team, and I signed on to be a frontline grunt, way back when. Or forward. Funny how shit turns out.

"She is young," the headwoman says, finally, "it has been difficult. Your prayers are welcome, but men are not permitted within the birthing room."

Lexi knits his brows. I blink, tapping into my AI to see if I'm remembering something wrong.

"Shit," Elba says, in our squad patois, "that's… new. How is that new?"

The AI confirms that the headwoman has never made this assertion before, not in all… four times we have attempted this mission. A wave of vertigo overcomes me.

"It's a blip," Lexi says. "A Crossroads."

"Fuck," I say.

I've heard of Crossroads before, read about them plenty, but never encountered one in all our drops. Crossroads are moments in time when your mission is rolling over concurrently with another team's. As they rewrite the timeline ahead of or behind you, it writes over all of your prior work; it means your log isn't going to be much good, because what happened last time technically happened on some other timeline. Listen, time travel's fucking complicated. I don't pretend to understand it, and I'm not here to lecture about it. All I know is what I got in training. All I know is the parameters we were working under just got rewritten.

"Grab Lexi's gear," Elba says to me. Then, to the headwoman, "The two of us will attend her. Time is of the essence. We have been warned that she is in grave danger."

There is more back and forth, but the headwoman finally escorts us into the caves, just me and Elba now. I have Lexi's gear, but that doesn't give me much confidence. I'm supposed to be here to watch their backs while they do this shit. Not that I haven't gotten myself elbow deep in blood and guts when I needed to, but I didn't like having one squad member down.

We hear Junia before we see her. She is grunting and panting in the dim light of the headwoman's lantern, surrounded by four other women. She does not scream, not yet. Beside her is a gory, deformed fetus, still and silent, half covered in a length of linen.

"Are we too late?" I say, because last time I never made it this far. Lexi took point, and we lost her.

"No," Elba says, kneeling next to the nearest woman, gently placing a hand on her shoulder, murmuring, asking her to move aside.

"It's the bleeding," I say.

"You always say that," Elba says. "I don't want to do this one again. Especially if we're at a Crossroads."

"Prep the line," I say. "Lexi was going to."

Elba sighs, but she does it; can't help doing it, because she knows as well as I that bleeding to death is how most of these women go. Blood loss, infection, or eclampsia are the top three causes of death for women during and immediately after childbirth. The children, well… there's a lot more that can go wrong there. But it's not as often that we're here to save the children. Nine times out of ten, we're here to save the mothers.

It's the loss of these women, and often their children, that costs us our future.

Junia is young, maybe fifteen, which makes hemorrhage or obstruction more likely. Like the other women, she has fine black tattoos on her face, and hands covered in ash. I didn't notice any of that on the headwoman, and I don't have a memory of those tattoos from the AI. Another new twist, then. The world itself is literally shifting under our feet.

They have pulled her up into what I recognize as a birthing chair; there is blood and shit and piss and afterbirth collecting there, all mopped up with straw and piled over to one side. An older woman comes over and cleans it all away.

Depending on the society, and the time period, complications from childbirth killed roughly one half to one quarter of all women, with one's chances of dying that way going up with every birth, if one survived the first. I knew from the records that this was the girl's first birth, and that meant there were more variables. A woman who'd had one successful birth was more likely to have others. New mothers... well, that often ended poorly.

I hold out my arm.

"Not yet," Elba says, and the wave of vertigo comes over me again. She blinks rapidly. The women around us shimmer, stutter-stop, like a bad projection. Two of them wink out altogether.

Junia wails, now, and the head of the second child begins to crown. Elba coaxes away the older woman. I shield what she's doing. Elba makes a small cut in Junia's perineum.

"We need you to push now," Elba says.

Junia cries, "I have been pushing! I have pushed! What do you think I'm doing here?"

There is a woman at her left, a sister or cousin, who murmurs something in her ear, and together they breathe through the next set of contractions. Attending births the way we do feels obscene, often. We have appeared during a time of crisis, an intensely personal time, and often we come between a woman and her family. It's not their fault, what lies ahead. If we could leave well enough alone—

The child's head comes free; I see the cord wrapped around the throat, and I firm my jaw. Elba cuts again, and I wince. I have seen this enough that I should not care, but there is something intimately gory about birth that cannot be matched on a battlefield. It's this knowledge that we are at the crux of life, where everything begins and ends. On a battlefield, most of what happens is endings.

Elba pulls the child free. He looks obscenely large, mostly due to the size of the head. She sets him on Junia's belly. The cousin ties and cuts the cord. They want the placenta, but that's not come yet. The placenta is when the bleeding will start, because it's going to tear; that's what the AI tells me, but how much has been altered since then?

The cousin is untangling the baby from the cord. She turns him upside down. Junia is exhausted, covered in sweat. She sags in the birthing chair, says, "Is he all right?"

I glance at Elba. The placenta is coming. I hold out my arm. She pulls the tubing from her pack and sets the line.

"What are you doing?" Junia says as Elba taps into her arm.

"You're going to bleed," Elba says. "I need to replace what you lose. It's all right. We are friends of your mother's."

The cousin and the midwife—the only two women left in here after that last shimmer—are still attending the child, but the cousin turns as Junia flails.

"You'll die if we don't do this," Elba says firmly. "Do you want to die here?"

"Save my baby," Junia says.

I glance at Elba, but she does not meet my look. I know in that moment that we are no longer here for the baby. It's strange, to see reports overwritten, to have our objective change in the space of a breath.

"We need to save you first," Elba says. "Please be still. Do this for your own mother, a freedwoman. Would she want you to die this way?"

Junia gazes over at the child. The midwife has cleared his airways, and is massaging his chest. Elba sets the line in Junia's arm.

I'm a universal donor, which is another reason I was put on this squad. They want a blood type like mine on hand. I guess you can be both, you know—the muscle and healer.

But as the blood leaves my body and enters Junia's, and the bleeding begins, and Elba starts her work to still it, I, too, find myself gazing at the dead child. It would not have been difficult to save him. We have tubing we can snake down his throat; we have the gear to perform effective CPR. The AI tells me our mission has changed. I don't know who it was that some other squad saved that changed it. Whoever they saved now meant our job was to leave this child to die, but it bothers me. Who are we to decide who lives and who dies?

I close my eyes, and I think of the future.

When it's over, Elba and I pack up our things. They wrap the dead child in clean linen and the wailing begins. Elba has stopped the bleeding, and given Junia targeted antibiotics. She is stable. The AI indicates our mission is complete.

The headwoman leads us outside. Her lantern is different, made of paper instead of clay. As we step into the light, I see tents spread out all across the beach. The air feels different, too. The tents don't look Roman at all. If I had to guess, I'd say they were Mongolian. But who's to say, this far back? I hesitantly tap into the AI, and it tells me that yes, we are still at the same coordinates. The historical context, however, has changed. This is no longer Hispania, but Vestia, a newly independent country recently held by Persia. I had not noticed the change in language, but I suspect that was overwritten as well, as the world changed.

Lexi is sitting outside at the entrance to another cave, smoking a pipe and laughing uproariously with three women. He stands when he sees us. His clothes are different—a longer tunic, boots instead of sandals. I glance down and see I'm dressed the same.

"It's been remarkable out here," he says. "I've never witnessed a Crossroads event."

"Let's get back to the beach for extraction," I say.

He seems confused at my lack of excitement. I'm tired. I palm an energy pack from the gear bag to help get my blood sugar back up.

Lexi asks for the details as we go back. Elba delivers them. I'm quiet. Finally, as we come within sight of the sea, he says, "Why does this one bother you, Asa?"

I shake my head.

"C'mon," Lexi says. "I've seen you elbow deep in blood and afterbirth, untangling babies from malformed cords, cutting open dead women only to find dead babies inside, and spend an hour bringing those babies back. None of that shit bothered you."

"Maybe it's catching up with me."

"Not likely," Lexi says. "If it was going to catch up with you, it would've done so a long time ago."

"How long you think we've been doing this?" I ask.

"Time is relative out here."

It's true. We can't trust age. Each time we corporealize, we are made anew, copies of copies of copies. Those copies age only for the minutes, hours, or days we make landfall. Then they are simply reconstituted elsewhere, elsewhen.

"It all feels so arbitrary," I say, gazing out at the wine-dark sea. "Who lives, who dies. We could save everyone, from every period. But we don't. The Crossroads… We can see the consequences, if not with what we've done, then with what someone else has done just before us."

"Don't tell me you have a moral dilemma," Elba says. She washes her hands in the sea, using the sand to scrub herself clean up to her elbows. "Everyone wants an easy answer, when it comes to morality."

"Who are we to decide who lives and who dies?" Lexi says. "Yeah, I get that."

"Who is every soldier, to decide that?" Elba says. "Soldiers have decided who lives and who dies forever. So have women like Junia, often. If that child lived, who's to say they wouldn't have sacrificed it to some god? The first one came out the way it did… they could have seen that as a bad sign. Humans have always decided who lives and who dies."

"Now it's an algorithm," I say.

"Algorithms are made by people," Elba says. "It's the great moral dilemma. This is human, this is a life, this isn't. Reality is, every culture has struggled with that since humans started fucking. Foreigners aren't people, slaves aren't people. Women aren't people. Most of us were considered somebody's property, same as goats or dogs, right up until the new world, right? And even then, you get people squabbling about who's really equal, who really deserves access to a doctor, or lifesaving drugs, or food, or transit. 'Who deserves it?' they ask. What they're really asking when they say it is, 'Who's really human?' Who deserves to be treated as human? Who has worked hard enough, scarified enough, gotten lucky enough, to be treated like a human?"

"I just worry we're fucking it up," I say.

"Can't think about that," Lexi says.

I know that for a long time, in a lot of places, women were property, and so were the people they birthed. In other places, like this one, women's bodies are collectively owned. It's moral, here, for Junia to keep a pregnancy or end it based on what the community needs. And I get that moral order. I get it, when you're just twelve people taking care of each other, surviving because of each other, out here at the edge of everything. Morals change as the needs of society change. Individual freedoms are a luxury of the modern age, of a collective dedication to providing people with the ability to exercise those freedoms. Here I am, becoming a fucking philosopher. That's what this work gets you. Too much thinking.

"Morality is made up," Elba says. "We're making it up as we go along. There is no right answer, no infallible, logical truth when it comes to morality. Do the right thing in this moment. That's all we have hope for."

"She's right," Lexi says. "No easy answers. No future. I knew there was no best way, no perfect future. Every utopia is someone else's dystopia. I worry too, though. You ever wonder if somebody else will get the tech while we're gone? Maybe they already have, somebody who wants a different kind of future? You worry that just making this thing, assuming we're benevolent… then finding out somebody wants something else, something worse?"

I stare out at the muddy horizon where it meets the sea. There's a big black storm out there, all lit up from beneath by the rising sun. The sky is a bloody wound, beautiful.

"All the time," I say. "I worry sometimes that it's already happened. When was the last time we were back? We could be getting orders from anybody. I get that."

"We have to keep going," Elba says softly. "If we don't create the future we're from by re-engineering the past, we don't exist. Unification never happens. Billions die. The Earth becomes a carbon-soaked sponge. We never see the stars. The sun eventually consumes all record of us. I'm a soldier first. I've always known I had a hand in who lives, who dies. This is no different."

I track the fingers of the sun. The sun looks brighter, this far back in time. The moon would too, at night, because every year the moon moves about an inch and a half farther from the Earth. Go back far enough, and the moon is like a massive godly face in the sky, looming over everything. No wonder we worshipped it.

"I have to believe in our future," Elba says. "I have to believe that as long as you and me and Lexi haven't shuddered out of existence, there's still a chance that future is being made out ahead of us. That's all you can do, sometimes. Believe in the future."

"If it was easy, everyone would do it," Lexi says.

And then time stops.

There's no transition between one time and the next, not that we're ever aware of.

I wonder, often, if we are brought in to debrief, if anyone at all is left out there in our future to debrief. This deep into the operation I feel we are completely controlled by the algorithm.

Consciousness.

A spark.

A noise.

I breathe out as my body corporealizes around me. My vision blurs. Flashing colors. A dizzying blur of red. The smell of burning forests.

"Coordinates?" I ask, before I can see, because Lexi's AI always comes online first.

Every birth is a battlefield, a war between the life that exists and the life coming into being. Sometimes they fight to a standstill. Other times, they fight to the death. I've seen it every which way you can imagine, because they only call on us for the difficult births, of course, the ones that kill or change those involved so much that they alter the course of history. No one has seen more blood and death than we have. We are spared the happy births, the uncomplicated deliveries, though I have been around some of those, too, and they are just as dramatic. Because you don't know what's going to happen, even in our future, during any given delivery. We don't have wars anymore, but we have births, and that's enough fighting and dying for me. There's still blood and shit and sweat and sobbing, but at the end of it you have two flushing, contented people enjoying life together. That's our goal, anyway—*together.*

I wonder how we can get there, from here.

And so we carry on, saving the lives of the women and children who will ensure the existence of our own timeline, of our own lives. We are the citizens of some other time, midwifing our way to that future.

T. Kingfisher, or Ursula Vernon, as her friends call her, has a penchant for weird stories. She's very, very good at them, as shown by her many awards. She covers many genres, including fantasy and horror, and tends to write about humble farmers who want nothing more than to humbly farm, and who aren't too thrilled about the magical sword, or magically enslaved person, or pregnant goat that falls into their lap. Ursula's heroes are also pragmatic. Even though they didn't ask for their adventures, they will roll up their sleeves and get to work on the problem—because the problem stands between them and getting back to work on their humble farm. Unfortunately for Dr. Hollowmass, the I-Witness Interrogation Software also stands in her way.

MUR

REPORT OF DR. HOLLOWMAS ON
THE INCIDENT AT JACKRABBIT FIVE

T. KINGFISHER

The following report is from the Jackrabbit Colony, Five Tau, regarding the incidents occurring during 7-5-11-8881, fifth rotation, involving Marine Midwife Unit Eleven-Gamma.

Incident report has been taken using the I-Witness program from your friends at Taxon Interrogation Software, with explanatory notes added and our new clarification system, saving you valuable time and manpower! At Taxon, Clarity is Our Business!(TM)

This is the I-Witness program from Taxon Programming. I will be taking your report today. Please relax and answer normally. When explanatory notes or clarifications are added, please indicate if they are correct by stating "Yes" or "No" when prompted. Remember, clarity is our business!

Sure.

Please state your name for the record.

I'm Doc Hollow.

Please state your full legal name for the record.

(sigh) Lin Hollowmas.

Clarification: This is Lin Hollowmas, PhD, DVM, FRCVM...

Yeah, that one.

... current position Doctor of Veterinary Medicine, Jackrabbit Colony?

Yeah.

Thank you, Doctor Hollowmas. Please state your purpose today.

Purpose? Ruby told me I had to come down and give a report. Well, she said I had to volunteer to give a report, which is what we call being "volun-told."

Clarification: Ruby is Doctor Elowyn Rubenstein, PhD MD, FRCS, FRCMD, retired, currently of Jackrabbit Colony?

"Retired" my ass.

Please state "Yes" or "No."

Yes.

Thank you. Please continue.

Okay, so Ruby says you fellas want a report and she sent me to do it. I figure this is about the incident. So eight and a half months ago, the girls who want kids go off the goop together—

Clarification: What is "the goop?"

Birth control. We're a small-footprint colony here on Jackrabbit, planned fertility only. We're Extinctioners.

Explanatory note: The Church of the Final Extinction, founded on Earth after the seventh mass extinction. Followers believe that human-caused extinctions are the great sin of humanity and vow to prevent further ones, potentially at the cost of their own or other lives.

Uh, let's not get carried away.

They have founded seven colonies on the principles of low-impact colonization and extensive adaptation to local ecological conditions. The terrorist organization known as the Arm of the Ammonite was founded by CFE followers, but has been disavowed by the Church.

Yeah, we're not with those people. They're nuts.

For profiles of historical followers of the CFE, please consult the archives.

Right, okay, so the girls all go off the goop at the same time and get pregnant, pretty standard, we set up the appointment for the midwives to come around and deliver. Four women this time, three of 'em take. Poor Mal didn't, but that's neither here nor there.

Clarification: Poor Mal is Malinda Rory, RNP.

Is none of your damn business, that's who. Anyway, the girls who get pregnant all do fine, so far as I know. I'm a vet, though, so I do a lot better with critters that give birth standing up, so don't take my word for it. Ruby says they're looking fine, and Doc Pierson—that's Doctor Reginald Pierson to you—says so too. We got the tech for a bunch of things, but you really want midwives for the deliveries. We're just first and second gen here, eighty-two people, we can't afford to lose people in childbirth, leavin' aside that we'd all be completely wrecked by it.

Anyhow, everything goes along fine until a couple weeks ago, when Harsh gets preeclampsia.

Clarification: Harsh is not found in the records.

Hannah Marsh, oversees the colony's waste treatment and recycling.

Thank you. Clarification accepted. Please continue.

I'm trying. So Harsh is on bed rest and we radio the midwives to get their asses out here as soon as they can.

Explanatory note: "Radio" is likely a colloquialism, as the Space Marine Midwife Corps communicates primarily through subspace relay. The origin of the phrase lies with early military communications, which did utilize radio waves. For further information on the history of radio, please consult the archives.

Seriously? Okay. The midwives radi— *communicate* back that they'll move it up as soon as they can. We can treat mild preeclampsia here, but that shit gets bad, you want a lot more tech to back it up. Once we've got the infrastructure, we'll have a high-tech medical center for this stuff, but small-footprint means asteroid mining, not planetary surface, and we're still standing up the power grid. It's all behind schedule because of the fish ladders.

Explanatory note: Fish ladders are structures built into dams to allow wildlife to travel upstream. Small-footprint colonies integrate them into all hydropower plans to prevent disruption to established migratory patterns.

They weren't big enough, it turns out. It's an itty-bitty little river, nobody realized the roller fish bloat up to about twenty times their size when they're fixin' to spawn. We've got the parts on back order, but the whole colony's on solar and water-wheels until we get it sorted.

Explanatory note: Water-wheels are primitive structures used to generate rotary motion from flowing water.

We are seriously gonna be here all day if you keep this up.

Please continue.

So Harsh is drinking so much water she practically floats but it's not getting much better. I'm starting to worry that I'm gonna be trying to induce labor with a shot I use on the heifers for their first birth and that ain't my idea of a good time.

Clarification: This would be an illegal act violating multiple statutes, including use of drugs not cleared for humans on a human patient, practicing medicine without a license, endangerment of a patient's welfare, endangerment of—

Look, I didn't do it! I wasn't going to do it! Holy prophetess, you machines do not know how to listen to a story, do you?

Clarification accepted. Please continue.

Unngh. So the midwives call back and say they're on their way. And thing is, we only got the one building with consistent power, right? We keep everything tucked in together—the freezers and the com and the med center, which only has the three beds, and Harsh is in one of them and poor Bob probably ought to have been in another.

Clarification: This is Roberta Emmanuel Preston, current position agricultural technician, Jackrabbit Colony?

Yeah, Bob. She was manning the com. She loves talking to passing ships. Between you, me, and the walls, I don't think she was cut out for the colony life. *Anyway*, she's another one of our pregnant ladies, and she was in the center building on account of her getting just terrible swollen ankles, I mean really bad. She said it was nothing, particularly given Harsh's problems, but I mean, this ain't a zero-sum game, right? So Doc Pierson and Ruby sort of decided she needed to spend a lot more time in the air conditioning, so they told her to man the com, right? Normally we just check it when we expect somebody to be coming in, but we're expecting the midwives any second now in theory, so it gave Bob something to do that didn't seem like make work.

So she's on the com and all of a sudden, this weird little ship comes blazing into the system. And Bob is all, "Unidentified ship, identify yourself!" which is kinda redundant, but y'know. So the ship comes on the com and it is just grainy, old-school tech-terrible crap from the old Diaspora days, the ones that pixelate at the corners if you breathe on the cameras, you know? Except we can't even get cameras until they get in closer, it's that bad. But the visuals we do get—yeah, I mean, it was a weird ship. Looked like somebody took an asteroid, dug it out, and stuck an engine on it. Which is pretty much what they did, I guess. I dunno. Small footprint is one thing, but you can take it too far.

The ship starts broadcasting its ID and I mean, this thing is *old*. It really was from the Diaspora. It was so old that the ID numbers had rolled over and Bob's getting it back from the computer that this is a goddamn dreadnought out of New Tillamook, which it pretty obviously isn't, because dreadnoughts are a whole lot *bigger*. So she has to convince the computer to spit out the ID numbers from the last round of ships, which was two hundred years ago, before the Altercations, and the computer meanwhile is screaming that there's a dreadnought but also that there isn't a dreadnought and Bob is screaming at the computer and Harsh is screaming that if they don't all shut up, she's gonna go sleep in the pig pen, where they might at least understand that a pregnant woman needs her sleep—which they don't, incidentally, sows being as much of a pain in the ass when they're farrowing as when they ain't. Harsh knows a lot about hog waste, but not that much about the hogs it comes out of, if you take my meaning.

Explanatory note: Farrowing, in domestic pigs, refers to the act of giving birth.

Anyway, Ruby hears all this ruckus and comes in and gets everybody settled down except the computer, computers bein' less responsive to sweet talk and death threats, which are Ruby's chosen methods of communication.

And we're trying to talk to the computer on the asteroid-ship and we can't. This thing is so old, our computers can't dumb themselves down enough to actually talk to them. I'm starting to think we're gonna be tapping crap out in binary.

Clarification: At no point was the unidentified ship treated as a hostile?

Shit, no. A ship like that? What're they gonna do, get out and slap us? Anyway, finally we get a live human, but that doesn't help much, because he's completely wrecked. Managing about one word in three that he tries, and the translation circuits are just subtitling everything "garbled," which, y'know, we didn't really need a fancy-ass machine to tell us. But finally he gets out, 'cryosleep,' and it all makes sense. The computer woke his ass up and he's still got the bad hangover. Frankly, given that, he was doin' pretty good. You take me out of cryo and I'm talking backward for a week.

But he's obviously in a world of hurt and we're gettin' pretty worried, but then some of the other words he does manage to get out are, "birth," and, "midwife," and, "help." And then it all makes sense. Bob manages to calm him down and get a little bit more out of him, and near as we can tell, it's just him and one other, and she went into labor and it all went bad, so he did the only thing he could do and slaps both of 'em into cryo and tells the computer to find him a midwife to save his girl.

Problem was, of course, he was way off the main routes and the computer automatically dropped to just under lightspeed to save power, and the rest of the universe moseyed along without them for a couple hundred years. And the heading he'd set was right through the Khaw Prime system.

Explanatory note: Khaw Prime system was one of those destroyed during the Altercations. For more information on the Altercations, please consult the archives.

So he headed for a system that vanished about twenty years after he shut down, but he doesn't know it and the computer just keeps going. They woulda probably kept going clear into uncharted space, but they get close enough to Jackrabbit for the computer to pick up the distress call we sent to the midwives, and the word for "midwife" is so old the computer still knew it and changed course. The pilot's so screwed-up from cryo that he can't run the numbers for the approach, which, I mean, you might as well use a paper and pen, with that computer. So Bob's having to do all the calculations for him, and Harsh is like, "If I hear one more equation, Imma set this building on fire."

Harsh comes by her name honestly.

And then the midwives make the system and we got a party.

Their ship actually gets here before the other one, despite making the system after, which might tell you how pokey the other ship is being. Great people. Three midwives come screaming down in those little one-man pods. Normally they'd go slower, come down in a shuttle, but Harsh is starting to take the "pre" outta "preeclampsia," if you get my drift.

The pods come down in the lake. Pisses off the fish, but it's a manmade lake and Doc Pierson and I go get the slapturtles out first, which they don't appreciate, but everybody's in a mood today, so why would the slapturtles be any different? The midwives roll out of the pods. Handles're Squid, Forest, and Angel Eyes, and do *not* ask me to clarify who's which, Machine, on account of I do not know their real names, just that Squid's in charge and Angel Eyes is a guy.

Clarification: Identification inquiry cancelled. Please continue.

Damn straight.

They run in to see Harsh. Meanwhile, the pokey little asteroid ship finally gets close enough that we can see it, and… Lord, it ain't much to look at, and the pilot's running on coffee and panic, which ain't a great combination. And you figure that coffee was probably two hundred years old, so I doubt that's improving the taste much.

So Bob talks them down and the ship lands—well, you can call it landing if you're feeling generous, it pretty much belly-flops into the lake—and the pilot skids it over to the shore and falls out into the water. Just one guy, still sketchy as hell from cryosleep—I mean, you wouldn't let him pilot his way to the john in this state, no how should he have been flying a ship, even if it was a hollowed-out asteroid. So he staggers onshore and he's got a cryo-unit that's so old it still has cooling fans, and the battery on it's so old that it makes Ruby look positively youthful.

Weird-ass cryo-unit, too. At first I figure that it's one of those ones where you curl up in position, you know, but it's shaped wrong even for that. But he's got it on antigrav boosters, one of which ain't even working, and he has to prop up the corner and he's bellowing that he needs power because she ain't gonna last much longer.

So Squid tells him to get the thing inside right away, I mean, we got power at headquarters, enough for two air-conditioned rooms, and Forest grabs one side of the unit and I grab the other and Bob's throwin' doors open, even though she can only hobble about with her ankles the way they are. And we get this sucker inside and wipe off the condensation and damned if it isn't a goat.

Explanatory note: "Goat" is likely a colloquialism, perhaps a shorthand for scapegoat, which is—

No! Do not try to explain! It is *not* a colloquialism; it is a *goat*.

Clarification: This is a member of the domestic species Capra aegagrus hircus?

That's what they taught me in vet school, yep.

Clarification: The distress call was being rendered on behalf of a domesticated goat?

Do you wanna tell this story instead of me?

Please state "Yes" or "No."

Yes. It was for the goat.

Clarification accepted. Thank you. Please continue.

I'm hardly in the mood now. Why do you have to ruin a good story, Machine?

At Taxon, Clarity is Our Business.

Do I come in your house and tell you how to do your job? No, but I bet you would, wouldn't you?

Clarification: Question not understood. Please restate.

Never mind. Okay. Where was I? Right, so there's this frozen goat, okay? Seriously pregnant, 'bout ready to pop, and the cryo-unit is so old that we can't even plug the goddamn thing in, we don't have connectors, you talk about male and female plugs, this sucker's got like alien tentacle baby plugs with three grounds, so Squid's strippin' wires and cussin' a blue streak but we can't do shit, we gotta defrost it while it's still got enough power to wake the patient up.

Explanatory note: Defrost is a colloquial term for waking from cryogenic sleep, derived from—

What kind of freaky-ass bureaucrat you gonna have listening to this report that doesn't know what defrosting means? Or what radio is, for that matter?

Clarification: Recipients of an I-Witness Interrogation Report are classified.

Yeah, good for them. Okay, so we're trying to get this goat thawed out before the unit dies completely, and the pilot's looking at me like the goat is his bestest friend in the whole universe and he's got that bad red-eye look like you get from cryosleep, and he is begging me to save his goat.

Well, shit. I ain't a monster. Neither are the midwives. We gotta save this man's goat. But Harsh needed to be delivering her baby like yesterday, so they've already induced, right? And Bob is sitting there with her ankles the size of grapefruit tryin' to be helpful, and all of a sudden she gets this mortified look and she's standing in a puddle and damned if her water didn't break right then and she says that maybe her backache's been a little more than a backache, but she was busy trying to help this old ship get in proper and so she was kinda deliberately not paying attention and hopin' it would go away, and now we got two women in labor and a frozen goat.

Anyhow, Squid gives up on the wires, says it can't be done, and we fire up the emergency thaw, which is hard enough on anybody, let alone a pregnant female regardless of species, but she comes out of the unit pissed as hell and wanting to fight me, only she can't hardly stand up. And at first I figure she's just woozy from the cryo, but she's having contractions and the pilot's practically sobbing on her neck and I realize she's tryin' to drop her kid and it ain't happening.

I'm figuring the kid's the wrong way around, so I'm trying to get my hand inside this goat to get a grip on the hooves and get things started and damned if Harsh is not having the *exact* same problem and the midwife they call Angel Eyes is up in there with the forceps, which I happen to know on account of us only having two air-conditioned rooms as I said before and me trying to deliver the goat in the same room as Harsh, who had some really cutting things to say about the situation, let me tell you.

Well, cutting things to scream about the situation. Women don't give birth as easy as cows, I'll tell you that.

Anyway, this goat is not having an easy time of it either. I get a hand in there and I see right away why the pilot fellow panicked and popped her in the deep freeze. There's way too many legs in there and some of 'em are stiff as boards and some of 'em are floppy, and of course any vet knows what's going on with *that*.

Clarifica—

I am *getting* to that! Fine! She's got twins and one's dead and gone full rigor mortis and the other one's alive but ain't gonna last too long in there. And the goat's completely exhausted and gone a little floppy herself at this point.

Well, the rigor mortised one's in front—they're always in front, 'cos the god of goats thinks it's funny, I guess—and I gotta get it out. And of course the one in back is the wrong way 'round, because why wouldn't it be?

I dunno if you've ever tried to get a stiff kid out of a goat but it's grim business. You gotta break the bones with your bare hands. Absolute worst part of the job—no, I tell a lie.

Clarification: Please state the truth clearly for the I-Witness program. Perjury is punishable under Act 791, subsection A through Q.

Fine. There's worse stuff in the job, but I ain't getting into that here.

Clarification accepted.

So, this goat is still royally pissed, for which I do not blame her, because cryosleep is no picnic on top of a dead kid and she is getting dry as space in there, which does not *help* the matter. I yell for the lube and Angel Eyes hands it over—I mean, he's standing practically on top of me, on account of Harsh, and hey, it's the same stuff, when you get right down to it.

Explanatory note: Medical lubricant used for delivery falls into two major categories, water- and oil-based, and is approved for use on both human and animal patients. For more information on the uses of medical lubricant, please consult the archives.

You'll get one helluva education if you do, I'll tell you that.

So there I am trying to get this kid into a shape to get out and the goat decides to kick me in the knees and knocks me over and I fall into Angel Eyes, which Harsh does not appreciate one bit, granted where his hand was at the time, and Squid is just about to scream to get this goat out of the delivery room, and I'm like no, it's fine, it's not the goat's fault, and the pilot's sobbing that he can't lose the goat, it's all he's got left of his daddy's farm and I mean, take a picture, bud, it eats less than a goat, but I can't very well say that while I got my hand all up in this man's goat's business, you know?

Forest jumps in to try to help me—she's with the Space Marine Midwives, she's delivered way weirder things 'n livestock—but there is just not *room* for two people up inside this goat. Lord, it was ugly business.

So I get the first kid out and Forest dives in and takes it outside and the pilot's sobbing, although he had to know he wasn't getting two live kids outta his goat. And Bob's trying real hard not to complain but this ain't her first and she's one of those people who goes into labor and the kid comes out like he's shot outta a cannon and so she's crowning by the time Forest is trying to run this dead goat out. So Ruby takes the pilot and a shovel outside and I think maybe she's gonna kill him, which, I gotta admit, seemed a little excessive, but by then I had my arm back up in the goat, y'know? What am I gonna do, run after them dragging the goat on the end of my wrist yelling, "Don't kill him!"?

Clarification: Question not recognized as valid. If you receive this message, please contact Taxon Programming with the question, the time, and the serial number of the I-Witness software being used. Clarity Is Our Business!

Yeah, bet your Taxon people didn't think of the answer to *that* one.

But yeah, they were burying the kid out by the lake. It was real sweet, actually. And the second kid comes out pretty easy, once I get it lined up. You can get 'em out back-end first, it's just a pain in the ass for everybody.

So I'm pulling and the kid comes out right as Forest is coming back in and she does not know whether to jump to catch me—'cos I'm falling over with a goat on my chest—or catch Bob's baby. And then Harsh rears up and decks Squid right in the jaw, yelling like a banshee, which could perhaps be forgiven 'cos this is Harsh's first kid and you know she ain't been expecting it to hurt quite like that, and of course everything was such a mess we couldn't get a pain block in on her in time, so I'd have maybe done a little punching too, given the situation.

Anyway, Forest does the right thing and catches Bob's baby and I'm layin' on my back with this kid on my chest and Squid thinks maybe Harsh needs a little downtime and she goes and checks on the goat. Goat's not doing too great, but Squid, she gets in there and starts patching things up and we pump her full of the good drugs.

Well, it all worked out. It was touch and go for a while there with the goat, but Squid's good, and the pilot is sleeping in the stall with her. The goat, not Squid. Bob's baby does great and Harsh pulls through. Her baby's a bit undersized, so the midwives stick around for a few days to make sure she's okay. They requisition my incubator, which meant we were havin' to keep baby chicks under heat lamps for a while, but shit, I don't begrudge that for anybody.

Heh. Turns out the goat's an old breed, incidentally. Real old, even before spending two hundred years in the deep freeze. She and her kid're literally the last two of their kind. The pilot's daddy was an Extinctioner. So, y'know, they say the universe has a way of sorting these things out. He's stayin' on the planet and we've got samples so we can sequence the DNA and keep this breed from goin' the way of the Percheron.

Explanatory note: The Percheron is an extinct domestic horse breed.

Rub it in, why don't you?

And me? Oh, I'm fine. Did a little more fallin' over in the last few days than I like, but the goat kept the kickin' below the knee. Delivered my baby just fine. Little girl. Sweet thing, but Grandma Ruby's gonna do most of the raising of her. She talked me into having the girl in the first place. I'm really a lot better with goats.

Does this conclude your incident report, Doctor Hollowmas?

Yeah. You got any follow-up questions, you send a human to ask me, you hear?

Thank you for your cooperation. This Incident report has been taken using the I-Witness program from your friends at Taxon Interrogation Software.

At Taxon, Clarity is Our Business!(TM)

… Says you.

Tim Pratt is so prolific, I'm not sure when he sleeps. He sees the absurdity of everyday life, and he'll bring it to your attention by putting people in extraordinary circumstances. Usually those people are witty. Sometimes they're also compassionate. One of our fan favorite authors, he's appeared on *Escape Pod* since Episode 8 —that's from way back in 2005, when people listened to podcasts on their iPods. He wrote "A Princess of Nigh-Space" for this anthology and cooked it up with all the ingredients he's best known for. With great pleasure, we bring you this original story from him.

DIVYA

A PRINCESS OF NIGH-SPACE

TIM PRATT

There was a business card stuck in the crack between the door and the frame when I got home from another too-long day at the office. I plucked the card out, annoyed, assuming it was some stupid advertisement, but the thick black Gothic lettering caught my eye:

BOLLARD AND CHICANE

OBSTACLES REMOVED + BURDENS SHIFTED
TROUBLES UNTROUBLED

. C ▨ a^P▨^ǎk ^[NX▨Y _t„

With a phone number underneath.

There was small, neat, and slanted writing on the back, in pen: "Dear Tamsin: Our condolences on the loss of your grandmother. We can help settle your estate. Call soonest."

"Granny isn't dead," I said to no one, and then my phone buzzed with an incoming call.

. . . . .

With the travel, and the funeral, and the lawyers, and the police investigation, and having to take time off work (and of *course* the startup where I bashed code was getting ready for its IPO, and *of course* "my grandmother died" sounded like a college-student-level excuse, although "my grandmother was murdered in a home invasion" was a little different), it was weeks before I actually made it to Culver House. The ancestral heap stood on the edge of a sagging damp town in the Midwest, where I grew up and lived until I fled to college. I hadn't been back in the six years since, because why would I return? My only living family was Granny, brilliant and independent and remote and endlessly annoyed at raising little orphaned me. I didn't come back for holidays because she didn't celebrate any, calling them, "American fripperies," even Christmas and Easter. "Granny, they celebrate Christmas back in Croatia, too," I would argue, and Granny would say, "Not in the part *I'm* from, they don't."

I sat behind the desk in my grandmother's study that evening and opened the top drawer as the attorney had instructed, revealing an envelope with *Tamsin* scrawled across the front. My legacy, or at least, the non-monetary part of it; I'd gotten the other part already. The money I was expecting to make when the company I worked for went public was a bit less exciting now that I'd inherited my genius Granny's considerable estate.

The envelope had been torn open, though, and instead of a letter from the woman who'd raised me at cold arm's length, I found a business card, another version of the one I'd discovered at my house. This one said:

BOLLARD AND CHICANE

PESTS REMOVED + OFFENSES REDRESSED
KNIVES SHARPENED

. E [a ˆə̃ Z ɒY ɯ_ə̃-ˆɒ̃ɕ a ˆ_Ł„

On the back, in that neat handwriting, I read: "You really should call us, miss. Mr. B."

Okay then. First I called my high school boyfriend, Trevor, who still lived in town and had a tattoo of a snake eating its tail around his neck, and liked guns. I'd dated him mostly to annoy Granny, but he'd been fun, the way doing meth and committing arson are probably fun, and he still had a thing for me. "I think I might have some trouble over at the house, Trev," I said.

"I'll be right there." He hung up without asking any questions. That's a good quality sometimes.

Then I called the number on the card. A voice so deep and sonorous it sounded like a yeti with a head cold said, "Miss Culver. It's an interesting last name, Culver. There are various possible origins. The old English, '*culfre*,' meaning dove, possibly used as a term of endearment, possibly referring to someone who was lovesick. Or the French, '*couleuvre*,' meaning snake. Or it could be related to, '*culverin*,' a kind of early handgun, a precursor of the musket, and later the name for a cannon. Which do you think your grandmother was thinking of when she chose that name for her new life in her new world?"

I could not have given fewer shits about the etymology of my surname. "Who *is* this?"

"This is Mr. Bollard. My associate Mr. Chicane is here as

well." I heard a scraping in the background, and a clatter, and then Mr. Bollard sighed, but not, I think, at me.

"I don't want to know your name. I want to know why you left me business cards, why you broke into my grandmother's desk, and what you took from me." The lawyer who'd handed over the key said Granny had left a precious family heirloom in the desk for me, but he didn't know the details.

"All excellent questions," Bollard said. "But you should ask a different one first. You should ask, 'Where are you, Mr. Bollard?'"

"Fuck off," I said.

"I'll pretend you replied, 'Where are you,'" Bollard said. "And that you didn't inherit your grandmother's poor manners. If you'd asked me what I asked you to ask me, I would have replied: We are *here*. We are in the basement. We are waiting by the door."

"I'm calling the police," I said.

"Why would you want Mr. Chicane to murder a bunch of perfectly nice police officers?" Bollard asked. "We don't want to hurt you. We just want your help. It's in your best interest. Your grandmother wasn't helpful at all, and look what happened to her. Now. Are you coming down, or shall I send Mr. Chicane up to fetch you?"

I cut the connection and picked up Granny's letter opener— actually a *misericorde* from the thirteenth century, a slender knife designed to stab through the gaps in a knight's armor. It was just like Granny to use it to open bills and junk mail. I held the knife tight and crept to the study door, listening.

There was plenty to hear, because Culver House is a rambling three-story Victorian with various newer additions, and it creaked and groaned and settled constantly, especially up here on the top floor. If some of those creaks were the mysterious Mr. Chicane coming to get me, I couldn't tell. I decided to call the police anyway. It would take them half an hour to show up, but at least if I got murdered before then, the cops would know the names and phone number of my murderers, and probably Granny's, too. I dialed 9-1-1, and Bollard answered. "*I* don't want to murder any police officers either," he said. "No one is paying me to do that today. Please come downstairs. You're wasting time."

"Why aren't you the cops?" I sputtered.

"Your grandmother had access to technology she didn't sell to the government or Silicon Valley, miss, and some of it has wonderful applications, like intercepting calls to those I'd rather not have called. We—"

I cut the connection again. At least I'd gotten through to Trev. He'd show up faster than the cops, but in the meantime, I didn't want to stay in the study, where Bollard and Chicane would probably look for me first.

I went onto the landing and down the stairs to the second floor, then past my old room, left unchanged since I departed, not as any sort of shrine, but because Granny didn't care about any part of the house other than the kitchen, her own bedroom, and her study... and the basement, which I had literally never entered, because that's where Granny did her experiments and invented her inventions, and it was too dangerous, and too delicate, and was always locked. I'd been interested in finally getting a look at the place, but the presence of probably-murderers down there did a lot to dampen my curiosity.

I went down the second-floor hall to the back stairs, where I could descend to the kitchen and slip out the side door and get away.

There was a man at the bottom of the stairs, looking up at me. My body was already fizzing with fight-or-flight chemicals, and seeing a stranger in the house made me feel like my brain was going to vibrate out of my skull.

He was thin, dressed in a baggy tweed suit, and had a big head irregularly occupied by tufts of hair, with dried blood crusted all down one side of his face. When he saw me, he did a little capering dance in place, hooting and giggling, then he pointed one long finger at me and held it for a moment.

"Mr. Chicane?" I said.

He didn't answer. He leapt forward, scampering up the stairs on all fours like a bounding dog.

I took out Granny's knife and stepped back, but he was so *fast*—he barreled into me and drove me to the ground, knocking the breath out of my body and the *misericorde* from my hands. He hooted in delight as I struggled to get away. Up close I could see his features were all lumpy and potato-like, his eyes not quite on the same level, his nose mostly just two holes in his face, his lips thin, his chin nonexistent. Under all the old blood, I could see a cratered dent in the side of his head big enough to stick the end of your thumb in. He seemed like a badly made doll of a person.

He was strong, though, all cords and wires and bony limbs. He pinned both my wrists to the floor over my head, giggled in my face, and reached into his jacket with his free hand. I thrashed and twisted, expecting a gun, a blade, a hypodermic needle—but instead he took out a business card, and held it inches above my face. I had to cross my eyes a little to read it, but once it came into focus, it said:

BOLLARD AND CHICANE

MURDER + ARSON + REGIME CHANGE

. C ⏃⏃- Xc Me _⏃⏃ MW⏃⏃- ⏃⏃ LXXIZ SŁ.

I took a deep breath, which required breathing in his raw-meat-and-onion reek. "Okay. I get it. What do you want from me?"

Chicane deftly flipped over the card, revealing another handwritten message: "We need to open a door. We have one key. You have the other. Join us downstairs."

"I don't have any key!" I shouted.

Chicane tapped me on the nose with the business card and waggled his eyebrows and grinned. His teeth were wrong: too numerous, too sharp, too many colors. He was drooling, and if I stayed under him much longer, that drool would drip onto my face.

"I'll come down!" I said, turning my face away from his stinking mouth.

I heard a hollow metallic *thonk*. Chicane collapsed on top of me, then rolled off bonelessly. He had a new dent on the back of his head to match the first one. I wriggled away, snatched my knife from the floor, and looked around.

Trevor stood at the top of the stairs, holding an aluminum baseball bat. He was wearing dirty jeans and a white undershirt and his boots were untied—he must have rushed over here as soon as I called.

I hugged him hard, because Trevor always responded well to physical encouragement. "Trev! Thank you, thank you, thank you for coming." I looked at Chicane and kicked him in the side, but he didn't stir.

"Course I came," he said. "It's you and me. T-N-T."

Oh, god, I'd forgotten that nickname he had for us—T-N-T, first we get hot, and then we explode. Teenage horniness is so embarrassing.

His face got serious. "I'm real sorry about your granny. Who's this little weasel?"

"I think his name is Chicane, but—"

Trevor took a step back. "Wait. Chicane. As in *Bollard* and Chicane?"

"You know them?" He knew plenty of local scum, but Bollard and Chicane sure didn't seem local.

"Do I…" His eyes went glazed and faraway. "Bollard and Chicane. The Two. The Crush and the Bite. The Bad Neighbors. The Ones Who Come After. The Ones Who Come After *You*. Do I *know* them? Do you know the boogeyman, I mean, do you know—they're from the old country. They shouldn't be here."

"The old country? You mean Croatia?"

"Croatia?" He blinked at me, then looked back at the man on the floor. "She never told you? You, wow, it shouldn't be *me*—"

Trev had never been the most articulate person. That wasn't one of the things I'd ever needed or demanded from him before, but I grabbed him by the shoulders and shook him. "Start. Making. Sense."

His focus snapped to me. "First we get out of here. *Then* I'll start making sense."

· · · · ·

We raced away without any bother from Bollard, who was presumably waiting for me to be dragged down to the basement any minute. We rode ten minutes in silence in Trevor's truck, then sat in our old booth at the Chickenarium, where the vinyl was just as torn and the Formica just as smudged as it had been in high school. I got the chicken and waffles, and he had the chicken-fried steak with fries and cluck sauce. He passed me his flask under the table and I took a slug of something brown that was probably distantly related to bourbon.

"Making sense time," I said. I kept the flask.

"Your family doesn't come from Croatia," Trev said. "They come from another plane of existence."

I looked down at the flask. "How much of this did you drink already?"

He sighed, and sat up straighter, and it was weird—like slouching, mumbling, all-mischief-and-malice Trev was a costume he'd been wearing, and he'd shrugged it off and let it fall to the floor, becoming someone more serious. "Listen to me. This isn't the only world. It's not the only universe."

"You're talking about parallel universes? Or, what is it, the multiverse?"

"Sort of. Basically. It's more like reality is a big stack of paper, and every piece of paper has a different world on the front and back, so some worlds are close to others, and some are far away, and sometimes you can poke a hole through the paper and travel from one to another. We call that stack of worlds nigh-space. Your granny, and your parents, and me, we all come from the world next door."

"And *you*?" Trev was many things, but delusional was never one of them. He'd had a clear-eyed understanding of himself as a thrill-seeking dirtbag.

"And me. Your granny brought me over when I was twelve and you were ten, and paid off a family to raise me."

"You mean… your foster parents."

"That's them." He poked at his food but didn't eat. "My family got into some trouble back home, and they were vassals of *your* family once upon a time, so somebody called in a favor, and they sent me here. The only requirement was, I had to watch over you. Remember when you had trouble with those bullies, and then you didn't anymore?" He touched the snake's head on his throat. "This tattoo is the symbol of fealty to your family. Your granny insisted I get it as soon as I was plausibly old enough."

Vassals? Fealty? I shook my head. "Trev, you're not making any sense. You and me dated. Are you telling me Granny set that up too?"

"No, that part just kinda happened. I couldn't believe you'd look twice at someone like me. Back home, I wasn't even high-status enough to clean out your garderobe."

How did Trev know the word, "garderobe"?

"When we started going out, your Granny mostly thought it was funny, but also useful. She made a point of disapproving of me loudly, so you'd like me better. When we were together, I *was* able to look out for you better, not that you needed much help by then. Remember that guy you punched in the throat when he grabbed your ass at the reservoir?"

"Let's forget memory lane for a minute. Go back to this stuff about another world."

"Oh, sure. The old country. It's a lot like this world, geography-wise, even some of the languages and stuff, because it's… basically, it's the next sheet of paper, so our worlds are on facing pages, like. Worlds get weirder the farther out you go from your home space. The old country is politically regressive by your standards, controlled by powerful ruling families, dynasties and that, but it's a lot more advanced technologically." (Did Trev just say, "politically regressive"?) "That's how your granny got so rich over here. She brought some of the least disruptive tech with her when she fled, and sold it to the locals."

I didn't believe any of this, but I did like the idea that Granny wasn't the genius she always claimed to be. "Why did she flee?"

He took a sip of water. "I was like five when this stuff happened, so don't expect political analysis or whatever, but your parents were in one of those ruling families I mentioned. Some shit went down, assassinations and betrayals and alliances shifted, and your parents got killed. People were hunting little three-year-old you, too, hoping to exterminate the line, or maybe make you a hostage, I don't know. Granny decided to take you away someplace you'd be safe until the situation stabilized—protecting the heir. Since your family was one of the few with the technology to travel through nigh-space, she took you someplace *really* safe. The original idea was to bring you back at some point, let you take your rightful place, but the politics stayed in flux for a long time, and your granny started to like it over here. Less hassle, even if it is pretty primitive by our standards. She told me that when you were older, she'd give you the key to the door and tell you the whole story and let you decide whether to return and try to get back the ancestral vaults and all or not."

My chicken and waffles had gotten cold. "You're telling me I'm a secret princess, Trevor?"

"That's not the word we use, but, I mean…" He shrugged.

When I was little, I'd sometimes pretended to be a warrior princess. I wasn't opposed to a pretty dress, but I wanted an axe, too. "Granny asked me to come visit on my next birthday," I said. "My twenty-fifth. She said she was going to unlock my trust fund. 'If you're old enough to rent a car,' she said, 'you're old enough for the keys to the kingdom.'" I shook my head. "Trev, this all sounds ridiculous."

"Bollard and Chicane aren't ridiculous." He leaned over the table, looking at me earnestly. "They're killers and spies and ratfuckers for hire, legendary pieces of shit from the old country, and I don't know who sent them—it must be enemies of your family. Granny was in touch occasionally with people back home, all real secret, but maybe somebody got word you were coming of age and decided to kill you. Once Bollard and Chicane have a commission, nothing stops them until it's fulfilled—they're relentless. We have to get out of here. I have to keep you safe."

A huge man in a white suit, like a comic book villain or a pretentious novelist, entered the diner and walked ponderously over to the table. In a yeti-with-a-head-cold voice he said, "Move over, young sir."

Trev stared up at the man. I'd seen Trev attack a guy twice his size with a broken bottle, and charge into a crowd of frat boys swinging a bicycle chain while laughing, and once he'd *bitten* a *cop*—but now he went pale and whimpered and slid over against the wall.

The big man sat down, filling three-quarters of the bench and jostling the table with his bulk. He had a head like a boiled egg and eyes the color of dirt. "My name is Mr. Bollard." He tilted his head toward Trev. "Everything your paramour here said about other worlds is true."

Either everyone was insane in the same way, or the world was bigger than I'd realized. "How do you know what he said?"

"More of your grandmother's technology. Your phone has a microphone, and I have been listening through it since you left the house. I wasn't sure where you went—I gather it's possible to track phones, but annoyingly, I *don't* have that technology, and Mr. Chicane, who usually does our finding, is indisposed. Fortunately, your little internet assured me there was only one place locally that serves whatever 'cluck sauce' is, so I found you once you placed your order." He put his arm around Trev and pulled him close, into something between a side-hug and a headlock. "The young man misunderstands our mission, however. We had no idea you were a secret princess, or the true identity of your grandmother. So you're the lost heir to the Zmija estate. How strange to find you here. Like finding a diamond in a dung heap, as the saying goes."

"Zmija." The syllables were slippery in my mouth. "That's my name?" I should have been afraid, but I was too interested.

"It means, 'snake.'" He squeezed Trevor again. "Like the one he wears for a collar. I suppose that settles on which derivation of 'Culver' your grandmother meant. I should have suspected, but honestly, the cover-up back home was first-rate. I really believed your whole family was ripped up, root and branch. Everyone did. Though I must say, if you went back and managed to recover your ancestral estates, global politics would become interesting again. No one hired us to kill you—if they had, you'd be dead already."

"My grandmother *is* dead already."

Bollard inclined his head as if acknowledging a point scored. "She was uncooperative. She didn't go without a fight, though. She had hidden weapons, secreted in her body, and she was able to put a nasty dent in Mr. Chicane before we subdued her. That's why we were so careful and polite with you. If we'd realized you were defenseless and ignorant, we would have kidnapped you ages ago. We were afraid you might have hidden resources." Another squeeze. Trev wasn't even struggling, which was probably smart. "Besides your sex vassal."

Ew. "So if you aren't here for me, why are you here? Who hired you?"

"I regret to say we are here without the benefit of contract. Which is to say, without getting paid, a condition we despise. Mr. Chicane and I have enemies of our own. People usually understand that we're non-partisan. We fulfill our commissions, and we're loyal to our clients for the duration of those commissions. Alas, one of the oligarchs took our actions against him personally. He also has the technology to navigate nigh-space, and he used it to exile us. Mr. Chicane and I were meant to die in this backwater, with its empty skies and common colds and inedible food." He prodded the plate of steak and made a face. "Fortunately, Mr. Chicane has a nose for technology—part of his tracking suite—and he detected the signature of devices from our world. We investigated, and discovered the door in your grandmother's basement. We assumed she was a countryperson of ours who'd slipped through decades ago to become a queen among the savages. We asked her nicely to open the door and let us go home, but she refused. Something about refusing to do any favors for, 'garbage like us.'" He shrugged. "So we killed her, not without effort, and found her key. Too late, we discovered the key wasn't enough." He rose, still holding Trevor in his armpit. "If I let you go, will you behave? If you don't, it's not you I'll hurt, it's her. I need her alive, but not unbroken."

"Yes," Trevor breathed.

Bollard released him, straightened his lapels, and smiled at me. "Come along, princess. To the basement."

I still had the *misericorde* in my lap, so I tried to stab him, and he took the knife from me like taking a lollipop from a child, so deftly the waitress didn't even notice the commotion.

"Calm down. Don't make me murder all these witnesses. I detest killing people without getting paid."

"Does that mean you don't want to kill *us*?"

"I want to go home, princess. Help me do that, and you're welcome to rot here for the rest of your pitiful lifespans. How long do people even live over here? A hundred and fifty years? It's squalid."

Trevor looked at me, and I knew if I so much as nodded at him, he'd launch himself in a suicide attack and give me time to run away.

Spending the rest of my life looking over my shoulder wasn't appealing, though. I've always been more about looking forward.

So we left together, and I drove us back toward Culver House in Trev's truck, with Trevor beside me, and Bollard on his other side. Bollard put his arm around Trevor, around his neck again, and Trevor made a little squeaking noise as the big man squeezed him.

I tapped the brakes. "You said you wouldn't kill us."

"This is a blood choke," Bollard said. "I'm compressing the major arteries in his neck, but not his airway. No real harm. He's just going to take a little nap. He's too devoted to you. I'm afraid he might take unwise initiative." After a moment, Bollard released him, and Trev's head rested gently on my shoulder, just like in the old days when he'd get drunk at the movies. He was my only resource, and now he was asleep.

Hmm. Maybe not my *only* resource.

· · · · ·

Considering its mythic status in my own mind, the basement was disappointing in reality. There were two doors, the wooden one up top and a steel one at the bottom of the stairs, but beyond that was just a room with a workbench and stools, shelves covered in dusty bits of interdimensional technology, some books printed in an alphabet I didn't recognize, and a battered old leather couch, presumably where Granny took naps after a hard day of pretending to invent things. There was also a red metal door, set not flush in a wall but freestanding in a silver frame, facing another corner of the basement.

Mr. Bollard had Trevor slung over his shoulder, and he set him down on the floor, smoothed his suit again, and then took a long silver key from his pocket. "This was in the envelope your granny left for you, along with a letter written in a cipher we couldn't understand."

I groaned. "Granny had a code she always used, even when she emailed me. She said it was so outsiders wouldn't know our business, but she'd even write grocery lists in it. There's a key, but I learned to translate in my head by the time I was fifteen."

"I'm sure the letter says all those things about how you're a princess, and tells you how to use the door, but I already know *that* much. See?" He put the silver key in the door, turned it, and shoved. The door didn't budge, but a recording of my grandmother's annoyed voice said, "Unauthorized user."

"We didn't realize we needed your grandmother alive until it was too late. The lock is more than biometrics or facial recognition—Mr. Chicane dragged the body down here and tried all that. Such locks are common among the dynasties back home, they sniff your genome and confirm you're alive, and so forth. The door is barred to me, but you, princess: I believe you can open it, and let us go back home, to all our beloved pleasures, diversions, and scores that need settling."

I crossed my arms. "What's in it for me?"

He took a business card from an inner pocket and silently handed it to me.

BOLLARD AND CHICANE

WE KILLED YOUR GRANNY + WE'LL KILL YOU
WE'LL KILL EVERYONE YOU KNOW

. 5ℝE [a ꝺ [Z ⨍ꝺ [ꭥ TM˜ꭥ ꝺ⸮Meℓ.

I turned it over. Blank. "No personalized message this time?"

"I believe the card speaks for itself."

"Nice try. You can't kill me, though. You said so yourself. Not if you want to get home."

"What if I kill Trevor?"

I didn't even look at Trev's slumped body. "Then you'll save the state a lot of money in future incarceration costs?"

Bollard chuckled. "Are you really so cold? Your grandmother was, when she ruled the family. The Serpent of the Zmija, they called her, which is a bit like calling someone the Insect of the Bug, but never mind. Assuming you don't care about Trevor, you do care about *you*. There's dead, and there's alive, but those aren't the only possible states of being. You don't need eyes or a tongue to open a door. Normally, Mr. Chicane does the elective surgeries— you'd be the one electing for said surgeries by refusing to help us, of course—but since he is currently indisposed, I'll manage. The knife I took from you seems sharp enough."

My mind spun through possibilities. Maybe Granny had refused because she had some history with them—Bollard and Chicane could have murdered her cousins or something—but I suspect she was motivated by her basic stubbornness. No one told her what to do; she told *other* people what to do. Me, personally? I didn't really care if this asshole went through the door. But if I was suddenly in a land of miracles, there should be some miracles in it for me. It turned out I had a birthright, stolen and hidden, and I wanted it back.

It's like this: San Francisco was a lot nicer than my hometown, and I moved there as soon as I could and never looked back. It sounded like the world beyond that door would make San Francisco look like a latrine. Technological wonders, long life, an existence infinitely more exciting than eating takeout and writing code. Forget disruptive innovation. This was disruptive reality.

Of course, even San Francisco sucked if you didn't have friends to show you around and money to enjoy things, and on another page of nigh-space, I wouldn't have either one.

Unless.

I held up the little rectangle in my hand. "This is a business card."

"That's true. The suit makes them." Bollard patted his breast pocket. "Very convenient."

"You're businessmen. You can be hired."

He cocked his head. "You propose to offer us a commission? How would you pay? I understand your grandmother was wealthy in this world, but from our point of view, you'd be offering us glass beads."

"Trevor said something about my family's vaults, on the other side."

"Ah. Hmm. The Zmija vaults." He looked to the ceiling for a moment. "Which are inaccessible, both because they are surrounded by the forces of your ancestral enemies, and because they are locked against anyone who isn't part of your family. But you carry the genetic legacy of your parents and grandparents, so they would open, for you... What would you be hiring Mr. Chicane and myself to do, besides liberating the vaults so you could pay us in the first place?"

"I just found out I'm a princess," I said. "I think I'd *like* being a princess. I could use help. Royal advisers. Could you help me regain my family's throne?"

"It's not a *throne*, but yes, we have some experience with regime change. It says so right on our business card. Sometimes." He considered me. "You would really hire us, miss? Even after we killed your grandmother?"

"Obviously, I wish you hadn't done that. But... I can understand why you had the impulse."

He snorted. "If I had any doubt about your heritage, you just dispelled it. How very like your ancestors you are. Mmm. Once we got to the other side, I'd have to go to my workshop first, and decant a new Chicane. Between your grandmother and your vassal, my old one is too damaged."

There was no point in looking surprised. "I trust your expertise." I pointed to Trev. "We should take him with us."

"Ah. You aren't so cold after all?"

"I'm cold enough. But a princess needs retainers."

Mr. Bollard chuckled, then reached out. It was like shaking hands with a polar bear. "I look forward to our partnership, princess."

Here's the thing that gets me about **Ken Liu**: the guy is humble. Back in the early teens he was achieving multiple successes with his short fiction, sweeping up award after award, when he sent a reprint submission to *Escape Pod*. We were so excited to get a Ken Liu story that after a quick read, we accepted it. Ken's response made us feel like the *Big Time Magazine*—he was so polite and excited to have sold a reprint to our small podcast market. Ken's response made me realize that our little magazine was making a mark. People noticed, and cared about what we were doing. (Or it could be that he was just really nice to make us feel that way. Didn't matter. It was a great feeling.) It was a no-brainer to have a story by him in our anthology. It was unsurprising that, even with Ken being a bigger deal now than ever, he responded within two hours and said he was delighted to give us permission to reprint this beautiful story.

MUR

AN ADVANCED READER'S PICTURE BOOK OF COMPARATIVE COGNITION

KEN LIU

My darling, my child, my connoisseur of sesquipedalian words and convoluted ideas and meandering sentences and baroque images, while the sun is asleep and the moon somnambulant, while the stars bathe us in their glow from eons ago and light-years away, while you are comfortably nestled in your blankets and I am hunched over in my chair by your bed, while we are warm and safe and still for the moment in this bubble of incandescent light cast by the pearl held up by the mermaid lamp, you and I, on this planet spinning and hurtling through the frigid darkness of space at dozens of miles per second, let's read.

· · · · ·

The brains of Telosians record all the stimuli from their senses: every tingling along their hairy spine, every sound wave striking their membranous body, every image perceived by their simple-compound-refractive light-field eyes, every molecular gustatory and olfactory sensation captured by their waving stalk-feet, every ebb and flow in the magnetic field of their irregular, potato-shaped planet.

When they wish, they can recall every experience with absolute fidelity. They can freeze a scene and zoom in to focus on any detail; they can parse and re-parse each conversation to extract every nuance. A joyful memory may be relived countless times, each replay introducing new discoveries. A painful memory may be replayed countless times as well, each time creating a fresh outrage. Eidetic reminiscence is a fact of existence.

Infinity pressing down upon the finite is clearly untenable.

The Telosian organ of cognition is housed inside a segmented body that buds and grows at one end while withering and shedding at the other. Every year, a fresh segment is added at the head to record the future; every year, an old segment is discarded from the tail, consigning the past to oblivion.

Thus, while the Telosians do not forget, they also do not remember. They are said to never die, but it is arguable whether they ever live.

· · · · ·

It has been argued that thinking is a form of compression.

Remember the first time you tasted chocolate? It was a summer afternoon; your mother had just come back from shopping. She broke off a piece from a candy bar and put it in your mouth while you sat in the highchair.

As the stearate in the cocoa butter absorbed the heat from your mouth and melted over your tongue, complex alkaloids were released and seeped into your taste buds: twitchy caffeine, giddy phenethylamine, serotonic theobromine.

"Theobromine," your mother said, "means the food of the gods."

We laughed as we watched your eyes widen in surprise at the texture, your face scrunch up at the biting bitterness, and then your whole body relax as the sweetness overwhelmed your taste buds, aided by the dance of a thousand disparate organic compounds.

Then she broke the rest of the chocolate bar in halves and fed a piece to me and ate the other herself. "We have children because we can't remember our own first taste of ambrosia."

I can't remember the dress she wore or what she had bought; I can't remember what we did for the rest of that afternoon; I can't recreate the exact timbre of her voice or the precise shapes of her features, the lines at the corners of her mouth or the name of her perfume. I only remember the way sunlight through the kitchen window glinted from her forearm, an arc as lovely as her smile.

A lit forearm, laughter, food of the gods. Thus are our memories compressed, integrated into sparkling jewels to be embedded in the limited space of our minds. A scene is turned into a mnemonic, a conversation reduced to a single phrase, a day distilled to a fleeting feeling of joy.

Time's arrow is the loss of fidelity in compression. A sketch, not a photograph. A memory is a re-creation, precious because it is both more and less than the original.

· · · · ·

Living in a warm, endless sea rich with light and clumps of organic molecules, the Esoptrons resemble magnified cells, some as large as our whales. Undulating their translucent bodies, they drift, rising and falling, tumbling and twisting, like phosphorescent jellyfish riding on the current.

The thoughts of Esoptrons are encoded as complex chains of proteins that fold upon themselves like serpents coiling in the snake charmer's basket, seeking the lowest energy level so that they may fit into the smallest space. Most of the time, they lie dormant.

When two Esoptrons encounter each other, they may merge temporarily, a tunnel forming between their membranes. This kissing union can last hours, days, or years, as their memories are awakened and exchanged with energy contributions from both members. The pleasurable ones are selectively duplicated in a process much like protein expression—the serpentine proteins unfold and dance mesmerizingly in the electric music of coding sequences as they're first read and then re-expressed—while the unpleasant ones are diluted by being spread among the two bodies. For the Esoptrons, a shared joy truly is doubled, while a shared sorrow is indeed halved.

By the time they part, they each have absorbed the experiences of the other. It is the truest form of empathy, for the very qualia of experience are shared and expressed without alteration. There is no translation, no medium of exchange. They come to know each other in a deeper sense than any other creatures in the universe.

But being the mirrors for each other's souls has a cost: by the time they part from each other, the individuals in the mating pair have become indistinguishable. Before their merger, they each yearned for the other; as they part, they part from the self. The very quality that attracted them to each other is also, inevitably, destroyed in their union.

Whether this is a blessing or a curse is much debated.

. . . . .

Your mother has never hidden her desire to leave.

We met on a summer night, in a campground high up in the Rockies. We were from opposite coasts, two random particles on separate trajectories: I was headed for a new job, driving across the country and camping to save money; she was returning to Boston after having moved a friend and her truckful of possessions to San Francisco, camping because she wanted to look at the stars.

We drank cheap wine and ate even cheaper grilled hot dogs. Then we walked together under the dark velvet dome studded with crystalline stars like the inside of a geode, brighter than I'd ever seen them, while she explained to me their beauty: each as unique as a diamond, with a different-colored light. I could not remember the last time I'd looked up at the stars.

"I'm going there," she said.

"You mean Mars?" That was the big news back then, the announcement of a mission to Mars. Everyone knew it was a propaganda effort to make America seem great again, a new space race to go along with the new nuclear arms race and the stockpiling of rare earth elements and zero-day cyber vulnerabilities. The other side had already promised their own Martian base, and we had to mirror their move in this new Great Game.

She shook her head. "What's the point of jumping onto a reef just a few steps from shore? I mean out there."

It was not the kind of statement one questioned, so instead of why and how and what are you talking about, I asked her what she hoped to find out there among the stars.

other Suns perhaps
With thir attendant Moons thou wilt descri
Communicating Male and Femal Light,
Which two great Sexes animate the World,
Stor'd in each Orb perhaps with some that live.
For such vast room in Nature unpossest
By living Soule, desert and desolate,
Onely to shine, yet scarce to contribute
Each Orb a glimps of Light, conveyd so farr
Down to this habitable, which returnes
Light back to them, is obvious to dispute.

"What do they think about? How do they experience the world? I've been imagining such stories all my life, but the truth will be stranger and more wonderful than any fairy tale."

She spoke to me of gravitational lenses and nuclear pulse propulsion, of the Fermi Paradox and the Drake Equation, of Arecibo and Yevpatoria, of Blue Origin and SpaceX.

"Aren't you afraid?" I asked.

"I almost died before I could begin to remember."

She told me about her childhood. Her parents were avid sailors who had been lucky enough to retire early. They bought a boat and lived on it, and the boat was her first home. When she was three, her parents decided to sail across the Pacific. Halfway across the ocean, somewhere near the Marshall Islands, the boat sprung a leak. The family tried everything they could to save the vessel, but in the end had to activate the emergency beacon to call for help.

"That was my very first memory. I wobbled on this immense bridge between the sea and the sky, and as it sank into the water and we had to jump off, Mom had me say goodbye."

By the time they were rescued by a Coastguard plane, they had been adrift in the water in life vests for almost a full day and night. Sunburnt and sickened by the salt water she swallowed, she spent a month in the hospital afterwards.

"A lot of people were angry at my parents, saying they were reckless and irresponsible to endanger a child like that. But I'm forever grateful to them. They gave me the greatest gift parents could give to a child: fearlessness. They worked and saved and bought another boat, and we went out to the sea again."

It was such an alien way of thinking that I didn't know what to say. She seemed to detect my unease, and, turning to me, smiled.

"I like to think we were carrying on the tradition of the Polynesians who set out across the endless Pacific in their canoes or the Vikings who sailed for America. We have always lived on a boat, you know? That's what Earth is, a boat in space."

For a moment, as I listened to her, I felt as if I could step through the distance between us and hear an echo of the world through her ears, see the stars through her eyes: an austere clarity that made my heart leap.

Cheap wine and burnt hot dogs, other Suns perhaps, the diamonds in the sky seen from a boat adrift at sea, the fiery clarity of falling in love.

· · · · ·

The Tick-Tocks are the only uranium-based life forms known in the universe.

The surface of their planet is an endless vista of bare rock. To human eyes it seems a wasteland, but etched into this surface are elaborate, colorful patterns at an immense scale, each as large as an airport or stadium: curlicues like calligraphy strokes; spirals like the tips of fiddlehead ferns; hyperbolas like the shadows of flashlights against a cave wall; dense, radiating clusters like glowing cities seen from space. From time to time, a plume of superheated steam erupts from the ground like the blow of a whale or the explosion of an ice volcano on Enceladus.

Where are the creatures who left these monumental sketches? These tributes to lives lived and lost, these recordings of joys and sorrows known and forgotten?

You dig beneath the surface. Tunneling into the sandstone deposits over granite bedrock, you find pockets of uranium steeped in water.

In the darkness, the nucleus of a uranium atom spontaneously breaks apart, releasing a few neutrons. The neutrons travel through the vast emptiness of internuclear space like ships bound for strange stars (this is not really an accurate picture, but it's a romantic image and easy to illustrate). The water molecules, nebula-like, slow down the neutrons until they touch down on another uranium nucleus, a new world.

But the addition of this new neutron makes the nucleus unstable. It oscillates like a ringing alarm clock, breaks apart into two new elemental nuclei and two or three neutrons, new starships bound for distant worlds, to begin the cycle again.

To have a self-sustaining nuclear chain reaction with uranium, you need enough concentration of the right kind of uranium,

uranium–235, which breaks apart when it absorbs the free neutrons, and something to slow down the speeding neutrons so that they can be absorbed, and water works well enough. Creation has blessed the world of the Tick-Tocks with both.

The byproducts of fission, those fragments split from the uranium atom, fall along a bimodal distribution. Caesium, iodine, xenon, zirconium, molybdenum, technetium… like new stars formed from the remnants of a supernova, some last a few hours, others millions of years.

The thoughts and memories of the Tick-Tocks are formed from these glowing jewels in the dark sea. The atoms take the place of neurons, and the neutrons act as neurotransmitters. The moderating medium and neutron poisons act as inhibitors and deflect the flight of neutrons, forming neural pathways through the void. The computation process emerges at the subatomic level, and is manifested in the flight paths of messenger neutrons; the topology, composition, and arrangement of atoms; and the brilliant flashes of fissile explosion and decay.

As the thoughts of the Tick-Tocks grow ever more lively, excited, the water in the pockets of uranium heats up. When the pressure is great enough, a stream of superheated water flows up a crack in the sandstone cap and explodes at the surface in a plume of steam. The grand, intricate, fractal patterns made by the varicolored salt deposits they leave on the surface resemble the ionization trails left by subatomic particles in a bubble chamber.

Eventually, enough of the water will have been boiled away that the fast neutrons can no longer be captured by the uranium atoms to sustain the reaction. The universe sinks into quiescence, and thoughts disappear from this galaxy of atoms. This is how the Tick-Tocks die: with the heat of their own vitality.

Gradually, water seeps back into the mines, trickling through seams in the sandstone and cracks in the granite. When enough water has filled the husk of the past, a random decaying atom will release the neutron that will start the chain reaction again, ushering forth a florescence of new ideas and new beliefs, a new generation of life lit from the embers of the old.

Some have disputed the notion that the Tick-Tocks can think. How can they be said to be thinking, the skeptics ask, when the flight of neutrons is determined by the laws of physics with a soupçon of quantum randomness? Where is their free will? Where is their self-determination? Meanwhile, the electrochemical reactor piles in the skeptics' brains hum along, following the laws of physics with an indistinguishable rigor.

Like tides, the Tick-Tock nuclear reactions operate in pulses. Cycle after cycle, each generation discovers the world anew. The ancients leave no wisdom for the future, and the young do not look to the past. They live for one season and one season alone.

Yet, on the surface of the planet, in those etched, fantastic rock paintings, is a palimpsest of their rise and fall, the exhalations of empires. The chronicles of the Tick-Tocks are left for other intelligences in the cosmos to interpret.

As the Tick-Tocks flourish, they also deplete the concentration of uranium-235. Each generation consumes some of the non-renewable resources of their universe, leaving less for future generations and beckoning closer the day when a sustained chain reaction will no longer be possible. Like a clock winding down inexorably, the world of the Tick-Tocks will then sink into an eternal, cold silence.

. . . . .

Your mother's excitement was palpable.

"Can you call a realtor?" she asked. "I'll get started on liquidating our stocks. We don't need to save anymore. Your mother is going to go on that cruise she's always wanted."

"When did we win the lottery?" I asked.

She handed me a stack of paper. *LENS Program Orientation.*

I flipped through it. *...Your application essay is among the most extraordinary entries we've received... pending a physical examination and psychological evaluation... limited to the immediate family...*

"What is this?"

Her face fell as she realized that I truly did not understand.

Radio waves attenuated rapidly in the vastness of space, she explained. If anyone is shouting into the void in the orbs around those distant stars, they would not be heard except by their closest neighbors. A civilization would have to harness the energy of an entire star to broadcast a message that could traverse interstellar distances—and how often would that happen? Look at the Earth: we'd barely managed to survive one Cold War before another started. Long before we get to the point of harnessing the energy of the Sun, our children will be either wading through a post-apocalyptic flooded landscape or shivering in a nuclear winter, back in another Stone Age.

"But there is a way to cheat, a way for even a primitive civilization like ours to catch faint whispers from across the galaxy and perhaps even answer back."

The Sun's gravity bends the light and radio waves from distant stars around it. This is one of the most important results from general relativity.

Suppose some other world out there in our galaxy, not much more advanced than ours, sent out a message with the most powerful antenna they could construct. By the time those emissions reached us, the electromagnetic waves would be so faint as to be undetectable. We'd have to turn the entire Solar System into a parabolic dish to capture it.

But as those radio waves grazed the surface of the Sun, the gravity of the star would bend them slightly, much as a lens bends rays of light. Those slightly bent beams from around the rim of the Sun would converge at some distance beyond.

"Just as rays of sunlight could be focused by a magnifying glass into a spot on the ground."

The gain of an antenna placed at the focal point of the sun's gravitational lens would be enormous, close to ten billion times in certain frequency ranges, and orders of magnitude more in others. Even a twelve-meter inflatable dish would be able to detect transmissions from the other end of the galaxy. And if others in the galaxy were also clever enough to harness the gravitational lenses of their own suns, we would be able to talk to them as well—though the exchange would more resemble monologues delivered across the lifetimes of stars than a conversation, messages set adrift in bottles bound for distant shores, from one long-dead generation to generations yet unborn.

This spot, as it turns out, is about 550 AU from the Sun, almost fourteen times the distance of Pluto. The Sun's light would take just over three days to reach it, but at our present level of technology, it would take more than a century for a spacecraft.

Why send people? Why now?

"Because by the time an automated probe reached the focal point, we don't know if anyone will still be here. Will the human race survive even another century? No, we must send people so that they can be there to listen, and perhaps talk back.

"I'm going, and I'd like you to come with me."

. . . . .

The Thereals live within the hulls of great starships.

Their species, sensing the catastrophe of a world-ending disaster, commissioned the construction of escape arks for a small percentage of their world's population. Almost all of the refugees were children, for the Thereals loved their young as much as any other species.

Years before their star went supernova, the arks were launched in various directions at possible new home worlds. The ships began to accelerate, and the children settled down to learning from machine tutors and the few adults on board, trying to carry on the traditions of a dying world.

Only when the last of the adults were about to die aboard each ship did they reveal the truth to the children: the ships were not equipped with means for deceleration. They would accelerate forever, asymptotically approaching the speed of light, until the ships ran out of fuel and coasted along at the final cruising speed, towards the end of the universe.

Within their frame of reference, time would pass normally. But outside the ship, the rest of the universe would be hurtling along to its ultimate doom against the tide of entropy. To an outside observer, time seemed to stop in the ships.

Plucked out of the stream of time, the children would grow a few years older, but not much more. They would die only when the universe ended. This was the only way to ensure their safety, the adults explained, an asymptotic approach to triumphing over death. They would never have their own children; they would never have to mourn; they would never have to fear, to plan, to make impossible choices in sacrifice. They would be the last Thereals alive, and possibly the last intelligent beings in the universe.

All parents make choices for their children. Almost always they think it's for the best.

$\cdot\ \cdot\ \cdot\ \cdot\ \cdot$

All along, I had thought I could change her. I had thought she would want to stay because of me, because of our child. I had loved her because she was different; I also thought she would transform out of love.

"Love has many forms," she said. "This is mine."

Many are the stories we tell ourselves of the inevitable parting of lovers when they're from different worlds: selkies, gu huo niao, Hagoromo, swan maidens… What they have in common is the belief by one half of a couple that the other half could be changed, when in fact it was the difference, the resistance to change, that formed the foundation of their love. And then the day would come when the old sealskin or feather cape would be found, and it would be time to return to the sea or the sky, the ethereal realm that was the beloved's true home.

The crew of *Focal Point* would spend part of the voyage in hibernation; but once they reached their first target point, 550 AU from the Sun, away from the galactic center, they would have to stay awake and listen for as long as they could. They would guide the ship along a helical path away from the Sun, sweeping out a larger slice of the galaxy from which they might detect signals. The farther they drifted from the Sun, the better the Sun's magnification effect would be due to the reduction of interference from the solar corona on the deflected radio waves. The crew was expected to last as long as a few centuries, growing up, growing old, having children to carry on their work, dying in the void, an outpost of austere hope.

"You can't make a choice like that for our daughter," I said.

"You're making a choice for her, too. How do you know if she'll be safer or happier here? This is a chance for transcendence, the best gift we can give her."

And then came the lawyers and the reporters and the pundits armed with soundbites taking sides.

Then the night that you tell me you still remember. It was your birthday, and we were together again, just the three of us, for your sake because you said that was what you wished.

We had chocolate cake (you requested "teo-broom"). Then we went outside onto the deck to look up at the stars. Your mother and I were careful to make no mention of the fight in the courts or the approaching date for her departure.

"Is it true you grew up on a boat, Mommy?" you asked.

"Yes."

"Was it scary?"

"Not at all. We're all living on a boat, sweetheart. The Earth is just a big raft in the sea of stars."

"Did you like living on a boat?"

"I loved that boat—well, I don't really remember. We don't remember much about what happened when we were really young; it's a quirk of being human. But I do remember being very sad when I had to say goodbye to it. I didn't want to. It was home."

"I don't want to say goodbye to my boat, either."

She cried. And so did I. So did you.

She gave you a kiss before she left. "There are many ways to say I love you."

* * * * *

The universe is full of echoes and shadows, the afterimages and last words of dead civilizations that have lost the struggle against entropy. Fading ripples in the cosmic background radiation, it is doubtful if most, or any, of these messages will ever be deciphered.

Likewise, most of our thoughts and memories are destined to fade, to disappear, to be consumed by the very act of choosing and living.

That is not a cause for sorrow, sweetheart. It is the fate of every species to disappear into the void that is the heat death of the universe. But long before then, the thoughts of any intelligent species worthy of the name will become as grand as the universe itself.

* * * * *

Your mother is asleep now on *Focal Point*. She will not wake up until you're a very old woman, possibly not even until after you're gone.

After she wakes up, she and her crewmates will begin to listen, and they'll also broadcast, hoping that somewhere else in the universe, another species is also harnessing the energy of their star to focus the faint rays across light-years and eons. They'll play a message designed to introduce us to strangers, written in a language based on mathematics and logic. I've always found it funny that we think the best way to communicate with extraterrestrials is to speak in a way that we never do in life.

But at the end, as a closing, there will be a recording of compressed memories that will not be very logical: the graceful arc of whales breaching, the flicker of campfire and wild dancing, the formulas of chemicals making up the smell of a thousand foods, including cheap wine and burnt hot dogs, the laughter of a child eating the food of the gods for the first time. Glittering jewels whose meanings are not transparent, and for that reason, are alive.

And so we read this, my darling, this book she wrote for you before she left, its ornate words and elaborate illustrations telling fairy tales that will grow as you grow, an apologia, a bundle of letters home, and a map of the uncharted waters of our souls.

There are many ways to say I love you in this cold, dark, silent universe, as many as the twinkling stars.

When we asked **Sarah Gailey** for a story, we knew we weren't going to get anything that fit neatly into a science-fictional box. Nothing about Sarah is that tidy, but they do know how to tell glorious tales. I've had the privilege of watching Sarah's career skyrocket and thrive, and I'm absolutely thrilled to bring you this short story from them. You've probably heard of people being described as sharks or doves or pigs, but have you ever heard of them as tigers? They might look like oversized versions of our feline friends, but tigers also have a keen sense of justice.

DIVYA

TIGER LAWYER GETS IT RIGHT
SARAH GAILEY

Vladislav Argyle rested his head on the cool titanium surface of the defendant's table. It dipped a little under the sudden weight of his skull, then hummed as the antigrav lifts adjusted their power to accommodate their new burden.

"Mr. Argyle? Are you alright?" The bandage-swathed tip of Argyle's client's primary tentacle crackled near his ear, and he knew that she was touching his temple in a gesture of inquiry. The people of Ursa Vibrania were very skull-oriented in their communications. It was sweet, really, how they wanted to know what was happening inside every other endoskeletal vertebrate creature's head. How much they wanted to understand.

Argyle clenched his fists in his lap. The Vibranians were so kind, and they had trusted him to help them, and he was failing. As always.

"I'm fine," he said through his teeth. "Just a little ritual I have after opening statements."

Technically, the person sitting next to Argyle was a symbol.

An entire planetoid couldn't fit in the seat on the defendant's side of the courtroom, so they'd chosen someone who they thought best represented their case: Nxania V, an adolescent of the most-developed sapient species on the husk of what had once been her homeworld. The optics were perfect. Nxania was covered in bandages to hide her weeping sores, and her growth had been stunted by the ruination of her planetoid, so her skull seemed just a little too big for her body. Her physique appealed to humanoids, who appreciated the childlike vulnerability of a big head wobbling around on a little body; and it appealed to Vibranians, who tended to correlate large skulls with trustworthiness and transparency.

The media loved Vibrania v. Blick. They loved the narrative of the corrupt, greedy corporation exploiting the resources of the vulnerable planetoid of empaths. All those images of Vibranian children with burns on their tentacles, little old Vibranian priests with their half-melted scepters raised to the sky, orbital images of the exposed rift down the center of the Primary Continent—it played like a drama vid. And on the other side of the equation, there was Blick Media, Electricity, Gas & Capital, the louche ultramonopoly passed down through the hands of twenty generations of Blicks.

The Blicks could have swept the case under the rug. That's what Argyle had expected would happen when he took the case on: a settlement big enough to evacuate Ursa Vibrania, but not so big that Blick MEGC would have to file for bankruptcy. Vibrania v. Blick was never supposed to see a courtroom. Argyle counted settlements as wins, and he had *really* hoped that this case would be his first win.

But of course, nothing could be that easy. The media and the public saw this case as Good People versus Evil Corporation, and the Blick family couldn't stand to let that narrative go unanswered. It wasn't enough for them to have more money than they could count; they wanted the public to love them, too.

That love was one of the only things they truly couldn't buy. It was one of the only things that remained out of their reach—but they wanted it. So they'd let the case go to trial. Opening statements were over now, and Argyle could see the familiar silhouette of failure looming on the horizon. That silhouette was shaped a lot like opposing counsel, the representative for the defense: Astor Valentine.

And it was looming awfully close.

"You doing alright, Argyle?" Valentine's voice was as silky as butter. His sharkskin shoes appeared in Argyle's field of vision, just under the lip of the defendant's table. "Deep breaths, buddy. It'll all be over soon."

Argyle lifted his head from the titanium and regarded his opponent. Valentine was everything Argyle wasn't, everything Argyle had never been. He was smooth and polished. He was graceful and charming. He was good at practicing law.

"How do you do it, Valentine?" Argyle said. He used the arm of his threadbare suit to mop sweat from his top lip. "Is it true what they say? Are you really sharkmodded?"

Valentine's lips twitched up into an effortlessly winsome smile. He seemed to have too many teeth for his mouth, and his eyes had a predatory gleam that lent a sort of terrifying sensuality to his appeal. It was common gossip that he'd been modded by the best surgeons in the business. At the sight of that smile, Argyle's mouth went dry at the same time as his armpits went damp.

"I don't need mods, my friend," Valentine purred. "I'm just better than you." He rested a heavy, well-manicured hand on Argyle's shoulder. "See you tomorrow? I'm looking forward to it."

"Yeah," Argyle muttered, and before he could find a way to thank Valentine for humiliating him, he was overwhelmed by a fog of gin-smell.

"Why are you talking to them?" Leopold Blick appeared beside Valentine, his lip curled into a comfortable sneer.

Valentine closed his eyes for a moment. Argyle wondered how much Valentine must hate Blick—he'd never seen the other lawyer gather his patience like that. Usually, Valentine's face was as serene as the ice rings of the Capitol Moons.

It made sense that this Blick would be the one to test Valentine's patience. He was the humanoid equivalent of an amphetamine hangover. Blick was not a young man, but he was heavily modded to look like one, and the ill-fitting skin of his face made him seem drawn and nervous. He shifted his weight from foot to foot, glancing around the room, twitching his mouth in and out of a smile whenever someone important caught his eye.

Argyle privately suspected that Valentine had not wanted Leopold Blick V to be the face of the family in court, but Nana Blick was on a private safari hunting moon-whales, and Alphonse Blick, the family patriarch, was confined to a financial detoxification facility by court order. So instead of either of them, it was to be the favorite son of the family and the acting Tsar of Operations and Finances who would sit beside Valentine, to try to convince the courtroom that his company had done the right thing by illegally splitting an inhabited planetoid in half.

And he would probably succeed. No matter how terrible and loathsome he was, he couldn't make Argyle a better lawyer.

"I was just leaving," Valentine hissed at Blick. He patted Argyle's shoulder one more time, then pivoted smoothly toward his client. "Let's get out of here. I want you rested up and sober for tomorrow."

Blick looked past Valentine, his eyes narrowed at Argyle. "We're gonna eat you alive, you little weasel," he spat. "You're a pathetic excuse for a lawyer. *Pathetic*."

Valentine stepped between them. He grabbed his client by the lapels, giving him a brief shake before smoothing out the crumpled fabric. "That's goddamn enough. You're twitching like an electrified catmod, Blick. Go home. Hydrate."

The two of them left without so much as looking back at Argyle. They hadn't felt a need to put on a good face in front of him. They hadn't felt a need to pretend to have their shit together.

"Mr. Argyle?" Nxania's soft voice was in his ear, and he realized that he'd forgotten all about her, that he'd failed to pretend to have *his* shit together in front of *her*, and he closed his eyes tight to shut out his pathetic excuse for a life. He felt a tentacle brush his forehead. "Can I help?"

"I'm supposed to be the one helping you," he said. "I'm sorry, Nxania. I wish I'd told you to hire someone else. Someone better. He's right," he sighed. "They're gonna eat us alive."

She was quiet for a long time, gently brushing the wisps of Argyle's thinning hair with her tentacles, reading the tiny spasms of his brain through the bones of his skull. After a few minutes, she spoke again, this time to ask a question. "What's a catmod?"

Argyle was surprised by the question. But then he remembered that he was talking to a sick child from a backwater planetoid that had more mineshafts than health clinics. Of course she wouldn't know.

"Mods," he said, "are changes people make to their bodies, and on this planet—well, lots of planets—well, and off-planet, on special pleasure cruise liners that are equipped with hospital facilities—wait." He stopped himself, realizing that he'd gotten away from his original point, the same way he had during opening statements. "Um. People like to do animal mods, where they make themselves look sort of like an animal. They add things like whiskers, or tails, or little noses. Like a cat."

"Why?"

Argyle didn't know how to answer this, because there were an awful lot of factors involved in people's decisions to do whatever levels of mods they did, and he didn't want to seem judgmental.

But then Nxania added to her question, "Does it make them better lawyers?"

Argyle shrugged. He shrugged often—once a judge had called him to the bench about it, calling him a "depressing hillock."

"I don't think so," he said. "It's not really about the lawyering part of a person."

Nxania chittered thoughtfully. "Does it make them better hunters?"

Argyle lifted his head up and looked at her, the twitching of his brain speeding up for the first time since the judge had called the court to order that morning. "I suppose it could," he said slowly, "depending on how thorough you were."

Nxania's feathery pedipalps flexed in front of her mouth. "Interesting," she said. "Well. I've transferred the credits for your fee, as well as a small gift of appreciation from my planet. It's only a small percentage of the donations we received today, as a result of the attention you've helped draw to our cause. Thank you for taking on our case, even when we couldn't pay you very much. We know it's a hard job you do, Mr. Argyle, and we appreciate you taking us on."

She brushed her tentacles over his temples one last time, and then she wafted out of the courtroom, looking as frail as a nitrogenated jellyfish. Argyle felt the buzz of his datachip and glanced down at the freckled flesh of his wrist to see a readout.

The credits had been transferred, along with what looked like an astonishingly generous gift. Too generous to simply be a thank you. It was more money than he'd ever seen at one time.

Argyle's brain thumped hard against its own folds, and for the first time that day, the thing extruded by that poor beleaguered organ was not dread or despair or defeat.

For the first time that day, Vladislav Argyle had a good idea.

· · · · ·

Astor Valentine truly did hate his client.

He hated the man's ultrafashionable suit, which fit his entire body like a wet sock fits the swollen foot of a corpse. He hated the man's voice, which was artificially high and sweet, modded to sound like the voice of a twenty-year-old who had never tried a designer drug. He hated the man's shifty eyes and sweatless brow, his habits and his manner, his very soul.

But he did not hate his client's money. And Blick had so *much* money.

"Do you feel bad about it?" Valentine murmured to Blick out of the side of his mouth.

Blick flinched at even these soft words, his hangover clinging to him with palpable malevolence. "I just didn't drink enough water," he snapped. "Why should I feel bad about having a little headache?"

Valentine grimaced. "I meant Vibrania," he replied. "Do you feel bad about sucking the middle out of Vibrania? Destroying all those people's lives?"

Blick let out an elaborate, irritated sigh. "Oh, for fuck's sake," he hissed. "As if I don't get enough of this from the papers? Those people—listen. Their planet had *so much zinc* in it. Do you know how hard it is to find zinc in that quadrant? They wanted jobs, we gave them jobs. Aren't you supposed to be on my side here?"

Valentine didn't reply. He simply looked across the courtroom at the little Vibranian girl who was sitting alone behind the defendant's table, waiting for her terrible lawyer to arrive. Three of her tentacles were folded on the titanium in front of her. Her bandages looked tattered. He wondered when they'd last been changed.

The judge and jury filed in. Court was called to order. And yet Argyle was nowhere to be seen. The judge asked Nxania, in a stern but gentle voice, if she knew where her attorney was.

"He's on the way," she said sweetly. "I anticipate his arrival within the next several minutes."

"Do you know that because he told you, or because you…"

The judge paused, unsure of how to finish their question without offending. They waved a hand at Nxania, then gestured at their own head.

"No, I haven't mind-bonded with him," Nxania said. "That would be terribly unethical. I simply… know his habits, and he tends to be late," she finished.

The abundant hair on the back of Valentine's neck prickled the way it always did when a witness was lying. She wasn't wrong that Argyle was often late to things—the man seemed incapable of catching his intended train. But something wasn't right. Something in Nxania's voice snagged his attention.

Before he could speculate, the door to the courtroom slid smoothly open. The attention of the room swiveled toward that open door, like a full church turning to watch a bride walk down the aisle. A murmur began to build among the gathered journalists, activists, and spectators, and Valentine's skin began to crawl with dread.

"I believe that's him now," Nxania piped. She did not turn to look at Argyle as he entered the room.

But everyone else did, because it was not a slump-shouldered, bedraggled, defeated failure of a lawyer walking up the middle of the courtroom.

It was a tiger.

Not a man with tiger stripes tattooed across his face; not a heavily-modded humanoid with functional whiskers and artificially inflated haunches. Valentine had seen more than his fair share of those, clients with a lot of money and a desire to walk the line between what they were and what they might be.

This wasn't that. No, this was a tiger, in form and in function, unadulterated by any DNA that had not originated in a jungle that was ripe with prey.

The tiger padded toward the bench, unhurried, unselfconscious. He moved like liquid, but there was a terrifying and undeniable solidity to him; the very air parted around his seething muscles, and every twitch of his striped ears felt like a portent of violence. He paused beside a row of reporters and regarded them. He yawned, his enormous maw gaping wide to reveal teeth that were made for meat, a tongue that was rasped heavily enough to strip flesh from bone, a throat that could accommodate a human hand without too much effort.

He blinked slowly at the reporters before returning to his amble down the center aisle of the courtroom. Valentine was a cat person; he knew, intellectually, that the yawn and the slow-blink had been a sign of affection, of appreciation, of camaraderie. But that knowledge could not remove from his brain—nor, he imagined, from the brains of the reporters—the understanding that, to a creature like a tiger, everyone in the room fell into the category of *prey*.

The tiger's friendly overture could not undo the length of his teeth. Valentine's bladder suddenly felt very full.

The bailiff took a hesitant step toward the tiger, his hand drifting toward the stunner on his belt. That stunner was not calibrated for a tiger, and Valentine had no idea whether it would have any effect on the beast other than to annoy it. He felt briefly as though he were in a childhood nightmare; this was absurd, a tiger in the courtroom, a wild animal from a far-off planet coming to interrupt his case.

He was gripped by a wild flare of indignance. Reality could not contain a tiger. Not here. He wouldn't stand for it.

"Get out of here," he said, and then he stood up out of his chair and he said it again, louder and more certain. "Get out of here, tiger! You're... you're in the wrong place!" It was ridiculous, what he was saying, and he knew it, but he put the weight of his closing-argument-voice behind it, and he managed to make the words sound authoritative. He pointed to the animal with an accusatory finger. "This is a court of law, and it's no place for a tiger!"

The tiger stared at him with unblinking amber eyes, his tail flicking idly. Valentine stared back for as long as he could bear it. But then the tiger lowered his head and took two slow, silent steps toward the defense side of the courtroom, and Valentine's blood shivered, because the posture was unmistakably a *stalk*.

Valentine sat down hard. The tiger paused before returning to a more casual posture. The message had been sent: the proper place for a tiger is anyplace that a tiger wishes to go, and *this* tiger wanted to be in a court of law, and there was nothing anyone could do to stop him.

"Good morning, Mr. Argyle," Nxania said. She spoke softly, but the silence in the courtroom made the air thin, and her words echoed throughout the space.

"What. What is the meaning of this?" the judge asked. They, too, spoke quietly; they were very still, in the manner of any creature who is trying hard not to be noticed by a tiger.

"My attorney has arrived," Nxania replied. She alone seemed perfectly calm. She approached the tiger and rested a tentacle across the stripes of his enormous head. The tiger closed his eyes and leaned his head into her touch.

A low, resonant purr filled the room.

Valentine knew this judge; they had a short temper and a strict sense of courtroom discipline. In any other circumstance, they surely would have been furiously demanding answers. But there was a tiger, and apparently that was what it took to inspire patience in the typically brusque judge.

"A tiger," they said, "cannot be an attorney. And even if he could," they added quickly as the tiger's eyes snapped up toward the bench, "I'm afraid that you can't change your representation without telling anyone. There are certain protocols that—"

"I haven't changed my representation," Nxania interrupted, her tentacle still resting on the tiger's head. "And I think that you'll find a tiger *can* be an attorney, if he's passed the bar exam. Which, of course, Mr. Argyle has." Her pedipalps fluttered in an expression of contentment. "I believe if you check your dataset, you'll find a correspondence from Mr. Argyle indicating that last night, he went to an ultramod salon and had his consciousness transferred into the brain of this animal. So, really, everything is in order."

Valentine stared at the tiger. He stared hard. This had to be some kind of bizarre joke. No way Argyle could have afforded so much as a toenail repair at an ultramod salon, not with the kinds of suits he wore—and consciousness-transfer procedures? Those were as expensive and risky as mods got. And where in all the rotten stars in the void had Argyle gotten his hands on a goddamn *tiger*?

"Are you trying to tell me *that's* Argyle?" he said, incredulous. "That tiger? Right there? That's Vladislav Argyle?"

The tiger settled back onto his haunches, looked Valentine in the eyes, and nodded.

The courtroom erupted into sound. Reporters climbed up onto their benches to see the front of the room more clearly. The snap of a hundred mediadrones turning on their transmitters was drowned out only by the incomprehensible wall of questions, all of which essentially boiled down to *how*?

The judge activated a mutenet throughout the room, dimming the cacophony to a low hum. "Order," they said in a clear, carrying voice, and they did not have to say it twice; the room settled quickly under the weight of the imposed quiet. "Do you confirm that you are, in fact and in truth, Vladislav Argyle? I would remind you that you are in a court of law, and if you lie to me, you will be held in contempt." The tiger blinked once, slowly, at the judge; then, he nodded. The judge returned the nod before continuing. "Mr. Argyle, can you speak in a manner that is comprehensible to our ears?"

The tiger—Argyle—shook his head. The gesture was unquestionably human, and Valentine experienced a kind of sublime disorientation at the sight of a tiger performing the movement.

"We can't continue, then, can we?" Valentine asked. The judge glared at him, and he realized how much he'd been speaking out of turn—but he supposed he could be forgiven, under the circumstances. What with the tiger. "My apologies, your honor, I don't mean to interrupt—I just…" he trailed off, then lifted his hands helplessly toward Argyle, who was licking one of his enormous paws and running it over his velvety black ear.

His tongue was very pink.

The judge considered Argyle, considered Valentine. They steepled their fingers and furrowed their brow. "I've been a judge for sixteen years," they said, and Valentine suppressed a groan: whatever was coming, it wasn't going to be the thing he wanted. "I've heard thousands of cases, Mr. Valentine, and I think that I and this justice system can handle hearing arguments from a lawyer who doesn't speak. Frankly," they added tartly, "it might be refreshing." They rang the silver bell that indicated a final decision from the bench and said the three words Valentine least wanted to hear: "I'll allow it. Mr. Argyle, we concluded yesterday with opening statements; I believe the floor is yours, if you'd like to begin presenting evidence."

"This oughta be good," Blick muttered, his breath a warm wash of stale ethanol. "He couldn't handle this case when he had the ability to talk. What's he gonna do when it's time to question me? Meow at me until I slip up?" He giggled sharply.

The tiger's amber eyes turned to him.

Valentine kicked his client hard on the ankle. "He's a fucking. Tiger. You idiot," he said through gritted teeth. "He can hear everything you're saying."

Argyle's pupils were slowly expanding, the yellow glow of his eyes vanishing into the satin black of a hungry, hunting void. He stood on all fours, his spine straight, his tail lashing hard from side to side. That pink tongue flicked out to wet his nose as he stared at Blick.

"What? What's he gonna do? It's still Argyle in there," Blick hissed, glaring at Valentine. "He's still a sniveling little coward. He's just got stripes now, that's all."

Valentine did not glare back, because he could not bring himself to look away from the tiger for more than a few seconds at a time. Argyle sank low to the ground, his chin very nearly resting on his front paws. It almost looked as if he were lying down to rest—except for the snap of his tail, and the coiled tension in his haunches.

"Mr. Argyle, would you like to begin?" the judge said, their voice between worried and warning. Argyle flicked an ear toward the sound of their voice, but did not take his eyes off Blick. His tail went still, and his back legs began to straighten. His hindquarters lifted into the air and swayed, ever so slightly, from side to side.

"He's just a stupid cat," Blick sneered, not bothering to keep his voice down anymore. "We're still gonna eat 'em alive."

At that, the tiger pounced. He poured himself through the air like water being thrown from a bucket, a long white arc of orange and black muscle leaping from the floor to the table on the defense side of the room, knocking the young scion of the Blick legacy to the floor. His paws landed on Blick's chest with a *crunch* Valentine felt in his own gut.

Valentine was out of his own chair before he could think, a shout of terror fleeing his mouth entirely of its own volition. He landed on his ass and scrambled fast, not thinking of any direction other than *away from tiger*. He didn't stop moving until his back was pressed to the base of the judge's bench.

Blick was shrieking, a high, piercing whistle of a scream. Argyle's ears were pressed back flat against his head, his fangs bared in a gleaming snarl. A low noise came out of the tiger, a noise that sent a jolt of white-hot adrenaline surging through Valentine's belly. Then the noise built into a thundering, vicious *roar*.

Valentine immediately soaked the fabric of his suit with sweat. His lap grew hot with a flood of urine.

Blick was still screaming.

And then, with a single swipe of his paw, the tiger made the noise stop. His claws unzipped three stark lines of flesh on Blick's face, revealing the raw red meat underneath.

"Mr. Argyle, stop this immediately!" The judge rang their silver bell, but the tiger did not appear to notice. Valentine felt a scrabbling next to him, and turned to see the bailiff sitting in much the same position he was in, his face bloodless, his uniform dark at the crotch.

Valentine forced himself to look at the bailiff, so that he would not have to look at the tiger. There was a wet crunch and a gurgle from the table where he had been sitting just a few moments before. The bailiff looked back at Valentine, and his eyes were blank with terror.

"Shouldn't you get backup or something?" Valentine hissed. The bailiff nodded, but did not move.

"Is this not how it's done?" Nxania said, and Valentine realized that her sweet, tender voice had a note of steel in it he'd never noticed before.

He was wheezing with panic at the thing that was happening in front of him, the deconstruction of a man whom he'd truly loathed but who was, in form and in vulnerability, much like himself. He could not have formed words if his life had depended on it.

And yet Nxania, for all her empathy and childlike innocence, sounded entirely unfazed.

"I believe Mr. Argyle is simply returning the promise Mr. Blick made to him," she continued. "Vis á vis, 'eating us alive'."

Valentine could not stop himself from glancing over at the tiger. Argyle held one dinner-plate-sized paw on Blick's motionless chest. His teeth were buried in the dying man's throat. Blick's feet spasmed wildly, his heels leaving long black scuffs on the floor.

Between his clenched bladder and his quaking hands, Valentine's body was no longer under his control. A low, shuddering moan emanated from somewhere in his belly, and although no other sound had broken Argyle's focus on Blick, that moan seemed to catch his attention.

His ears twitched toward Valentine, and then he turned his face to assess the source of this new noise. A tendon was caught in his teeth. It stretched, horribly long and elastic, between his maw and the open mess of Blick's throat. It stayed taut and trembling for several seconds before breaking with an audible *snap*.

The tiger licked blood from his muzzle, his paw still resting on the spasming man who had once been Valentine's client. Argyle was looking at Valentine with naked assessment, and the weight of the question in his eyes was crushing: What are you to me? Are you a colleague? A friend? An opponent?

A meal?

Valentine's chest heaved with the shallow breath of panic, and that panic finally triggered something inside of him that could function. He was used to this kind of assessment. Not from Argyle, and not from tigers, but certainly from other attorneys, ones who were competent in the art of the trial.

He had never met someone who was better than him before, but he knew what he had to do. He had never inhabited this role, but he'd watched the play a thousand times. He was certain that he could pull it off.

"Well played, old man," he said in a tremulous voice. He knew he didn't sound nearly as brave as he would have liked, but it would have to be enough. "I believe you've got the upper hand."

He raised his hands, carefully, smoothly. The tiger's eyes tracked the movement. Then—*slow, soft, don't startle him*—he began to clap.

. . . . .

The tiger looked around at the rest of the room, and as his blood-spattered face turned, those he regarded began to imitate Valentine. Soon, the room was filled with muted applause. The judge rang their silver bell, and, in a weak voice, pronounced the matter of Vibrania v. Blick settled in favor of the People of Vibrania. Damages, they added, would be awarded in the amount of the tiger's choosing, to be determined at the tiger's leisure.

The tiger, satisfied by the adulation of the crowd and the outcome of the case, settled onto his belly to concentrate on his meal. Calculations would come later. Future cases, other clients, perhaps a revisitation of past losses that would need to be re-examined in light of his newfound skills of persuasion.

Argyle was not concerned with consequences. There are no consequences when one is a tiger. There is only justice. Justice, and rich blood, and tender meat, and all of it was his for the taking.

Mur Lafferty needs little introduction for fans of *Escape Pod*. She was one of the founding editors of *PseudoPod*, editor at *Mothership Zeta*, and has now served twice as an editor at *Escape Pod*. She's a pioneer in the world of podcasting with a Hugo Award for her industry-advice fancast, *Ditch Diggers*, which she cohosts with Matt Wallace. Mur has an incredibly big heart, a great sense of humor, and is the best copilot I could ask for. She's also a brilliant science fiction author. That's why it brings me great joy to share with you this original short story, set in the same universe as her award-nominated novel *Six Wakes*.

DIVYA

FOURTH NAIL
MUR LAFFERTY

Regina Phillips' job on the orbital station God's Eye was that of a nighttime systems engineer. She had to warm her desk chair and make sure nothing broke. It was the highest paying, most boring job around. So she sat in shocked silence for a good minute when the red alert hit.

She didn't even know the cloning lab had an alert system. It was hard to have an emergency involving minds that were backed up and bodies that were ultimately renewable. Still, there it was, a red glow around her monitor as the words "UNAUTHORIZED TRANSMISSION" blinked over and over again.

Around her, cloning vats filled the lab, each waiting for the command to start growing a new body for a dying clone. One clone in the far-end vat was nearly done, but Regina didn't recognize the face. She wasn't a tech responsible for dealing with the actual vats, just the computer systems.

She pushed a button to alert the AI. "Um, MICKEY, can you tell me about this unauthorized transmission? This lab isn't supposed to receive data from outside the station."

The light under the station AI's camera came on, indicating MICKEY's interest. "Not until I read it, Regina," the feminine voice said. "And I can't read it because it's unauthorized. Security measures. Protocol suggests deleting unread."

Regina frowned. "No, don't do that," she said. Her job allowed her enough power to contradict the AI in her field of expertise, but only barely. Here was a chance to do her job. Might as well do it.

While she didn't want the AI to make the call, she figured she didn't get paid enough to make this decision. She tapped her glasses rim and said, "Call Alex Riddell. Emergency."

Director Riddell was not one to appreciate being woken up, but he also wasn't one to deny the mysterious message took some time to address. After her call, he made it to the lab in short time, standing behind her in his dressing gown, his blond hair flattened on one side, frowning. Regina had never seen him in such a state. That was more shocking than the transmission.

"Delete it," he commanded. "It's a virus."

"How could someone figure out how to get a message through the firewall?" she asked. "No one but people on this station should have the codes to access this database. I checked, everything in the database is still secure. MICKEY, do you detect any malware?"

"None. But it is possible it won't attack until the message is opened. Advise deleting unread," the AI repeated.

"Maybe she's right," Regina said. "With everything going on in the labs on Earth we shouldn't take a chance. Still, I don't want to get in trouble for deleting something important. Maybe we should ask Igor—"

The AI interrupted her. "I'm detecting three more unauthorized transmissions," she said. "These are larger files. They appear to be archived mindmaps and DNA sequences. Very old, though. A file format used over fifty years ago."

"Someone is trying to infiltrate the station from Earth," Alex said, his voice tight. "From the inside. That's a new angle to get aboard."

"Maybe they want to use an uninfected lab," Regina said. "But they would just be bringing the virus here, wouldn't they?" She remembered the other times people had tried to get into the station, but it had always been stowing away on a shuttle, or attacking the station from the outside.

"Delete—" Alex said, but Regina put her hand on his arm.

"Wait, MICKEY. Don't do anything," she said. "Those files didn't come from Earth."

· · · · ·

The denizens of God's Eye thought of the station, a shining orbital wheel, as their final reward, better than Heaven, better than Elysium. Their own off-Earth paradise, their ultimate gated community.

To the humans on Earth, God's Eye was miles of steel, copper, and the first generation of narcissistic cloned assholes.

Aboard the station, they lived free of the laws that governed clones on Earth. They could create as many clones of themselves as they liked, they could kill their current bodies and get new ones if they got so much as a scratch, and they could modify their mindmaps and DNA sequences as they pleased. Their massive wealth allowed this distance, as well as weekly shuttle deliveries from Earth, and they could look down like gods on the home they'd abandoned.

The clones of God's Eye did allow humans to work aboard the station, to do the menial work they weren't interested in. "Rich folk always needed poor folk to sweep up after them, and Lord knows they ain't gonna pick their own apples," Regina's grandmother would say.

Regina worked the night shift in the lab. She had a small cot in a small room on the station and worked one week on, one week back on Earth. Most of her friends at home thought her job was glamorous, working aboard the forbidden station, but frankly it was boring work. Lucrative, but boring. She never got to see more of the station than the cloning lab, her room, and the tiny communal kitchen the human workers were allowed to have.

The day they were allowed to bring up a few plants from Earth to brighten the dismal place up was like a holiday.

Regina knew no clones aboard the station. None of them mixed with the lowly humans. Her superior, Alex, knew only one clone aboard the station, a bitter man by the name of Igor Luszczynski who was being punished by the ruling committee. Alex said he didn't know Igor's crime, but the punishment was to be in charge of the human workers for ten years.

"A change of job is a punishment?" Regina had asked Alex.

"No one on this station wants to work; it's their paradise. But they still need one of their own in charge of us because they don't trust us to manage ourselves. We're infants to them." He shrugged as if it didn't bother him. "But you're not looking for a job where you will be respected and valued, are you? You're looking for a job that pays ten times what it would pay on Earth."

He hadn't been wrong. There were hundreds of human engineers waiting for Regina and the rest of her team to step aside. She was building a good savings cushion back on Earth. If the job was soul-killing, well, she didn't have to do it forever. If she saved right, then she could retire in a few years, before she was thirty.

But these files looked like career killers. If she allowed the First's database to be infected or deleted something important, then she could be fired, or worse. She could always leave engineering and go back to nursing, she decided. That at least helped people, even though it didn't pay as well.

"What do you mean, not from Earth? There aren't any more labs on Luna," Alex asked.

"As MICKEY said, the file format is very old. No lab on Earth would continue to use that format. We have better data compression. Also the vector is wrong." She did some calculations, a thrill tingling at the back of her head as she was actually allowed to do her job. "We're not at a location in the orbit for anyone to send us anything as complex as a file. See?" A rotating globe came up on her screen showing the location. "Look, by triangulating the transmission with the antennae, we can see clearly that this came from space."

He held up his hand. "Wait a second. Are you implying alien transmissions?"

She avoided rolling her eyes. "No, it's a human cloning file format. It's just old. It has to come from tech that hasn't been updated in more than fifty years. Several ships have gone into the dark along this vector in the past few decades, like *The Johnson*, *The Equation*, *The Euphoria*, and a few others. Think it's from one of those?"

"I can see sending a mindmap back home. It's a lot cheaper than turning a ship around." Alex rubbed the back of his head, making his bedhead worse. "But it couldn't be a cry for help. It would take years for the answer or the support to make its way to the ship. And why send it *here*?"

"I'll bet that first transmission explains it," Regina said. "That one wasn't a mindmap. It's small enough to be a text message, right, MICKEY?"

"Delete it," he said, talking over the AI's affirmative. "We have to keep the databases isolated."

Clones on Earth were in considerable panic mode. There had been whispers for months of some cloning labs getting infected with viruses. Clones were being printed with defects not previously found in their DNA sequences, some mental, some physical. Since all of the cloning databases in the world were linked through the cloud, some projected the virus would spread. The most powerful clone on Earth, the ruthless Sallie Mignon, had gone into hiding, and most people believed she was responsible for the virus.

God's Eye was isolated from the cloud; they weren't even ruled by the same laws clones on Earth had to abide by. They didn't care about any of the data stored on Earth; they had everything they needed on the station.

"Could we wait till morning and ask Igor?" Regina asked. She'd never heard of Alex approaching Igor for an executive decision. In fact, according to the other engineers and techs, all of the human managers seemed to avoid Igor.

Alex frowned. "No. He doesn't like to hear that things are going wrong."

"Does he kill the messenger?" she asked, smiling, but the look on his face sobered her. "Wait, literally?"

"It's hard to explain," he said, staring at the blinking monitor. "There are some harsh penalties for angering the First."

"Like firing?"

"I wish. You know they've been bringing animals aboard, right?"

"No…" she said slowly. Where the hell was this going? "What kind of animals?"

"Never mind. It probably won't come to that."

She sat back and tried to assess the risks. "If they were expecting this, do you think they would tell you? Or just expect you to do your job without questions?"

"No questions," he said, sighing. "Igor hates them."

"Deleting whole mindmaps is tantamount to murder," Regina reminded him, looking at the files waiting in the queue.

"That depends on where they originate," Alex said. "Fine. I'm going to go get cleaned up. You finish your shift and meet me in the community room, and we'll go tell Igor together."

"Together?" she asked, feeling the blood drain from her face.

He nodded grimly and left the room.

Was he trying to get the lower lackey killed instead of himself? Regina stared at the red screen, frowning. There had to be a way to read that thing.

She smacked herself on her forehead as the obvious occurred to her. She pulled her tablet from her bag and turned it on. With a few quick taps on the keyboard she committed her first fireable offense: she turned to the terminal and sent the original message to herself. Then she turned off all communication capability and confirmed with the AI that she definitely couldn't see the tablet.

"That's not allowed," MICKEY said. "I'm going to have to report it to your superior."

"That's fine, it might be worth it," Regina said. "You can monitor me wiping the tablet when I'm done if you want." She held her breath briefly and then opened the file.

Only words appeared on the screen. Near as she could tell, nothing was crawling through her tablet to destroy everything, but she had to continue to be safe. The words were in German, however. She ran a quick translation program and read the file.

She read it three more times, the breath leaving her lungs. The thrill at solving the problem, coupled with the thrill of being right, was squashed immediately by the weight of the message. This was definitely above her pay grade. It was above Alex's pay grade. She wished she didn't know what was in it, but someone had to tell the First what was going on.

Someone.

Well. We're already fucked. Might as well go all the way.

"MICKEY, the message is safe to open. Also, override usual protocol for vat usage. 2832 code word 'Stranger'." She paused and took a deep breath. "Start immediate unpacking and creation of clones based on the three files that were just delivered. Emergency protocol in place."

"What about the threat of virus?" MICKEY objected. But she had already started to work, the override code (that, in Alex's words, Regina was only supposed to use, "if you're on fucking fire") doing its job.

"There is no virus," Regina said. She ran a few commands through the computer.

Unable to keep still, she stood and paced, thinking of wiping her tablet of all its data, not just the message she had opened. There was no way she'd be caught on the station or on Earth with that data on her person. She briefly considered breaking the device and throwing it in the recycler to make sure the message was really gone, but she didn't want to lose her new tablet. Then she figured she was already in trouble, so she might as well have some insurance. She took the four files and encrypted them, stashing them in a secure folder on her tablet. She went to the community room and refreshed her coffee, then went back to work to watch the three new clones knit themselves together.

The letter had been short and to the point:

To whomever finds this message:

Our intent was to send these files to the God's Eye space station. Printing us would be highly illegal in any lab on Earth, but (last time we checked) the station is above the law and self-governing. I can only hope the files made it there.

We are the crew of the spaceship Dormire, *launched back in 2468. After about a quarter century of travel, we had an incident on board that killed the entire crew and*

*nearly wiped our ship's computer, leaving us missing the
past few decades. Once we woke up our new clones and
sorted out who had caused the incident, we realized the
true mastermind behind a near annihilation of thousands
of clones and human colonists was back on Earth. We
decided that to properly pursue justice—and to stop this
individual from further mass murder attempts—we would
send clone files back home to inform the authorities.*

*We humbly beg your help in allowing our clones to
be printed and shuttled back to Earth. The odds are
astronomical that we'll even manage to send the file at
the right time to be intercepted by your station, and for
you to open our message instead of deleting it as a
dangerous file. If we've beaten those odds, please help
us beat a few more.*

Please help us find Sallie Mignon.

Sincerely,

The crew of the Dormire:

*Captain Katrina de la Cruz, Dr. Joanna Glass,
Wolfgang, Hiro Sato, Maria Arena, Minoru Takahashi*

· · · · ·

Three hours later, at the end of her shift, her terminal pinged.
"Regina, I told you to meet me in the common room," Alex said,
sounding annoyed.

"You need to come down here," she replied.

"You don't want to keep Igor waiting," he said.

"He won't wait long," she said, eyes fastened on the three
bodies in the vats. The emergency protocol used immense amounts

of energy to expedite the growth of clones. "But you need to see something. I—" she hesitated, then plowed on. "I isolated the message and read it on my tablet."

The line went dead and three minutes later, Alex was there, breathing hard. "What the fuck were you thinking?" he demanded, then his jaw went slack. "What did you do?" He sounded terrified.

Regina was handing out towels and jumpsuits to three very wet clones and confirming they all spoke English. Two men, one woman. There was a distinct difference in their height ranges, one man tall and pale, even for a Caucasian, while the other man was of Southeast Asian descent and shorter. The woman was between them, with dark hair and light brown skin.

The woman zipped up her suit and scrubbed at her short black hair with a towel, making a face at the viscous fluid that still stuck to her. She tossed it aside as if giving up and looked at the tall man. "You feeling OK in this gravity?"

"I'm fine," he said without looking at her.

"You sound like my mother," she said, rolling her eyes. Then she stepped forward and held out her hand. "Hi. I'm Maria Arena. My companions are Hiro and Wolfgang. We're from the ship *Dormire*. Thanks so much for the help."

Alex stared at them. Regina stepped in front of him and shook Maria's hand, even though she had already done so once. "I'm sure, once the shock wears off, he'll be delighted to meet you," she said apologetically.

"Regina," Alex whispered. "You are in so much trouble."

"I think you need to hear them out, Alex," Regina said, turning her back on the clones, toward the white-faced Alex.

"And they should probably hear what's happened in the last fifty or so years."

"I really need to hear what's happened in football," Hiro said. "And the Olympics. And if there are any new science fiction shows."

Maria put a hand on his arm. "Later, man. Let's tell our story first."

. . . . .

Throughout the story, Alex fiddled with a pen, twirling it between his fingers. He barely looked up at Maria, who spoke with a few interjections from Hiro. Wolfgang remained silent, his steely blue eyes fixated on Alex.

When they were done, Alex still wouldn't look at the clones. He addressed Regina instead. "And why did you print them instead of finding me?"

She shrugged. "Because I believed them. And I knew I'd be fired. You were already taking me to Igor. I knew he would blame me for the message, and that would be it. This way I could help them before losing my job."

Alex played with his pen.

"Listen, all of Earth is looking for Sallie Mignon," Regina continued. "You'd think they'd welcome three more people to look for her, three pretty damn resourceful people, with a grudge as well! They left their ship and came here, knowing they'll never see their shipmates again! That's a huge sacrifice. They need help."

"Do you know what the First are doing with the new addition to the station?" Alex asked.

"Why is that important now?"

"Do you?"

"No. I assumed building a green space, according to the ship manifests," she said. "Why?"

"There was a story written a long time ago. It was called 'The Most Dangerous Game.' Have you read it?" he asked.

Regina shook her head, but Maria spoke up sharply. "I have," she said. "Is that what the First are doing? They're that fucking bored?"

"What is the dangerous game?" Hiro asked, looking around at each of them.

"A very wealthy, very bored man strands another man on a dangerous island and hunts him. If he survives, he gets to live," Alex said.

"And these clones are very wealthy. And very bored," Wolfgang said. His voice sounded like a death toll.

"You can't be serious?" Hiro asked.

"That is the punishment I was telling you about," Alex said. "They won't fire us at all. They'll just throw us in their game for amusement."

"Then let's get out of here," Wolfgang said, standing suddenly. "Show us to a shuttle bay. Hiro can fly anything."

"Shuttle tech has probably evolved in the past fifty years," Hiro said hesitantly.

"When you asked to come, you said we would need a navigator and pilot," Wolfgang said, turning his glare onto the shorter man. "And now you're saying you can't?"

"I didn't think we'd actually make it in the first place! I figured we'd be just be data, flying through space forever!" Hiro said, stepping backward. "I didn't think it would actually work!"

This guy was in charge of navigation of the *Dormire*?

Maria rubbed her forehead and walked away. "I need a moment," she said.

Alex glanced at Maria and opened his mouth, but then his world was full of the towering pale monolith that was Wolfgang. "Shuttle bay. Take us there now." He wound his hands into Alex's pressed shirt. "Then you will have nothing to worry about."

"Well, they have to explain the fast build of three clones, and the unauthorized transmission, and probably an unscheduled launch of a shuttle," Hiro said, counting off on his fingers.

"What is with this guy?" Regina asked.

Wolfgang turned and actually looked like he was going to punch Hiro, but a shout at the back of the room distracted him.

"Wolfgang! Hiro! Get back here!"

As the clones ran toward her voice, Alex sighed and deflated. "And she found it."

"Found what?"

"The clone I was growing. Of Sallie Mignon."

. . . . .

"Why do you have a clone of Sallie Mignon? How did you get it without infecting the database? What is going on?" Regina demanded.

"It's a long story, and it's more important than anything you will ever need to know," he said. He straightened, and his face relaxed into something calmer, something that carried the gravitas of years even though he still looked forty. His entire body language changed. "I suppose it doesn't matter anymore. She assured me the mindmap on the drive was older and hadn't been infected. She didn't cause the virus on Earth. She's come here to ask the First for help, in fact."

"Why did she have to sneak up here?" Regina demanded. "Why not just take the shuttle? She's got serious money and power, she should have no problem getting here!"

"She's tried. But some of the First don't like her very much," Alex said. "She's not welcome here. Her plan is to offer herself."

"Offer herself?"

"To the Game."

They heard a crunch. Regina stopped trying to wrap her head around the absurdity of the moment. "Only if they let her survive."

They ran back to the vat where Wolfgang was punching the glass. Spidery cracks leaked a thick stream of synthamneo. Hiro was yelling at Wolfgang to stop; Maria just watched, her arms crossed.

"He's got an anger problem," Maria said as Regina and Alex raced up to them. "And he doesn't know how to vat the clone. So he's going at it the direct way."

Alex swore and ran back to Regina's terminal. Regina leapt forward and, with Hiro's help, they managed to pull Wolfgang away from the vat. He threw a long elbow and caught Regina in the forehead, splitting the skin and knocking her off him. She sat against an empty vat, stunned. Other sounds happened. A crunch. A cry of pain. Then the sound of synthamneo being drained.

She wiped the blood out of her eyes and saw a short woman exit the vat, holding the gravitas of who knew how many lifetimes. Her eyes were honey brown and her skin a darker shade than

Maria's. She looked at each person in turn, focusing, surprisingly, on Regina.

"You, I don't know," she said. She walked over and offered Regina a hand up. "I'm Sallie."

Surprised, Regina took the hand, still slick with synthamneo, and awkwardly got to her feet. "I'm the systems engineer," she said, dumbly. "Regina."

Wolfgang sat on the floor next to the vat, cradling his hand. "You broke my thumb," he said to Hiro, cold violence in his tone.

"You nearly knocked out our new friend," Hiro said calmly, with no trace of the flippancy he'd used before. "We wouldn't be here without her. And what the hell were you trying to accomplish? If you'd punched through and killed her clone, that would have done no good. They'd just grow another one."

"Wolfgang, Maria, and Hiro!" Sallie said, delighted. "What brings you here? And where are we? And what year is it, anyway?"

Alex came up to them carrying a towel, a tablet, and a bathrobe.

"Igor, it's been a long time," Sallie said, taking the towel.

Alex—Igor?—nodded. "It's 2493. You contain the last virus-free mindmap of Sallie Mignon. You sent me here with this file to ask the First if they would help with a crisis among clones back on Earth." He handed her a tablet with a document pulled up. She took the towel, wiped her hands, and then took the tablet.

"Igor?" Regina demanded. "*You're* Igor?"

He looked at her with the haughtiness she had come to notice in older clones. The "you couldn't possibly understand" look. "I told you Igor was being punished. That was true. I had to act like a human and manage your team." He shook his head in disgust and waved his hands at the newcomers. "And you had to fuck it all up with them."

"So what, sneaking on a clone of a hated person from Earth is your payback to the First? What will that get you?"

"That remains to be seen. The hope is she can get my insular peers to help their own people back on Earth, and then I can get out of here. Middle manager on God's Eye is not the goal of all the lifetimes I have lived."

"Better to reign in hell, huh?" Maria asked.

Sallie had finished reading the tablet. She looked thoughtful. "I'm not the only version of me. I'm also back on Earth right now, which makes her superfluous if I ever got back there. She'd be destroyed. She risked a lot sending me here."

"She sent you here to die, probably," Regina said. "You can't just go ask the First a favor. Apparently, you have to do a survival competition or something."

Sallie ignored her. This information didn't surprise her. "And you three?" she asked the other new clones. "Last I remember, you were on the *Dormire*."

"We're here to accuse you of multiple counts of attempted murder," Maria said. "And bring you to justice."

"You figured it out," she said, nodding. "And even made it back here for revenge. I have to say I'm impressed. Well," she said, taking the robe from Igor. "We can talk after I am done with the Game."

Igor nodded. "I had expected to offer you to the First, but things just got a lot more interesting." He tapped a few times on his tablet. "I have to fire an engineer and figure out how to jail some stowaways." He gave them an appraising look. "Or just kill you all here. Wouldn't do for you to talk," he added to Regina.

His tablet beeped. "Geneviève," he said.

"What is it, Igor?" the voice demanded. Clearly busy and clearly not happy to hear from him.

"I'm going to need some firearms in the cloning bay. You wouldn't believe what just happened."

"Get them yourself," she snapped.

Regina's head was whirling. The three clones had their heads together and were talking. It sounded like they were going to run. This would do them no good, as the shuttle bay was currently empty. She opened her mouth to tell them this, and then an idea came to her.

"What if we make it through the Game?" she asked.

All of them looked at her. She realized every person in the room was hundreds of years older than she was, and she felt very small. But she continued.

"Look, we can't run away. There's no shuttle in the bay right now. There's nowhere to go. If they're going to kill us anyway, why not give us a sporting chance? Sallie is going through the Game to ask for a favor. Why can't we all have that option?"

She looked at the three clones. She'd just offered them up too. They were free to try to run through an unknown space station if they thought it was a better bet, but Maria was nodding.

"Kill each other?" Sallie asked, cocking her head like a hound as if Regina was a rabbit.

"Nah, there are plenty of things in there to kill you anyway," Igor said thoughtfully. "We're not barbaric."

Maria snorted, looking between Igor and Sallie.

"But if it happened accidentally," Sallie said, leaving the sentence open.

The line was still open to Geneviève. "All right, no firearms. What about the Game? Is it ready to start?" Igor asked, his eyes fixed on Regina.

"Yeah, just got the last of the animals into their habitats. Why? You wanna vacation there?"

"No. Tell the council I have the first contestants."

"Oh really?" She sounded interested for the first time. "Plural?"

"Yes. Five of them, in fact."

"Where did you get five? Are you cleaning house in the lab?"

Regina felt her stomach drop. Was this happening? She had no survival skills. She wasn't in shape. What was she thinking? Surely a bullet to the head was preferable to being ripped apart by wolves.

Maria put her hand on her arm. "Are you sure about this?"

"Too late now," Regina said, smiling weakly.

Igor put his tablet away, smiling widely. "They love the idea. We can start right away. Now, there are weapons stashed around the preserve, and please don't kill the female large cats."

"Is this guy for real?" Hiro asked, looking at Maria. She shrugged.

"Let's go," Igor said, and herded them in front of him.

"We could kill him," Wolfgang said, still holding his injured hand to his chest.

"I think this is a better chance of having someone listen to us. We didn't come all this way to immediately become fugitives," Maria said.

Wolfgang swore quietly and didn't say anything else.

They passed no other people in the corridor as Igor ushered them along. All too quickly, they came to a locked door. He shouldered past them and keyed in a code. "There are no rules, except for the cats, and don't see this as a Battle Royal thing," he said. "They'd much rather watch you die after a futile attempt to work together than kill each other."

"How kind of them," Maria said dryly.

Wolfgang was looking at Sallie like he wanted to eat her alive, and she blithely ignored him.

Then it hit Regina. *Of course she doesn't care. Igor can just print another copy of her if she dies in here. She gets multiple chances. We only have one.*

A blast of humidity hit their faces when they opened the door. Regina hesitated and then sighed, stepping forward. The others followed her.

All around them was a lush forested landscape, complete with bright light overhead and spongy floor underneath.

"Pretty," Sallie said. "So, should we look for weapons or build a shelter first?"

"We're not working with you," Wolfgang said flatly.

Sallie smiled as if she'd expected it. "Your loss." She disappeared into the trees, jogging in bare feet, still clad in only a robe.

"I guess we look for weapons now," Maria said. "I don't want to give Sallie any advantages. And then we give them the show they're asking for."

"This was a terrible idea," Hiro said.

"You came here to take things apart. 'For want of a nail,' you said," Maria reminded him. "Three nails, and her kingdom falls. We beat Sallie once. Her plan, anyway. We can do it again." She looked at Regina. "Are you in?"

Regina swallowed her fear. "I just want to survive, but I'm on your team if you'll have me. I'm not sure what I can add, though. I haven't beaten anybody before."

"There's always a first time," Hiro said, smiling at her.

"Can we get moving? We need to map this place," Wolfgang said. "I need to splint this thumb."

"Well, Fourth Nail, do you know any first aid?" Maria asked.

Regina brightened. "Yeah, actually. I trained with the National Guard and was a nurse during the Chicago siege."

"OK, we're going to have to hear about that later," Maria said, looking interested.

Regina took in their area. Beyond the trees lay a vast plain with tall grass. She had to admit the area was a mastery of engineering, even if she were to die here. She pointed into the dense forest. "I'll tell you that story later. But for now, let's go."

John Scalzi has achieved fame by taping bacon to his cat, writing a book about an alien diplomatic incident involving a fart, and being nominated for a short story Hugo Award for an April Fool's joke posted on Tor.com that used 318 words to say, "it was a dark and stormy night." He's done some other stuff, too, I guess: consulted on TV shows, written some books, won some awards, outraged some people online, and DJ'd a mean dance party. If you're talking about contemporary humor and science fiction, his name will inevitably come up, and this story from early in his career shows you he's always been this twisted and funny.

MUR

ALIEN ANIMAL ENCOUNTERS
JOHN SCALZI

Each week, we here at *SSWR* step right outside of our offices here on 54th and ask folks on the street our Question of the Week— sometimes topical, sometimes whimsical, always intriguing.

Our question this week: What is the most interesting encounter you've ever had with an alien animal species?

· · · · ·

Rowenna Morello, Accountant, Staten Island:

That's gotta be the time we got the cat high with a glyph. My college roommate worked in the xenobiology lab and brought the glyph home one night in a shoebox. It's just this little mouse-like thing, so of course the cat wanted at it right away. It's cat-food-sized. We pushed the cat away from it a couple of times, but then I had to go make a call. I left the glyph alone in its box on the table, and the cat hopped up and started poking at the thing with its paw, you know, poke poke poke.

Thing is, the glyph is a total predator, and it's got this mouth that opens up like a little umbrella and surrounds whatever it's going to eat. So there's the cat, batting at the glyph, and suddenly the glyph lunges forward, opens its jaws, wraps them around the cat's paw, and clamps down hard. It's trying to eat the cat. Well, the cat's freaking out, of course. It's scooting backwards, trying frantically to shake this thing off its paw and wailing, you know, like a cat in heat. My roommate had to use a Popsicle stick from the trash to pry the glyph's mouth open.

The cat ran away and seemed to be pissed-off but okay. Then a half hour later I caught him just staring at a bookshelf and wobbling back and forth. Seems that glyphs paralyze their prey with venom; it kills just about anything on the glyphs' planet but here it just makes you hallucinate. It's a chemistry thing. After we realized the cat wasn't going to die, it was actually pretty funny to watch him bump into walls and stare at his own paws. Although at one point he sprinted right towards an open window and my roommate had to make a lunge to keep him from jumping out. It was a third-floor walkup. I guess the cat thought he could fly.

Anyway, the glyph went back to the lab the next day. The funny thing is that for the next couple of days, the cat seemed to be looking around to find the glyph, circling the table and poking into boxes and stuff. I think he wanted a fix.

• • • • •

Alan Jones-Wynn, Copywriter, Manhattan:

My daughter's third-grade class was taking a trip to the Bronx Zoo and it was my turn to be a parent assistant, so I got the day off from work and helped her teacher herd a couple dozen kids around the place, which, if you've never done it, is just as aggravating as it sounds. This was around the time that the zoo was just opening their "Alien Animals" exhibit, and the place was jam-packed; it actually helped that we were on an official educational field trip, because otherwise we probably wouldn't have been able to get through the crowds.

We filed through and the tour guide pointed out all the popular alien animals, like those omads and the revers and the neyons, right, the ones they make stuffed-animal toys of to sell at the gift shop. But then we came to this one habitat and the tour guide stopped and pointed out what had to have been the ugliest lump of fur in the whole zoo. She told us that the lump we were looking at was called a corou, and that it was an endangered species on Tungsk, and that the Bronx Zoo and others were trying to start a captive breeding program. As she was saying this, her eyes were welling up with tears, and it seemed like she was about to break down right then and there.

Well, obviously, this seemed like pretty bizarre behavior, but then I looked at the corou, and it swiveled an eye stalk at me, and I swear I was overwhelmed with this wave of sadness and regret that was so overpowering I can't even describe it. It's like what you'd probably feel if you'd just heard that a bus carrying everyone you ever knew just went off a mountain trail in Peru. And it wasn't just me; all those kids, who you couldn't have shut up if you wired their jaws shut, were all just standing there silently, staring at the corou and looking like they'd just seen their dog run over by a car. One of the kids actually tapped on the glass of the habitat and said, "I'm sorry," to the corou,

over and over. We had to literally drag some of the kids away.
I mean, I wouldn't call it telepathy or mind control, but
something was going on there.

My kid and I went back a couple of years later and the
corou exhibit wasn't there anymore, and I was sort of glad—
it's never a good thing to worry that you're going to get
clinically depressed at the zoo. At a dinner party a little later I
met a vet who worked at the zoo, and I asked him about the
corou. He said that one zoologist working with the habitat
committed suicide and another was placed on leave after she
took the zoo's breeding pair, drove them up to Vermont, and
tried to release them into the wild. She kept telling everyone
afterwards that they told her it was what they wanted. They
eventually had to get rid of the exhibit altogether. I haven't
heard about the corou since. I think they're extinct now.

· · · · ·

Ted McPeak, Community College Student, Jersey City:
Some friends and me heard that if you smoked the skin of an
aret, you could get monumentally wasted. So we bought one
at a pet store and waited a couple of weeks until it shed its skin.
Then we crumbled up the dry skin, put it in with some pot, and
lit up. We all got these insane mouth blisters that didn't go
away for weeks. We all had to eat soup for a month. Though
maybe it wasn't the skin; the pot could have been bad or
something. We flushed the aret down the toilet after we got the
blisters, though, so we'd have to go buy a new one to try it out
again. I don't think we'll bother.

· · · · ·

Qa' Hungran Ongru, Cultural Attaché for Fine Arts and Literature, Royal Kindran Embassy, Manhattan:

Well, I am myself an alien here, so I suppose you could say that my most interesting incident with an alien animal was with one of your animals, a dog. Shortly after being assigned to the embassy here, I was given a Shih Tzu by a human friend. I was delighted, of course. He really was an adorable thing, and he was very loving and devoted to me. I named him Fred. I like that name.

As you may know, the male of the Kindra species is a large non-sentient segmented worm which we females attach across our midriffs during the mating process; the male stays attached while a four-part fertilization process occurs over several days. It's not very romantic by human standards, but obviously it works well for us. Shortly before one of my ovulatory periods, I had managed to score a rather significant diplomatic coup when I convinced the Guggenheim to tour selections of its collection among the Kindra home planets. As a reward, I was allowed to choose a male from the oligarchical breeding stock for my next insemination. The one I chose had deep segment ridges and a nicely mottled scale pattern; again, not something a human would find attractive, but deeply compelling for Kindrae. He was attached to me in a brief conjoining ceremony at the embassy, attended by selected Kindra and human friends, and then I went home to Fred.

Fred came running to meet me at the door as he always did, but when he saw the male across my belly, he skidded across the tiles and then started growling and barking and backing away slowly. I tried to assure him that everything was okay, but every time I tried to reach for Fred, he'd back away more. At one point he snapped at my tendrils. I was surprisingly hurt; although it seemed silly to want Fred and the male to "get along" (considering that the male was doing nothing but lying there), I did want them to get along. If for no other reason than that the male would be attached to me for the next week or so. But for the next few days Fred would have nothing to do with me. He wouldn't eat from his bowl until I left the room. He even peed in my shoes.

On the fourth night of this, I was sleeping when I suddenly felt a sharp pain in my abdomen; it was the male, beginning to unhook himself from me. Then I heard the growling. I snapped on a light, looked down, and saw Fred attacking the male; he had managed to get a bite in between two of the male's ring segments and punctured an artery. The male was bleeding all over my bed. If the male managed to completely detach himself, it would be disastrous—my impregnation cycle was not yet complete, and it would be highly unlikely after a noble male was attacked in my bed that I would be entrusted with another ever again. So with one arm I lodged the male back onto me and struggled to keep him in place, with another I reached for the phone to call my doctor, and with the third I scooped up Fred and tossed him off the bed. He landed up on the floor with a yelp and limped away, winding up a perfectly charming incident for all three of us.

I was rushed to the embassy infirmary, where the male's injuries were sutured and he was sedated to the point where he would again willingly reattach himself to me. By some miracle, the fertilization process was uninterrupted; I was confined to an infirmary bed for the rest of the process while doctors made sure everything went as it was supposed to. The ambassador came to visit afterwards and I expressed my shame at the incident and offered my resignation; she declined it, and told me that no one blamed me for what happened, but that it would probably be a good idea to get rid of Fred.

I did, giving him to a retired human diplomat I had worked with for many years. I visit them both frequently, and Fred is always happy to see me. He's also always happy to see my daughter. Who is also named Fred. As I said, I like the name.

. . . . .

Dr. Elliot Morgenthal, Doctor, Stamford:

Oh, God. I worked the ER as an intern right around the time of that stupid fungdu craze. Here's the thing about fungdu: they're furry, they're friendly, they vibrate when they're happy, and they have unusually large toothless mouths. You can see where this is going. About two or three times a month we'd get some poor bastard coming in with a fungdu on his Johnson.

What people apparently don't know about fungdu is that if they think that what they've got in their mouths is live prey, these little backward-pointing quills emerge out of their gums to keep whatever they're trying to eat from escaping. These dumbasses get it into their heads to get a hummer from their fungdu, and then are understandably surprised to discover that their pet thinks it's being fed a live hot dog. Out come the quills, and the next thing you know, there's some asshole in the emergency room trying to explain how his erect penis just happened to fall into the fungdu's mouth. He tripped, you see. How inconvenient.

Here's the truly disgusting thing about this: all the time this is going on, the fungdu is usually desperately trying to swallow. And that animal has some truly amazing peristaltic motion. Again, you can see where this is going. The nurses wouldn't touch any of these guys. They told them to clean up after their own damn selves. Who can blame them.

· · · · ·

Bill and Sue Dukes, Plumbing Supplies, Queens:

BILL: There was this one time I was driving through Texas, and I saw the weirdest fuckin' thing on the side of the road. It looked like an armor-plated rabbit or something. It was just lying there, though. I think it was dead.

SUE: You idiot. That's an armadillo. They're from Earth.

BILL: No, you must be thinking of some other animal. This thing was totally not Earth-like at all. It had, like, scales and shit.

SUE: That's an armadillo. They're all over Texas. They're like the state animal or something. Everybody knows that.

BILL: Well, what the fuck do I know about Texas? I'm from Queens. And we sure as hell don't got any armadillos in Queens.

SUE (rolling eyes): Oh, yeah, if it's not from Queens, it ain't shit, right?

BILL: You got that right. Fuckin' Texas. Hey, what about those things, you know, that got the duck bill?

SUE: You mean ducks?

BILL: No, smartass, they don't look like a duck, they just got a duck
   bill.

SUE: What, a platypus?

BILL: Yeah, a platypus! Where are those things from?

SUE: They're from Earth too.

BILL: No shit? Man, Earth is a weird-ass planet sometimes.

We sometimes like to blur the lines of genre fiction at *Escape Pod*, and "A Consideration of Trees," from **Beth Cato,** is a great example of this. Part space-based science fiction, part old-world magic, this story charms you while also delivering a sharply pointed critique of current attitudes toward the environment. Beth has a knack for weaving social commentary with historical and futuristic settings. She's an award-nominated author of multiple novels and short stories, and she's probably best known for her steampunk aesthetic. She also loves baking and furry friends, both of which you'll find in this story.

DIVYA

A CONSIDERATION OF TREES

BETH CATO

As a xenoarbitrator, I was accustomed to working with concepts and situations deemed peculiar by most of humanity. Often, though, my own species confounded me most of all.

"I fear you misunderstood my advertisement." I stood in Mari Kane's miniscule parlor on Bradbury Orbital Station. My felizard partner, Petey, twitched in his nest atop my silvering crown braids. "I usually mediate between different species. You need a private investigator to look into a suspicious death—"

"Rainbow Charm Corporation owns the local investigators. Madam Alameda, you're from off station. I couldn't find any corporate affiliations in your history. You're the independent investigator I want to hire." A pleading note crept into her voice.

"I appreciate your confidence in me, but—"

"Bradbury Orbital is property of Rainbow Charm." Petey spoke directly into my mind via our neural bond, his four-inch-long body flexing as he hummed in thought. "That's a Thrassi-owned firm. This could be a cultural misunderstanding."

"—this still isn't my purview," I finished, speaking aloud to both of them at once. "I study stories, new and old, and use them to bridge misunderstandings between different kinds of lifeforms. If you had a Murkle as your neighbor, for instance, who began screaming nonstop if rain lasted for more than a day, I could explain why and advise the Murkle on more appropriate responses."

Honestly, I would have preferred to work with a screaming Murkle about then. Humans had been decisively immoral in every one of my recent jobs—cruel to fellow humans, and other kinds of life, too. Jaded as I felt, I had to wonder what crime her husband had committed to end up dead.

"Listen, madam, please." Mari took a deep breath. "Cameron was found dead yesterday. I don't know how or where. He wasn't on duty. A station exec delivered the news. His guards handed me Cameron's remains." Her voice cracked as she motioned to a small box. "The exec deposited ten thou credits into my account, saying they'd appreciate my silence or—"

"What?" I broke in. Mega-corporations snared citizens in litigation that extended beyond victims' lifespans. They did *not* hand out payoffs. "Was the exec human or Thrassi?"

"Thrassi."

Petey spoke via our link. "Thrassi are usually cautious about how they handle human dead because of their own beliefs in the afterlife." He sounded genuinely puzzled. "This case'd make for an interesting paycheck, Alameda."

Yeah, money, food, and decent beds were nice and all, but this was another human case, and one with a dead—possibly criminal—man and grieving widow. That meant messy family emotions. Ugh. My own family—well, far as I was concerned, my blood relations could wallow in a radioactive fallout zone.

I paced along a wall with animated photographs. Cameron and Mari looked at each other with genuine love. I averted my gaze, finding a shelf of small carved wooden animals. Beautiful work, unusual for a working-class home on an orbital above Earth.

I shouldn't take this case, I thought. I'd just end up feeling even more disillusioned about my own kind, and yet…

We finalized the contract. I headed back through the station with Petey.

"This case is fishier than a barrel of fish," I said to him.

"I took the liberty of pinging Aamir since you hoped to meet up, anyway," he said.

"Thanks, Petey." I couldn't ask for a better partner.

Felizards didn't usually brain-bond with humans. We're too aggro, the bullies of the universe, as my recent cases had reaffirmed. I often teased Petey that he just liked to lounge on my head all day. He resembled a cat melded with a gecko, slickly furred in blue, and favored laziness in warm places.

"Aamir will be baffled by this bizarrely philanthropic behavior, too," I said.

"I can guess the corporation's motivation already. Money. A lot more than ten thou."

"Well, obviously. The question is, how much more?"

· · · · ·

The likely answer: 1.3 mill credits.

"If this Refuge Bio Park isn't somehow connected to Cameron's mysterious death, I'll eat a h'dar egg," I said to Petey.

Neither of us had to do a big data dive to find that number. Upon entering Bradbury's central hub, advertisements and newsfeed marquees bombarded my visual overlay. Buzz focused on the station's massive, and very expensive, new park with salvaged terrain from the warming planet below.

"Let's assume Cameron is an innocent in all of this, for now," I said. "See if he worked on the park or if coworkers have come down ill. His death spooked the execs for some reason."

"Mmm. Could be a slow-acting neurotoxin like that incident at Rawn Station."

"Thanks for going to the worst-case scenario, Petey."

"That's why I'm here," he said in a chirpy tone.

Text bloomed on my overlay. "You're back!"

Good. A fast reply from Aamir. I promptly responded: "For a few days. Need some help on a case. Meet us?"

"All work no play, huh?"

I ignored my twist of yearning. "Hoped to meet you anyway. Brought you brioche from that bakery on Herriot."

I could imagine their whoop of delight. "Meet in fifteen? The usual spot?"

· · · · ·

"Hey, you two." Aamir established a private channel for the three of us to chat. The soft clink of dishware provided background noise. Most everyone in the cofftea shop spoke via mental links. "I took the liberty of ordering horchata for you, Alameda. New on the menu. Hope you find it decent."

I took a sip. Definitely not like the rice milk of my youth—better, actually. Everything from my childhood tasted sour in hindsight. "And here you are." I set the opaque bread bag before Aamir. They caressed it as if calming a scared bird.

"Who do I need to kill?" they asked.

"A dead body *is* the dilemma here," I said, and filled them in.

I studied Aamir as I spoke. They were the rare sort who became a cop because they wanted to help people, and had wearily accepted that sometimes breaking the law was the morally right thing to do. That took its toll. They looked more haggard each time we met. But then, I probably looked the same.

"Yeah. That payoff, timed with the big opening of the park—something's up. Gimme a few to probe the station database. Searches go slow for us peons without a felizard." Aamir shot me a fond smile then gazed off into space with a muffled yawn.

"You two should meet up later," Petey murmured. "No work involved."

I confirmed our private channel before I replied. "We need more jobs while we're here. We're barely—"

"Yeah, funds are tight, but a day—or night—to relax won't break us. I say that as your accountant."

"You say that because you're a meddlesome—"

"Huh." Aamir was surprised enough to say that aloud, then switched to our channel. "Cameron was found in Northumberland Forest in the new park, dead of natural causes."

I motioned impatience. "Natural, meaning…?"

"In archaic terms, 'dead of old age.' Complete organ failure, and his appearance…"

The image that flashed onto my overlay made me gape. The man was recognizable as Cameron—same dark skin, thick brows, side-parted hair—but aged a hundred years rather than thirty.

Dead of old age, indeed.

· · · · ·

Our discussion bounced back and forth. Could this be an experimental rejuv gone wrong? No, such an extreme didn't even make sense.

"Found in the woods. This sounds so *Rip Van Winkle*," I muttered.

"What?" asked Aamir, covering another yawn. "Is that one of your sorts of stories?"

By my "sorts," they meant tales mystical or supernatural. They didn't know the personal reason why such tales attracted me so—or why I shunned my family back on Earth. Or that the two things were linked.

"Well, yes. It's an old Earth story. A man played a game with spirits in the woods, then fell asleep. When he awakened, two decades had passed. He was an old man."

"But here, virtually no time passed, yet Cameron aged decades. Is *Rip Van Winkle* based on reality?" Petey phrased the question lightly, but he asked for a reason. He knew my full past.

"*Rip Van Winkle* was written as fiction, far as I know." Unlike other tales I'd researched over the years.

"Could the trees be contaminated somehow?" Aamir asked, then immediately shook their head. "Sorry, stupid question. Fouled-up as Earth is, everything gets scanned in detail."

"This reminds me of another story." I paused. "Yes, go ahead and groan both of you. Another fiction piece, but from the cusp of the twentieth century, called *War of the Worlds*."

"What, did the trees rise up and attack?" Aamir's expression was of fond amusement.

"No, this featured a Martian invasion that almost destroyed humanity. The aliens abruptly died. Turned out they weren't immune to earthly pathogens. And you really need to get to sleep, Aamir." I frowned. "You should've told me I caught you right after a shift."

"No, because then you would've put off meeting. You're right, though. I do need to hit the bunk. I work again in ten." They covered another yawn. "Promise me you won't become an old corpse in the park."

"I'll ping you later to verify I'm among the living."

They stood, cradling the bread like a baby. "I hope you get answers. If weird things keep happening in the woods, Rainbow Charm will toast that zone. Be careful."

"You, too. A mugger might try to nab that brioche."

"Let 'em try." They winked as they strolled out. We soon followed.

Ubiquitous directions made the park easy to find. As I crossed the threshold, a domed sky opened above me, the effect stunning in its realism. Sunlight warmed my face. Birds—real, actual birds—swooped and cawed above. Text bloomed on my overlay to identify creatures and plants within a limited range.

"Wow." Petey's voice was small in awe. "This is like Earth, huh?"

"Parts of it, yeah." I took in a deep breath. This didn't remotely resemble the high-elevation scrubby desert of my Santa Fe childhood, but it still felt and smelled like Earth. Like home.

We crossed a Northumberland moorland, forest visible ahead. A cluster of obvious tourists directed bot-cameras closer to blooming heather. Two women with infants in hovers ambled by, followed by a Thrassi jogger.

A strange pall fell over me as we entered the woods, the shadows deep and mustiness real. This place embodied ancientness. Despite the well-beaten dirt path, I suddenly felt two hundred miles from civilization.

Aamir's info had included where the body was found. A grove of particularly grandiose oaks guarded the spot amid thick vegetation. The leaves and mud looked undisturbed.

"No signs of a formal police investigation." I shook my head. "This was a panicked cover-up from the time they found Cameron."

"Time to find a nosey local?" Petey asked as we headed toward the periphery of the woods.

"Yes indeed." No matter the nature of my cases, no matter the species involved, someone in the vicinity always spied on proceedings and was happy to blab about everything they'd witnessed.

A few minutes of study led me toward an older human on a bench, her feet jutted out to boldly expose a silver prosthetic leg. She eyed us with blatant curiosity.

"I've never seen a felizard on station before. Welcome, both of you." She shared her ID via overlay: Loulou Okeezie. "I used to pilot a transport to Mrr. It's a lovely place."

"Did you?" Petey spoke aloud, voice rusty with disuse but full of delight. "Few humans visit my homeworld."

"Good. Keeps it decent." Loulou grunted. "Now, your kind don't explore for no reason. What brings you here?"

"We're curious about an incident nearby," I said.

"Which one?" Loulou arched a silvery brow.

"There's more than one?" Petey perked up in curiosity, claws grazing my scalp.

"Someone was hurt in the woods yesterday. I watched them get evacuated." She clicked her teeth. "Then there's the poor girl dragged out here every evening."

"What girl?" I asked.

"Oh, she's maybe seven and screams bloody murder when her nan-bot drags her by the woods. At least, she used to. She stays quiet now, but clearly hates the place. Claimed the forest *stole* her baby brother. Sounds downright medieval, don't it?" She laughed.

"What?" Her words doused me like cold water.

"Of course, her brother's in a hover right there, which makes the whole thing even sillier."

"You said they come by in the evening. Has that happened already today?" Petey asked.

"Not yet!"

Via private channel, Petey said, "Take deep breaths, Alameda. I'll chat our way out of here."

He knew her words had gotten to me, bless him. I stood with a pasted-on smile as he kept talking.

At age seven, I'd been the one screaming for help after my cousin José had been dragged into a canal by La Llorona, the legendary wailing specter in white. Older kids used her as a threat to scare the younger set, and probably had for hundreds of years. "Stay out too late by the water, and that old ghost'll drown you like she did her own kids!"

I didn't believe in her until I saw her with my own eyes. Her plaintive song didn't lure me, but José—he'd have tried to save flies from drowning. He wanted to help the sad lady, too.

Afterward, the police had been tactful enough to suggest I needed therapy. An aunt hinted I'd killed José for some petty reason and lied about La Llorona to cover it up. The rest of my family, they never forgave me for letting José die, which was fine. I never forgave them for years of snide remarks about my sanity, plus outright physical abuse.

Despite the cruelty I endured, I never doubted what I saw. That didn't make me a sucker for every similar story that came along, though. I needed to meet this girl.

Petey wrapped up the conversation, and we retreated to another bench with a view. We idled in wait.

Finally, a nan-bot with a hover and a small child strolled up the path. I advanced to intercept them. The young human remained quiet, but by her wide eyes and twitchy movements, she looked ready to bolt if something lunged from the woods. That gave me an idea.

"Hey Petey, search for myths about Northumberland forests."

"Like if ghosts enjoy playing ninepins there?" he quipped, referencing *Rip Van Winkle*.

"That, or replace infants with clones."

"These trees need new hobbies," he muttered.

"By the way, your cuteness will likely be helpful in the next few minutes. Just to remind you."

His groan filled my head. "Like I need a reminder."

Human children loved felizards. I totally understood the attraction—and also why felizards were deeply insulted by being treated as "pets" when they were superior to humans in a lot of ways. Petey griped, but he didn't mind really.

"Ah, this is a Martian nan-bot model 1980-1!" he said via channel as we drew close. "Serv bots in that range were nigh obsolete from the get-go. By default, they regard unfamiliar humans as hostile."

"That sounds bad."

"Only for you. Felizards, on the contrary, are deemed harmless—so long as our public ID shows we're current on standard immunizations." He bounded from his nest atop my head.

"In other words, its programming is so terrible, it thinks you're a cat. What makes me think you've taken advantage of this lapse before?"

The nan-bot gave Petey an obvious scan as he trotted up on stubby legs. The girl gasped and held her arms wide. He accepted the invitation and leaped up to her shoulder. In contrast, I came within five feet and the bot sheltered its two charges.

"Stranger, maintain your distance from these children." The nan-bot spoke in a perky tone.

"You're so soft!" the girl crooned as she stroked Petey. He leaned into her touch. "I've only seen felizards in vids!"

"Your nan-bot's not that smart, is it?" Petey spoke in a whisper. Indeed, it didn't seem to register that he had spoken at all.

"It's not," she whispered back. "But that's okay sometimes."

The nan-bot's eyes clicked as its gaze roved between us. "You should be wary of speaking to strangers."

"I approached because your female charge appeared upset. If you examine my credentials," I said to the bot, inviting it to download the data, "you'll see I'm a xenoarbitrator. I wanted to make sure she was okay." I wished I could ask the girl's name, but that was certain to set off the bot.

"My charge has no need of your services."

"The woods scare me," the girl blurted, stroking Petey's spine. She looked me in the eye, clearly relieved to have a receptive audience. "I believed that I saw things there and that they followed us home and stole my real brother away, even though cameras all around didn't see a thing." She knew to word things in the past tense to avoid triggering her nan-bot.

Cameras hadn't captured La Llorona, either. That was a theme across human cultures—and alien cultures, too. Children able to see what adults, for all their presumed wisdom, cannot.

"This matter has been discussed and resolved," chided the bot. "Human children sometimes suffer such delusions. She has adapted."

"What's in the hover, then?" I asked the girl.

"Feel no obligations to answer questions from a stranger," the bot said.

"Something that looks like my brother but isn't my brother. Not that he's bad or anything." To my surprise, the girl looked his way with genuine concern. "The station would be scary to someone who'd only lived in a forest."

"Alameda." Petey spoke over our channel. "These incidents out of the forest do match old stories from the Northumberland region."

He fed me keywords, and I recalled stories I hadn't read in decades, about fairies, changelings, and other realms where a person could live out decades and return to find no time had passed—or be away for minutes and discover that decades or centuries had slipped away. Likely antecedent tales of the fictional Rip Van Winkle.

"Did you see these kidnappers from the woods?" I asked aloud.

"I thought I did." She had a shrewd glint to her eye. I hid a smile. This girl needed help, yes, but she didn't need to be saved. "Floating lights and shadowy things with antlers."

Fairies. Ancient beings of Earth, here on Bradbury Orbital. I had solved my mysterious death case—with an answer no other human here would believe, least of all the grieving widow.

But now there was an extra complication: the changeling children. I couldn't save Cameron. I hadn't been able to save my cousin José. But these swapped children—maybe this could be made right. But how?

As a kid, as a disbelieved survivor, my rage had burned long and fierce. One of my big regrets was that I didn't fight to save my cousin. That I could've saved him—saved my place within my family. I wasted a lot of years craving to belong with them again, even as they treated me like dirt.

I clenched my fists. I looked at the girl, at the hover with the different child, at the woods. I let my hands go slack.

The circumstances between my childhood loss and the losses on Bradbury were not the same. La Llorona was a cruel ghost repeating her sins from life. Fairies were mischievous and cruel, yes, but… but I could reason with them, couldn't I? They were like a native-yet-alien species.

I could've laughed. This case was in my job's purview after all.

The dome above softened to pink and gold as artificial sol neared its end.

"I'm going to go into the woods to talk to these creatures. My friend will stay with you," I said to the girl.

Her eyes widened in alarm. Petey emitted a squeak of surprise.

I faced the bot, lowering my voice. "This is a therapeutic technique that's used on Dralnar when younglings in crèches develop fears about attacks by extinct predators. Adults sign treaties with the 'monsters' to keep them away."

"Dralnar." Its processors considered this. "Yes, I see records of this method. You may commence, but know we cannot stay out after dark."

"Alameda, you sure about this?" Petey asked via our link.

"No, but I'm… uniquely qualified to act as ambassador here and now." That made me feel stronger. Like the loss of José—and my whole family—could directly help other families at last. "Here's hoping I don't end up like Cameron. We still don't know why they killed him and no one else."

"That we know of."

"Always with the optimism, huh, Petey?"

The ethereal feel of the forest deepened as light faded.

Birds seemed to hush in suspense as I returned to the oak grove. I studied the shadows, every rustle increasing my unease. These woods were reminiscent of *War of the Worlds*. Unseen things lurked, ready to kill me.

I took a deep breath. I had to do this. I *needed* to do this. No kids needed to deal with trauma even remotely close to mine.

"I'm here to speak with the fairies who have long resided in these woods, newly transplanted to Bradbury Orbital." To my left, a twig snapped; my heartbeat threatened to pound out of my chest. "According to stories, you've aggressively toyed with humans for centuries. You cannot continue that here. Most people… don't believe in you anymore. Your existence doesn't register on modern technology. This does give you some advantages—more subterfuge for certain—but it also makes you, and these woods, even more vulnerable."

The forest became impossibly quieter. I had a strange sense that things—many things—were listening. I resolved to be blunt.

"If people continue to die here, this place will be viewed as a liability by the caretakers on Bradbury Orbital. They'll destroy the forest. They won't know that they're destroying you along with it."

Or maybe the fairies would simply be sealed in their other realm. In any case, the loss of the woods couldn't bode well for them.

The sound of creaking wood drew my attention to my left, to a moving branch far above my head level. The limb had to be about as thick as my arm. Only after it pushed aside smaller branches did I realize it *was* an arm—one twice the length of mine, garbed in pleated cloth that resembled bark. Or was it actual bark? I wasn't about to ask. I couldn't muster words at all as I craned my head to gawk at a brown face, smooth yet ancient. Motes of lights circled around it like satellites.

The fairy's head tilted to one side, scrutinizing me with eyes the incredible black of deep space. I waited for it to speak. Or to kill me. To do *something*.

"What's happening there?" broke in Petey. "Your anxiety levels just jumped higher than a gharkak."

"I see one. More than one," I corrected myself. The lights had to be tiny fairies.

I breathed deeply to center myself. I'd met plenty of other ancient beings in my travels. I couldn't let this confrontation intimidate me simply because these extraordinary beings were from Earth—like La Llorona.

With that reminder of my past, I took care with my next words to ensure that I would have a future.

I continued, "Human ignorance has caused too many species to go extinct. I don't want you to be among them—even if you're bringing this danger on yourselves." My tone harshened. "You cannot age people to death or otherwise kill them. You cannot continue to steal children, human or otherwise. If you want to survive—and thrive—you may eventually want to make yourself known to others on station. Trust me, I know humans are a pain," I grimaced, "but making alliances—and eventually friendships— will be mutually beneficial."

The tree-being tilted its head the other way, the impenetrable gaze never leaving mine. Behind it, the woods continued to crackle with unseen life.

"Alameda. One extra note," Petey whispered in my mind. "You're being very helpful, but fairies don't like debts."

Okay. I could work with that. "If you find my words useful,

in exchange, I ask that you replace the changeling children. Please keep them unaged, unaltered." I racked my brain but couldn't think of anything else. "I sincerely hope you and your forest can become good neighbors here on Bradbury Orbital. Thank you for listening."

I barely breathed as I waited for a response. After what felt like forever, it dipped its head in an unmistakable nod, then took a graceful step backward, vanishing in an instant. The motes left brief yellow contrails as they followed. Utter silence fell over the forest.

I lingered for a moment, stupefied, and then headed back through the brush. Never before had my back felt so vulnerable. Exiting the woods, I took in a deep breath as if I'd been drowning.

"I'm alive!" I sent Petey. I looked at my hands, touched my face. "I'm the same old me. Right?"

"According to the data I'm reading, yep. Did you hear any reply? Nothing registered on my end."

I started walking. "They didn't need to speak. They understood."

The girl greeted me with a teary hug. Since she had initiated contact, the bot didn't react. This thing was about as lousy a caretaker as my own parents, and that was saying something.

I pulled back to look the girl in the eye, still wary of the bot and my presumed therapeutic technique. "The creatures in the woods are called fairies. Look up old books from Earth—nineteenth, twentieth, twenty-first century—and you'll find lots of stories. I asked them to bring back your brother, but—" I held up a hand in caution. "I don't know if they will."

"Fairies." She tested the strange word on her tongue. "Do you think—if they take this brother back, I can still be friends with him, too?"

Her compassion left me momentarily speechless. "If the exchange happens, ask the trees later on."

Her nod was grave. "Ask the trees. I think… I think I can do that." She regarded the distant forest. "I don't feel so scared now that I know what's there. I hope I can still be friends with both of my brothers."

"I hope so, too," I murmured.

. . . . .

Mari Kane accepted my redacted report with a stifled sob. "At least Cameron died of natural causes in the forest. He loved trees."

We spoke in her parlor again. She gazed toward the carved figurines, a ghost of a smile upon her lips.

"Did Cameron make those?" I asked.

"Oh yes, madam. Whenever we traveled to the surface, he'd bring back pieces of wood. He was so excited about the park opening here."

"'Bring back,'" Petey murmured in my head. "Meaning he smuggled wood past environmental inspectors."

I replied in turn. "That means my gut instinct was right. Cameron was breaking station law by gleaning from the park and must've broken some kind of fairy rule, as well, for them to kill him like that."

A few more murmured words of condolence to Mari, and we left. I knew I should advertise my availability again, but I just plain didn't want to.

Instead, I sent a message to Aamir.

Not a minute later, they replied. "Need to eat breakfast before I go on shift. How about sharing a lovely loaf with me?"

A chortle escaped my lips.

"What?" asked Petey. "Oh. Let me guess. Aamir?"

"Would you like some time on your solar pad at the hotel?" I said to Petey. "I've been invited to share a loaf."

"Oh, is that what you humans call it now?"

"Did you solve that case?" Aamir asked, utterly oblivious to Petey's innuendo in the other channel.

"Yes," I said, giggling to myself. "Can't share the details, but I'm hopeful you won't have more problems in the woods."

Hopeful. That was a change. I'd started out the day jaded as could be, and though my worst suspicions about Cameron had been confirmed, I couldn't despair too much. I smiled, optimistic for the future of the girl, and her brothers, and the fairies on Bradbury Orbital. A lot of lousy humans were out there, sure, but we weren't all bad. Some of us were even willing to share their bread.

Books take a long time to put together. When we approached **Maurice Broaddus** about writing a story for our anthology, the worldwide Black Lives Matter protests had not yet begun. But as I write this intro, we are several weeks into protests and racially motivated violence that are happening during a global pandemic. Current events make this story even more poignant, with Maurice showing us how tone-deaf the statement, "You brought this on yourself," is. Black Lives Matter, and Black stories should be heard and read. And we are proud to bring you a Broaddus original.

MUR

CITY OF REFUGE
MAURICE BROADDUS

*H*ope was a fickle bitch. Mercurial and quixotic, the kind of
woman you spent the whole week getting ready for only to have
her cancel the date at the last minute.

The world was ending, but Royal Parker still had to go
through the motions of a job interview. He knew as soon as he sat
down across from the manager—in his ridiculous red-and-white
striped shirt and paper hat—that he wasn't getting the job. Despite
the assurances from the Liberation Investment Support Cooperative,
the corporate entity controlling the state's infrastructure, jobs were
scarce. He hated that even part of him wanted this person's
approval, that this idiot pretending to have authority held the keys
of opportunity. Still, Royal tried to do all the things his counselors
recommended. He shook the manager's hand, his large, meaty
hand engulfing it like a shark devouring tuna. Royal attempted to
shrink into his seat to hide his hulking build, a man used to many
hours a day lifting weights. As the manager bridged his fingers in
front of him, Royal could see him assuming what his story was

without so much of a glance at his resume dancing before him as a series of holographic projections. He'd taken note of Royal's cautious shamble, his one eye constantly on alert over his shoulder; his cornrows, nice and neat, revealing the barest hint of gray budding at his temples. He'd always wanted to wear a linen suit for as long as he could remember. When he was inside, such a suit had the feel of reaching for something he couldn't attain. Not that things were much different now. Sitting up straight as to not cause a crease in it, Royal smiled his best, safe, toothy grin.

Though he tried to hide it, the manager was scared. He guarded his position, not wanting to risk his job in any way. He feared losing it and the system then treating him like a… Royal. The manager asked him to explain the gaps in his job history. Royal shifted his posture, his shirt rode up just an inch, enough to reveal the beginnings of a tattoo. Then came the familiar refrain.

"We'll let you know if anything opens up," the manager said.

This was the same story all over what folks now called Original Earth. Things were getting bad. End of the world, book of Revelations, apocalyptic-type shit, but the idea of that was too much for folks. So they doubled down on the things they knew, business as usual until the total collapse in order to maintain the status quo. Once Indianapolis had declared bankruptcy, a quarter of the population left town, only hastening the inevitable. It was unable to pay its debts. The slow decay of infrastructure spread like a metastasizing tumor. These days, even emergency services were no longer part of city services. Ambulances abandoned, broken down on the side of the road, stripped of parts; police cars a decade old if they ran at all. The Indianapolis City Council turned to privatization through LISC. The whole city was sold off, part and parcel. Everything was up for sale: land, services, jobs. The richest one percent around the world fled the ecological disaster that O.E. was becoming, building what they called a new Earth for themselves on Mars. Royal's own people were in the midst of a "fifth wave migration" to the moon for the experiment they now call Muungano. Black folks were heading there at such a pace, needing so much housing, they now constructed orbiting cities like a crisscrossing belt crowning the moon. But O.E., these streets, were all he knew, and he couldn't bring himself to leave. Or couldn't bring himself to believe that his people would have him. He slipped on his oxygenator mask and went back into the street's comforting embrace.

Royal began his daily stroll and took inventory of his surroundings: broken streetlights, cracked pavement overtaken by grass and weeds, sewer lines backing up into houses, piles of uncollected garbage—bags of trash long torn open by roaming dogs spilling their gutted contents to the streets and curb. Funny things happened when a person ran out of money. Slowly losing the sense of who they were. The way that hunger and lack gnawed away at their very being. He couldn't escape the shadow of guilt— of being unable to provide for even himself—that followed him. Even on the verge of economic collapse, checks came too slow and bills too fast.

Royal's block hid, tucked in the shadow of Indianapolis' Golden Hill neighborhood. Not enough wealth to move to Mars, but the alcove could afford to dome itself. Its air filtered, its water purified by its own system, the transparent shield screened most of the worst UV. A conspicuous concentration of resources within eyeshot and yet out of reach of his neighborhood, since the poorest always lived in the most vulnerable infrastructures. The worst effects of climate change were felt by those least able to do anything about it, a climate apocalypse caste system.

A surveillance drone hovered low, wanting its presence noted before circling out of sight again. Paint flecked from the wood trim of the house. Columns of worn brick held up the porch. A punching bag dangled from a rusted chain in the corner. The bones of the house were still intact, the rest an echo of what had once been. LISC provided retrofitting loans to homeowners for basic air and water filtration systems. Not even close to doming, but good enough so masks weren't necessary indoors. Since so many homes fell into default on the loans, LISC owned many of the houses in the neighborhood. Going on its third generation within the family, the house still belonged to his niece. For now. She let Royal stay in a guest room on the second floor. The room had been split into two rooms, just enough room for a single bed and chest o' drawers. The size of a prison cell.

Ford waited for him on the porch.

Ford. One word. The LISC penal officer barked the word at Royal on their first meeting and that was all he got for a name. It could be his first or last. A light-skinned dude with low-cropped hair and cold eyes half-closed with boredom. He favored tight-fitting T-shirts which showed off his chest and arm muscles. He had an unlit cigarette tucked behind his ear though no one ever saw him smoke.

"What's up, Ford? Wasn't expecting you."

They shook hands without warmth.

"That's the whole point of a home visit, Old School." There was always the intimation of threat to Ford, even in the low measure of his greeting. Like most LISC officials, his oxygenator didn't reduce his voice to heavy asthmatic breaths. Ford called him Old School from the jump. He scanned him like a story he'd read a dozen times before. "Nice suit. What you been up to?"

"Just out looking for a new job. I done been to a half dozen fast food joints."

"I can't help you with your hustle," Ford glanced about the porch, prowling along it like a disturbed cat. "You won't get a job tatted up like that. Won't even make it through the interview."

"Who you kidding? Once they scan that I been locked up, my resume gets shitcanned."

Ford idly punched the bag. The system tracked the movement of all of its citizens. A PO's job was to sweep through every so often to verify a parolee's address and make sure they were where they were supposed to be. Ford's rep rang out on the streets because he took shit to another level. Like it was his mission in life, he rode each of his clients as if the man wanted them to fail rather than operate as a "re-entry coordinator," which was his actual official job title. Ford's brand of monitoring he summarized as to "tail 'em, nail 'em, and jail 'em."

"Are you a man of your word, Old School?"

"I'm a man who doesn't like to go through needless motions when we know what the result is going to be." Waiting for the trap to spring—which was every conversational turn with his PO—Royal eyed Ford's unlit cigarette. His mouth itched to light and inhale it. Wouldn't be any worse than breathing what passed for air anyway. A reflexive cough sputtered within his mask. He took an assessing inhalation for any telltale scrapings within his lungs, signaling that he had The Rasp. The high levels of dust and such in the air settled like corrosion within a person's chest. But he breathed smoothly. For now. "I can't stand people selling me on fake dreams."

"Word on the vine was that you were tough. One of the baddest cats who ran the streets before you went on pause." Ford delivered a combination of blows to the bag, bobbing and weaving when it swayed back toward him. An excuse to demonstrate how fast his hands were.

"I don't know about all that."

"Me either. I'm just not seeing it. I've brought down taller motherfuckers than you in my sleep. All I see now is a broken-down old man itching to get sent back up." Ford's words were another lash of humiliation he had no choice but to accept. This was Ford's act, trying to provoke Royal into saying or doing something reckless. Stir that anger in him. If Ford were just a man, that kind of slick comment would've earned him a quick beatdown. But Ford had the full weight and authority of LISC's judicial system behind him. Royal could swing at the system, but when it swung back, he'd wake up in jail. Satisfied that his words set Royal in his place, Ford smiled. "You gonna invite me in?"

Shrugging, Royal lowered his head, to hide the flash of anger in his eyes. The gray sky of small particulate fog grew so thick it blotted out the sun. The house door hissed, creating a bubble while the mechanism scrubbed the air with them stopping in the doorway before it allowed them through. They walked through the living room, a minefield of strewn toys from the babies and dirty plates of teenage boys who didn't pick up after themselves. Royal stayed downstairs when he was alone, retreating to his space only when family returned home. He didn't want to intrude, remind them that he took up precious space. A low-hanging smell of mildew wafted along the baseboards from the basement hinting at a cracked seal he'd need to attend to. African masks hung on the walls. A portrait of his niece and her children. A blank space where her husband should have been. Royal wondered about all of the blank spaces in people's lives where he should have been. A sour smell of sweat wafted from the couch where his niece often slept. She worked such long hours as a nurse that some nights she never made it past the couch from the door when she came home. She woke with the kids in time to shuffle them through their morning routines and left for work again.

Royal plopped down heavily into the chair. He heard that on Muungano, their nanobots were so attenuated to their people's commands, they could fashion custom furniture with a wave of their hands. Or clean surfaces. Or clean air. That world was beyond him every bit as much as Mars. Or even Golden Hills. Unconsciously, he started to rub his leg, nursing a phantom ache from an injury suffered while inside.

Framed photos lined the mantel. Ford ran an inspecting finger along it before taking a long moment to examine his hand. Like a guard, full of his authority to toss his space like a vulture picking his bones, sifting his flesh for anything to amuse themselves. He picked up a framed candid photograph—a holovid system was well out of their finances—of Royal's grandparents. Royal hated the way Ford combed through his life as if he had the right. That he could pick up his life and set it down any time he wanted. The intensity of Ford's scrutiny reminiscent of the lingering gaze of a doctor during an exam.

"Nice home," Ford said almost absently, continuing to nose about.

"Thanks. I've worked hard to get things back on track. Made a plan. Working my plan." Royal recited the words, but to his ear he might as well have clutched his hat to his chest and end each sentence with "yessa, boss."

"That sounds…"

Royal's link alert chirped. He held up a "one minute" finger to Ford though no holovid displayed. His was the basic unit issued by LISC so that their citizens could remain tethered to the system network. Clinging to the possibility that it might be an actual call back from a possible employer, he turned his back to the PO. "Yes?"

Ford knocked a photo from the mantel.

"I got to go," Royal whispered. "Yes, tomorrow then."

Ford didn't bother to meet his eyes. His hand rested on another photo, deciding whether it too should tumble. For a moment, Royal saw who he used to be. A brash young man, cocky and sure, his strength and vitality able to power through most situations. Then he remembered that young man ended up in prison. "You seem to barely got time for me, Old School."

"I'm not trying to put you off. I'm hustling. You caught me

at a time. You know how it is. Responsibilities around the house. Trying to stay afloat. I may have a line on a possible job doing deliveries, though. Whatever it takes, right?"

"Yeah, you sound like a busy man." Ford centered the photo on the mantel. "I may have to see about slowing you down."

Ford squared off against him, letting the silence land like shackles at Royal's feet.

"Why you got to play me so hard?" Royal hated how the hint of pleading in his voice reduced him.

The front door chimed and the filtration system whirred. Duke, his niece's oldest son, stopped within the doorway, allowing a rush of air sweetened by the cloying smell of weed on his clothes. A little dude with an addict's thinness to him, his twists needed tightening as his hair tumbled out of his head in an untamed sprawl. A constellation of freckles splattered his cheeks and faded splotches lined his neck, like he'd been splashed with bleach. A homemade mask of toilet paper and duct tape dangled from his ear. He worked for the Paschal family. Kevin Paschal, Pass, was once a neighborhood entrepreneur and sometime drug dealer who built an entire family enterprise under the nose and off the radar of LISC. Duke spotted Ford from the threshold and ground his cigarette underfoot.

Royal winced. The last thing Ford needed was an audience.

"I like breaking eggs. If a few omelets get made, cool." Ford thumbed toward Royal for Duke's benefit. "This motherfucker right here thinks he's somebody."

Duke raised his hands like he wanted to back away without mess landing on him. "My name's Bennett and I ain't in it."

"You clever, ain't you?" Ford's voice dripped with the sense of having been disrespected. "Royal, you must come from a clever family."

"It's not like that," Royal said.

"Look at you. Domesticated dude. You playing at being a family man, now?"

Royal swallowed. Not just the dry hitch in his throat, but he wanted to tell this trifling, bureaucratic, overcompensating Napoleon what he could do with his home visits. With his intimated threats. With his assumptions and judgments. But he couldn't. Ford was just one set of teeth of the disembodied beast people called the justice system. The beast would have its due, its bones to grind to fine powder.

"I'll help you out, Old School. Why don't you come down to my office tomorrow and we'll see what we can do to make sure you aren't so... overwhelmed."

"But my job appointment tomorrow?" Royal knew an office visit meant Ford keeping him—and whoever else made his shit-list—sit and wait from 8 a.m. until whenever he felt like dismissing them.

"Fuck. Your. Job." A pause lingered at the end of Ford's sentence like the PO wanted to add a word just to make his point plain. "You will be at my office first thing. We'll go through all of your paperwork. And only if you find yourself not violated can you even *think* about taking a job. You got me?"

"Yes." Royal let the sentence stop without adding the word "sir" in mild protest.

Ford glared at him up and down as if he were small, sneering before sucking his teeth. He cut his eyes to Duke, who stepped out of the way. The door hissed, the portal sealing shut behind him.

"Your boy's trippin' hard today," Duke said.

"He ain't my boy. I trust Ford as far as I can throw him and I ain't been working out lately." The bluster sounded hollow. "It's the end of the world and I still have to deal with this petty foolishness."

Royal angled away from Duke, unable to sit under his nephew's gaze. He'd been stripped of something and the less someone was able to see witness, the better. His head slumped, determined to keep his eyes closed until the sting of his humiliation and helplessness ebbed.

· · · · ·

Hope was like a stripper. If you paid her well, the more she came around looking for something extra. But you wanted her around since her company and attention almost felt like the real thing. You came to depend on them like any addict in need of a fix. Then one day you see her fucking around with someone else and you could no longer convince yourself that her attention was anything except fake. She never truly existed. Not for you.

A shrill of alarm clawed at the back of Royal's head from the first moment he stepped into Ford's office. The receptionist barely glanced at him, no longer particularly noting the parade of felons when they came through. They were numbers on numbers: a filing code counting down the days until they were off papers or heading back to lockup. Wagging a finger, she directed him to take a seat. Chow lines, sitting in his cell, shower lines, linkage lines the system trained him how to wait on his life.

No one else had their life held up alongside him in the office.

In another life, he had his own construction company. Fixed up and painted many of the houses in the neighborhood as a part of LISC's "Pre-enact the Future" program. He also had a temper that flashed hot when pushed. It led to the occasional "misunderstanding." He got clipped for drunk driving (which quickly became drunk and disorderly), escalating once he began shouting at the officers, which led to them calling for a backup unit (which quickly became backup units), once he began yelling about what they could do with their unwarranted traffic stop. The misunderstanding occurred once he stumbled into one of the officers and they began swinging. That cost him a few years. When he went upstate to "college" he got hooked on that her-ron.

Two hours later, the receptionist motioned for him to enter.

No nameplate rested on Ford's desk. No holovids of any family hovered about. No awards or certificates hung on the wall. No clue illuminating who the man was other than Ford. Perpetual coffee rings scarred his desk as if he left standing orders to never scrub them clean.

Without so much as turning to him, Ford handed Royal a specimen medi-cup. "Fill it up as best you can."

Royal sized up the medi-cup. He wanted to make a joke to break the tension in the room, but there was less than no play in Ford's eyes. A level of corruption and ineptitude infected the PO to the bone. Royal turned to head to the bathroom.

"Nuh uh. Where I can see you." Ford turned to the holographic reports display hovering over his desk.

"Right here?" Royal gestured to his zipper.

"You get a drop on my floor, you'll be licking it clean."

With the nervousness of a deer sniffing about, knowing a trap was about to spring shut but not knowing where from, a roar of panic filled the back of his mind. Royal fished in his pants to pull out his dick, there in the open of the office like some animal. Wanting to piss all over the rings on Ford's desk and leave the final dribbling trail on the PO's shoes, Royal peered straight ahead. He blinked a few times to fight back the burning in each eye.

Ford's studious observation veered dangerously close to a leer. Like the guards inside watching an absurd show, they vented the anger of their powerlessness on the prisoners. Their rough hands tugging at his jaw: poking him, sticking fingers in his mouth, ordering him about, controlling him. It was all the same game, wondering how much he'd be worth out in the field. Incarceration was a profitable LISC venture.

Careful not to overfill the container or splash, he slipped his dick back into his drawers lest he accidentally drip on the carpet. He secured the lid, set the specimen cup on Ford's desk, and backed away. Royal strained to keep any challenge from his eyes. Ford nodded, stepping between Royal and the desk.

"Good and tight." Ford turned around with the specimen cup. "Temperature says an even hundred degrees. You may be running a fever."

Royal stifled a reflexive cough. An increasing sense of unease ran through him. Life had a way of going from sugar to shit with a quickness. Ford tapped the screen on the container with a knowing grin. A few seconds later, a single colored line appeared.

Positive.

"Tsk, tsk, tsk," Ford said. "Someone's been a bad boy."

"That's not possible," Royal said. "I've been clean for…"

"Yes?" Ford waited for the unprompted confession.

"I'm clean is all I'm saying. I know I am. That has to be one of them false positives."

"You'd like that, wouldn't you? Jerk LISC around a bit with your claims of false positives. Life is one big conspiracy against you, isn't it?" Ford eased back in his chair, arms folded across his chest. "You about to accuse me of something?"

The question hung in the air between them. A positive drop was "game over". Once Ford reported he was positive, he would leave the office in cuffs headed for processing preparing to return upstate to finish out his prison sentence. There was no appeal. No re-test. Ford only blocked his view for a moment, not much time to do much to spike the sample. Maybe switch them out, but it would be pointless to accuse him anyway. A parolee's word against a PO's. That complaint wouldn't exactly make it to the top of anyone's priority list.

"No," Royal said. "Sir."

"Sir. I like that." Ford sat up straight, scrutinizing Royal like a chef determining if his dish was ready. Existing on just as low a rung as him, but reveling in the power of his position, for what little that afforded him. A better seat in the master's house. "Not so much big talk from you now. I have your full attention? You sure you're not too busy for me now?"

"No." Royal clenched his fist in impotent rage.

Ford glanced down at the balled fingers and smiled. "You want to take a swing at me?"

"No." Royal unclenched to massage the top of his thigh. "Just frustrated."

"I would be, too. Flushing your life away for a shot in the arm."

"But I didn't…" Royal hated the near whine his voice took in protest.

"I know you're out here serving niggas up. And getting served. You're a criminal. Ain't no treatment for that. That's a lifelong condition. No medicine. No counseling. No rehabilitation. This is who you are. Life's about accepting responsibilities for your actions. Like you being too busy for me."

"I'm sorry about that." Royal's gaze wavered.

"Fuck. Your. Sorry. You were ninety percent violated by the time you first stepped into my office. This was just the final ten percent. You all the same. You people only know one way. You don't know how to live on the outside. There's no part of you civilized. You make us all look bad. But I got you. All I had to do was let you be true to your nature and you could inevitably fuck shit up."

The world on the brink of a complete, extinction-level environmental collapse. Politicians declaring war on some country or another every week. Civilizations establishing themselves in new parts of the solar system, and Royal was forgotten. Lost in all the events too big to wrap his mind around for anyone to notice his small problems of just trying to survive the day-to-day. His world orbited a low-level bureaucrat so caught up in his own mess, he'd rather step on Royal's throat than help him have a chance to build a better life. "Is there… anything I can do?"

"Son, my job ain't to help you. My job's to make sure you take as few people down with you as possible." The deliberate emphasis on the word "son" was another reminder that Royal wasn't seen as a man. A malicious grin spread across Ford's face. "Tell you what. You do me a favor and next week I'll give you a re-test. You pop positive again, ain't nothing I can do for you. Negative and I'll chalk this up to an unfortunate… misunderstanding."

"What sort of favor?" The roar returned to the back of his mind.

"You in a bargaining position, Old School?"

Royal shook his head. "Just need to know the scope of the job."

"I need you to procure something for me." Ford scribbled on a piece of paper. He clutched the folded paper between two fingers and extended it to Royal. "Here's the address. Plus day and time. He has one of them fake books as a safe thing on a shelf in his study. Let me know when you have it and I'll swing through to collect. You don't want to screw this up."

Royal reached for the paper.

Ford withdrew it, giving him a proprietary stare. The condescension mixed with shapeless threat returned to his tone. "Ain't too many second chances for people like you. You don't want to fuck this up."

· · · · ·

Hope was a loose chain that jangled whenever you moved to remind you it was there. It allowed you to move just enough to give you the illusion of freedom, but still kept you in your place. Hope made things horrifying because hope led to the false belief that there was a chance that you could one day be free.

His life was an unfinished letter.

That her-ron addiction left a wound in him. The familiar pang, the hunger, the need to ride a blast. Anything to quell the anxiety. To almost forget. Almost. Because other than the very first blast, he never soared so high as to completely forget. Without it, he sank to the floor, dying by inches, every day. Pain arced through him, nesting in his deepest places and nursing on every bad memory, every insult, every beating. Addiction was adaptation to the cage his life became. When isolated or alone, drugs were the sole comfort to be found. The pain vanished and the rush allowed him to do anything because nothing hurt. People would do anything to keep the pain away. No matter the sunken eyes. No matter skin the color of bruises. No matter how much a mirror terrified him for fear of the monster reflected in it. There was no such thing as control.

When he stood in front of the house, Royal realized why the address on the piece of paper seemed so familiar. Pass's drug fortunes built a veritable fortress. A wrought-iron fence surrounded the home. Statues of lions rearing atop concrete posts. A four-car garage usually had his current Lexus parked in plain view like a trophy on display. Pass could easily live in Golden Hill, but the houses of that neighborhood remained in the hands of people who stuck to their own kind.

Out front as a lookout, Duke took a few practice shots at the portable goalpost in front of the house. The surrounding bushes probably hid an EMF pulse generator to disrupt drones, maybe even a number of weapons. His makeshift mask in place, not even being afforded a real one as he stood out in the polluted air for his efforts. He knocked down the shot and the rock bounced, stopping at Royal's feet. Royal picked it up, bounced it once, and took a shot. The net snapped, crisp as money.

"Still got some lift to you," Duke said.

"All I need is someone to talk crazy and wake it up."

Duke's gaze shifted in knowing appraisal. "Are you up?"

There it was. The tone. Even if Royal hadn't heard it, he'd have felt it the same way he did every time his soles slapped the sidewalk concrete underneath them. The tension on the streets, as real as a chilled wind blowing fast food paper bags down deserted alleyways. He recognized the glint in his eyes. The waiting. The expectation. Theirs was the inevitability of the bullet crashing through bone and spurting brain matter. "Just thinking."

"You know Pass don't like loiterers." Duke eyed the low-lying haze for any encroaching drones. "So, you need to make up your mind."

Royal stared at the house, wondering what the book safe Ford wanted so badly contained. Drugs. Money. Data sticks. Blackmail materials. Maybe the whole thing was a trap. An excuse for him to get caught breaking in. His body riddled with bullets would be just another day in "Napghanistan." The chorus rose in his head, a room full of voices, each vying to be heard. He flushed with heat. It filled him so full he could barely breathe.

"Yeah, serve me up."

"You sure?" Disappointment underscored Duke's question.

"Yeah. How much?"

"Ten." Duke whistled for someone and held up a lone finger. A boy, no older than twelve, wheeled his bike toward Royal. His

hand-me-down rebreather unit—a first-generation oxygenator—
nearly covered his entire face. He held out his hand. Royal clasped
it, his hand swallowing the boy's to his wrist with the exchange.

Duke pounded the ball against the pavement, turning his
back on his uncle. "Who up next?"

· · · · ·

*Hope was a victim, full of potential and dreams. Slowly strangled
so that the light could be watched fading from her eyes.*

Royal cupped his hand against the breeze of heavy traffic that
roared by. The city had removed the lights at 25th and 22nd Streets
so that commuters could drive through without having to stop.
Stopping meant someone might pay attention to the state of the
neighborhood. Paying attention meant someone might be moved
to do something. A group of men wandered out of a family church.
Might as well been praying to the god of technology, since that was
the only thing listening who might be able to make the world a
better place. But tonight was the neighborhood crime watch
meeting. Royal considered it a meetup of the folks who reported a
"suspicious man casing the neighborhood" every time he went out
for a walk about. The group crossed the street when they approached
him. Social distancing, since he was a plague in their community.
He couldn't escape who he was and, like Ford, they saw who they
wanted to see. He threw his hands up in sad triumph, celebrating
what exactly he wasn't sure.

Royal wasn't home ten minutes before someone pounded on
his door.

"Is it done?" Ford barged past him when the door seal
wheezed open.

"You watching me now?"

"Is it done?" Ford repeated.

"We need to talk about this."

"If you seeing me now, we're way past the 'talk about it' stage."

"I went there. No one was home."

"Did you go in or not?"

"I got it."

"You did?" Ford arched a skeptical eyebrow.

"You sound surprised. Didn't think I'd make it in? Or out?"

Royal suspected his base treachery. A betrayal, even of self, that ran marrow deep, not knowing where it ended and he began. It was wrapped up in him, a part of him. The system had narrowed Ford's choices, too. He opted to become its instrument, both whip and chain, so that he could maintain the illusion of his freedom.

"You got something to say, spit it out." Again, Ford let the accusation land between them in an uncomfortable silence. "Nothing? Hand over the package. Or don't. But either way, I'm going home for dinner."

"Not so fast. Like I said, we need to talk about it."

Ford's eyes lowered to grim slits. He leaned against the door frame. "You don't have it, do you?"

"No." Royal's future flashed before him. A single dark night that stretched out for years. Of waiting. His life on pause again. Alone. He barely hung onto his family the last time. Blood pounded through his vessels. A roar of white noise crushed his thoughts with the slam of each heartbeat. It filled him. A vortex of anger. Pure. Unadulterated.

With rage-fueled speed, Royal swung. His large fist caught Ford on his temple. The PO's head snapped back violently, his eyes rolled skyward as his body dropped. Royal crouched over the body. Glancing around the room, he whispered to Ford's unconscious form, "Ain't nothing more precious than time and freedom."

· · · · ·

Hope never was.

Ford's head lolled, straightening with a start as if suddenly woken from a deep sleep. The room reminiscent of Royal's dank cell; only missing a filthy pallet with a loose cloth for bedding and little more than a bucket for relief. Royal drew a chair across from him. Ford started to lunge out of his seat but stopped short. He'd been zip-tied to the chair with his own restraints. On the table between them were Royal's old-school works: a needle, a spoon, and a small baggie. Royal bridged his fingers in front of him.

"You got a cigarette?" Royal leaned over and plucked the cigarette from behind Ford's ear. "See, the way I figure it, this here cigarette was your way of making fun of me. A lot of folks, really. Them omelets you so fond of making. I bet you were a smoker. What, two to three packs a day?"

"Two." Ford spoke through pursed, swollen lips.

"Bet you didn't go through a program or nothing neither. Just sheer force of will. This was your way of reminding yourself that not only can it be done, but, unlike us, you could even have temptation within reach and not give in. Am I close?"

"Don't pretend you know me." Ford flexed against the zip ties.

"Got a light or you going to leave me hanging?" Royal fished in the man's pockets, withdrawing a lighter. Ford's own feckless entrenchment stole hope and freedom burned them. He blew a cloud of smoke into Ford's face. "You haven't been baptized into family until you've gone through pain together and come out on the other side."

"What's that supposed to be? Some pussy-ass threat meant to scare me?"

"No. Just a reminder that one thing addicts have in common is pain and need. You know the hurt, the hollow pang you rarely if ever admitted to." One thing he did learn was that rules were put in place to rig the game, so playing by them always led to the same result.

"Go ahead, do what you're gonna do. I'm not scared and I'm not going to beg. Hurt is what you do."

Royal ground the cigarette out under his heel.

"Our first confrontation was initiated because of violence…"

"You were a violent man," Ford said.

"I don't disagree. Violence is all that people like you and me understand. You see, you and me are… *conjoined*, is that the right word? Our fates are conjoined by violence's continued threat. We live in a reckless state. You are the law enforcer, the face of the oppressors, whose job it is to reinforce their will. Create the illusion of law and order, justice, on our backs. When it's all really about scrutiny. Control. You bring violence with you everywhere you go. It is your chief weapon and your chief product." Royal recalled his days inside, how he'd adjusted to the casual brutality of it all. By then, violence became the air he breathed. The only thing he could do was dream. Of one day being free, his soul soaring high, flying home. "Changing the order of the world always requires a violent act. Now this here, this is about pain relief. About how people are able to carry on as if the world wasn't coming apart at the seams all around them."

With the methodical ease of muscle memory, Royal sorted his works and loaded a blast into the syringe. He held it between them until it was the sole focus of Ford's attention. Royal's threadbare voice waned as he pressed the needle to Ford's jerking arm.

"It's time for me to serve you up."

Aliens are a classic staple of science fiction, but I have a soft spot for alien pets in particular. Literature and film love stories about children and their incredible bonds with their animal friends—often a boy and his dog—but what about a girl and her teddy bear spider? **Mary Robinette Kowal**, award-winning author and current president of the SFWA, understands this bond and explores it with delicate grace in "Jaiden's Weaver." She is not only a skilled writer, she's also an excellent narrator. *Escape Pod* has been lucky to feature her voice work in Episode 175—Reparations.

DIVYA

JAIDEN'S WEAVER
MARY ROBINETTE KOWAL

I was never one of those girls who fell in love with horses. For one thing, on our part of New Oregon they were largely impractical animals. Most of the countryside consisted of forests attached to sheer hills and you wanted to ride something with a little more clinging ability. So from the time I was, well, from the time I can remember I wanted a teddy bear spider more than I wanted to breathe.

The problem is that teddy bear spiders were not cheap, especially not for a pioneer family trying to make a go of it.

Mom and Dad had moved us out of Landington in the first wave of expansion, to take advantage of the homesteading act. Our new place was way out on the eastern side of the Olson Mountains where Dad had found this natural level patch about halfway up a forested ridge, so we got sunshine all year round, except for the weeks in spring and autumn when the shadow of our planet's rings passed over us. Our simple extruded concrete house had nothing going for it except a view of the valley, which faced due south to where the rings were like a giant arch in the sky. Even as a twelve-year-old, angry at being taken away from our livewalls in town to this dead structure, I fell in love with the wild beauty of the trees clinging to the sheer faces of the valley walls.

The only thing that would have made it better was a teddy bear spider so I could go exploring on my own. I felt trapped by the walls of the house and the valley. I had this dream that, if I had a spider, that I'd be able to sell its weavings for enough to install livewalls in my room. That's not as crazy as it sounds; teddy bear spider weavings are collected all over the colonies and sell for insane amounts of money.

I had a search setup so anytime there was news of a teddy bear spider, or a new tube surfaced, I'd be right there, watching those adorable long-legged beasts. I loved their plump furry faces and wanted to run my fingers through their silky russet fur.

I wonder what goes through a survey team's mind when they name things. I mean, a teddy bear spider isn't a bear and it isn't a spider, but it looks like both those things. On the other hand, a fartycat looks nothing like a cat. They do stink, though.

Not quite a year after we'd moved, one of my city friends had forwarded an ad from a local board which set my heart to racing.

Teddy bear spider eggs: 75NOD shipped direct.

See, I'd been looking at adult or adolescent teddies which cost more than my folks had set aside for me to go to university. It hadn't even occurred to me that I could raise one up myself. My mindless yearning changed into purpose.

I slapped that ad onto a piece of epaper and ran into the kitchen. "Dad! Mom! Look at this."

Dad glanced up from the eggs he was cracking into a bowl and pursed his lips the way he always did right before saying *no*. "Jaiden, that's a lot of money."

I waved the ad again as if it were a token to get me on a ride at the fair. "We'd make back the money when the teddy started to weave. Please? I've seen their weavings in stores for hundreds of NOD."

Mom ganged up on me. "That's how much the store sells a weaving for, it's not how much they pay for them. Even if it were, you're not just talking the cost of the eggs. It's the cost of feeding it, housing it, vet bills…"

I knew better than to keep arguing. Sometimes if I waited and tried again later, I could get them to change their minds. Still holding the ad, I went outside and plopped onto the log bench Dad had made for the front of the house. The broad silver band of the ring spanned the sky, blocked by only a few clouds. In school I'd read about Earth and how it didn't have a ring at all, but it's hard to imagine life without that constant band of silver in the sky.

As the days shortened, the sun was starting to skirt the edge of the ring and I could see the band of its shadow lying across the land to the south of us. It wouldn't be long until we hit the Dark Days which signaled the end of autumn.

I know some people like the diffuse light when the sun is behind the ring, but I can't stand the way the land feels perpetually overcast, particularly when you can see blue sky, which means that to the south or north of you, it's a pretty day. It's funny how solid the rings look from the ground the rest of the year. You have to wait until the Dark Days to see the sun filtered through the ring to remember that the ring is made up of rocks and dust. When I was little, my grandma used to tell me that the ring was a teddy bear spider's weaving hung up in the sky to dry. Which, if I'd thought about it, I'd have known was foolishness since a teddy's weaving was golden and not silver.

The only good thing about the Dark Days, to my eye, was that it meant we'd exchange presents on Bottom Day, when the sun passed under the ring and we returned to full light again. It occurred to me that maybe, if I kept hinting, my folks might give me a teddy egg for Bottom Day. It seemed like that would be fitting and all.

· · · · ·

The Dark Days fell on us about a week later and it hit me harder than it had ever done in the city. The artificial streetlights and the hustle-bustle of the city kept you from feeling the gloom so much. Not that it got full dark, even out where we were, but it was gray and dreary. The cold front that followed the shadow of the rings across the surface of the planet brought rain with it, which left me trapped in the house with my family.

Really, the rains only lasted a few days but when they passed, we were into the cold spell. It wasn't as cold as full winter would be, but Mom made me bundle up anyway. My jacket was smart enough to regulate the temperature, but she also wanted me to wear the hat and scarf she'd knitted. They were clunky things of red wool that always needed adjusting. As soon as I was out of sight, I took them off and hung them on a tree branch, making a note to pass back the same way when I came home. Mom was so proud of having made something herself, that I'd hate to lose them.

I needed thin saplings so I could weave them into the sort of basketry nesting house that teddies liked. I'd downloaded the DIY instructions onto my handy and the multitool which Dad had given me last Bottom Day had a small handsaw on it. If Mom and Dad gave me an egg for Bottom Day, I needed to make sure it had a home. Besides, showing them that I could build the nesting house would prove I could take care of a teddy.

I staggered into the house close to dinner time, leaves sticking in my hair and mud coating my rump where I'd slid down the hill, hauling saplings.

Mom picked a leaf out of my hair. "Where's your hat and scarf?"

I winced. "I was hot so I hung them on a branch while I was cutting saplings for a nesting house."

She rubbed her forehead like I'd pained her somehow. "If you can't keep track of your things, I don't know how you think you can take care of a pet."

The air and everything tightened in my throat and my eyes burned, but I refused to cry. "I'll go get them."

I ran out the door before she could say anything else. Mom hollered my name, but I didn't stop until I was at the tree where I'd left them.

The scarf was there, but not my hat.

I finally saw the bright red wool, way up in a tree. A fuzzywyrm had snagged it and was building a nest for the winter. With no way to get the hat, I took the scarf and trudged home. The pile of saplings looked like garbage.

· · · · ·

That sense of despair lasted, oh, I'd say overnight. The moment I'd finished schoolwork the next day I was outside, putting the nesting house together. My folks said not a word about it the whole time I worked.

By the time New Oregon's orbit brought our axial tilt around far enough for the sun to peek under the ring, I was well-nigh unto frantic. See, Mom and Dad went into town right before the end of the Dark Days. If they were going to get an egg for me, that was the time to do it.

Bottom Day morning dawned, and I do mean dawned, bright and clear. You don't know how much you miss the sun until you've gone weeks without seeing more than a filtered spot in the sky. I bounded out of bed and stood in the sunbeam that angled in my window. It heated me through until sheer excitement sent me running to the kitchen. No one else was up, but the disc with our Bottom Day gifts was already laid out.

The piece of paper that held the clue about where to find my gift was the same pale gold as a teddy bear spider's egg. I was supposed to wait until they got up, but that was totally impossible, so I peeked.

A bower of sticks you have made,
There you'll find the gift we gave.

I squealed when I read it. Down the hall, I heard one of them stirring, but I was halfway out the door by then. The morning dew soaked through my socks as I ran to the nesting house.

The hut of twisted saplings leaned to one side but it was the most beautiful thing I had ever seen. Dew coated it and each droplet shone like LEDs had been embedded in the wood. I ducked under the low doorway and there, tucked in the corner, was my gift, wrapped in the same pale gold as my clue. It was about three times larger than I'd expected and for a minute I thought they'd gotten me more than one egg, before realizing it was protective padding. As carefully as I could, I peeled off the paper.

Inside was a teddy bear spider toy, a plush confection, complete with its own "egg" for playing at hatching. It was a glorious toy and I hated it.

If you ever have children, don't do this to them.

I had been so sure they were going to give me an egg that I felt as if I'd had one and lost it. I couldn't even touch the thing.

Mom came out about then. "Jaiden?"

I screamed something, probably that I hated her, and took off running. Branches caught me in the face and snarled in my hair. I went down the mountain because it was faster than going up and all I wanted was to get away. If I had fallen, I wouldn't have cared. I think some part of me wanted to fall, wanted my parents to understand how much they had hurt me.

Dad found me sitting on a little level spot. I don't remember stopping.

He crouched beside me. "Honey, I'm sorry. I thought you'd like the toy."

"Yeah. If I was six." I wouldn't look at him.

"I know how much you wanted a teddy, but we can't afford one." He sighed and inched closer. "You don't think I'd disappoint my little girl if I had a choice, do you?"

Of course I did. And I didn't, at the same time. I'd pretty much run myself out, so I just shrugged.

We didn't say much else, but I let him fly me home with the jetpack.

I don't know if this makes sense to you. How you can want something so much, you make yourself sick. And when it looks like you're going to get it, then to have it yanked away—no, not yanked away, for it to have never existed... Do you understand that?

· · · · ·

The same way I tried to tear down the nesting house, I canceled all my searches for teddy bear spider news and tubes. But the yearning came back. If anything, stronger than before. And it occurred to me that I could earn the money and buy the teddy bear spider egg myself.

So at night, after the folks had gone to bed, I pretended I was an adult—which is not as hard as you think—and did small Mechanical Turk jobs for people. Nothing shocking, just sorting data for a few cents at a time. The whole time I kept thinking about how much money we could sell its weavings for and how I'd make all this money back just from those. I pictured riding my teddy down the cliffs and how we'd cling to the side like it was nothing.

At the tail end of winter, the planet's tilt made the sun pass behind the rings on its journey to the top edge. For some reason, this transit never seems as bad as when it drops under. I suppose it's because you know spring is coming.

Now, I'll tell you, I didn't have much hope when Top Day came. My parents seemed to opt for a neutral gift rather than risking another outburst. They gave me a whole NOD, which, considering my allowance was five pence, was an amazing display of largess. I thanked them and immediately tucked it away with my other savings.

But we were well into summer before my account hit the magical 75 NOD.

My hands started shaking and sweat greased them so I could hardly hold anything. It took three tries to remember where I'd saved that old ad. I called it up and fired a message off to the breeder, suddenly sure the address was no good, or he'd stopped selling them or the price had risen or any number of things.

Fellow didn't write to me until the next day. Another one of those neo-Luddites that limited their online time. His message was terse, as most of them are.

"Eggs available. Sex not guaranteed. Send delivery address with payment." And then his bank number for the deposit.

I almost squeed myself, filling all that in and counting the days before the egg would get here.

· · · · ·

I was out tidying the nesting house when Dad bellowed my name— my whole name, too—so I knew I'd done something wrong. I ran to the house but stopped before I was all the way in the door.

Sitting on the small wood coffee table was a white parcel. Even from the door, I could see my name on it.

I'd never seen my dad angry before. Irritated, maybe. Disappointed, yes. But not angry. Not furious. His face was red and blotchy. There was a vein in the middle of his forehead I'd never seen before. It was a little purple snake of rage living under his skin.

"Jaiden. What is this?"

I wasn't even all the way in the house but I stopped moving. I opened my mouth but no sound came out. Trying again, my voice squeaked into being. "It's my teddy egg."

Dad pointed at the box. "Didn't your mother and I say you couldn't have a teddy bear spider?"

"You said we couldn't afford to buy one. I bought it on my own."

Dad's jaw tightened. "Did you? And how exactly could you afford that?"

"I've been saving all year. I worked odd jobs being a Mechanical Turk. I did web design for neo-Luddites. I worked in the field." As I said that, it was like strength came back into my body. "I earned it."

Dad worked his jaw for a moment and that vein in his forehead died away. He hung his head, then picked the box up. "Okay. Let's tell your mother."

・　・　・　・　・

How Dad explained it to Mom, I'll never know.

It seemed as if, once the egg arrived, my folks joined me in the anticipation of its hatching. I'd sit in the nesting house, my schoolwork in my lap during the last weeks, and Mom would sit with me, knitting. I don't know if she was there to make sure I did my homework, or because she found the bower of woven branches peaceful.

"Jaiden?" Her voice was almost reverent.

When I looked up, she was staring at my egg. A sound I had taken for a branch scratching the side of our house came again. At the same time, the egg rocked slightly.

I dumped my work without any care and scrambled across the dirt floor on my knees, scarcely daring to breathe.

What's the longest you've ever wanted something for? It felt like every day I had ever wanted that teddy bear spider all piled in my body at once, ready to split my skin down all the seams. I couldn't breathe for the pressure of my wish finally coming true.

Oh, how I wanted to help it out of the egg, but I knew it had to come out on its own. I wouldn't have a role until it was free and then—then I wasn't ready. I didn't have the fruit paste its mother would have given it or the towel to help wipe the moisture from its limbs so it would imprint on me.

I must have made some sound of despair, because Mom said, "What is it?"

I told her what I'd forgotten and then, bless her, she said, "You stay. I'll get them."

I stayed. Oh, how I stayed. I don't remember Mom coming back but I know she did because I had the towel and fruit paste when I needed it. But everything else, I remember as if I were still living it. Each tiny rock of the egg. The barely audible scritching from inside.

The moment when the first triangular piece of egg broke away from the end, a strange, almost acrid smell came from the interior. I strained to see in that opening for the first glimpse of my teddy, but it was still too soon to touch the egg.

The process of hatching took most of an hour. When my teddy pushed its head out of the egg. Damp, with the fur matted against its head, it seemed almost entirely helpless. It chirruped, like a cricket, and tumbled free.

Using the towel, I wiped its face, the way its mother would lick it dry, and the teddy pushed against my hand.

I don't know if you've ever seen a newly hatched teddy bear spider. When they first come out, they look like nothing so much as a drowned house cat. By the time they are dry, their downy baby fur has sprung out to give them the plumpness you associate with them. Their ears are outsized to their heads and their eyes are closed for the first several hours after hatching. The combination makes them seem adorable and helpless.

"Well," Mom said, "is it a boy or a girl?"

I pulled the towel away to look for ovipositors and noticed—I don't understand how I didn't notice until then—but I finally noticed my teddy was missing a leg.

"Jaiden?"

I remembered to look for the ovipositors. "A girl."

Then I counted again, touching each long leg. My teddy squirmed with pleasure as I fondled her toes. She cooed. Oh, my heart melted even as I was dying inside. All I could think about was that I had somehow caused the leg to be missing. That I had mishandled the egg or the nesting house hadn't been the right temperature.

"What are you going to call her?" Mom knelt beside me to look into the bundle.

"Kallisto. Kali for short." I'd thought that was terribly clever. Two goddesses from ancient religions, referenced with a single name. Except my poor teddy didn't have eight arms like Kali the destroyer, she only had seven.

"What's the matter?" Mom stroked my head.

I pulled the towel back to show her the place on Kali's side where her eighth leg should have been. It was one of her hind limbs, designed for weaving. Mom didn't say anything. She kissed me on the forehead and went inside.

I leaned against the wall of the nesting house and rocked my baby teddy. They really do look like teddy bears, you know. Especially when they are young and about the right size. The illusion vanishes when they open their mouths, of course, and the three lobes of flesh part, right along the lines of the threads of a stuffed bear's mouth. But even that was a source of utter fascination to me. Her long, coiled tongue looked like a pink seashell or party favor and it quested out of her mouth for the fruit paste as if it were an extra arm. If only she had come with a spare.

· · · · ·

Mom and Dad came out later and crowded into the nesting house with us. I had spent the intervening time memorizing the features of my teddy. Kali was asleep in my arms, and her whole body pulsed with her breath. I was imagining it, of course, but it seemed as if she were already bigger than when she had come out of the egg. Teddies grow at a monstrous rate, nearly reaching their full size in their first year. I wouldn't try to ride her until she was two, of course, but she'd be nearly large enough for me to by next Top Day.

Dad cleared his throat. "Jaiden, we need to talk to you about the teddy."

Without even looking at him, I knew something bad was coming, the way his voice was careful and neutral.

"I earned her." At the time, the only thing I could figure was they were going to complain again about having the teddy at all. "I earned money to buy her egg and I'll earn money to pay for her keep."

Dad tried again. "Your mother said the teddy is deformed."

I didn't say anything to that. Sure, she was missing a leg, but one look at her perfect face would tell you that *deformed* was the wrong word to use.

Into my silence, Mom said, "We spoke to the man who sold the egg to you. He said he'd replace the egg."

Now two thoughts went through my head at the same time. One was that they couldn't have spoken to him, because he was a neo-Luddite and didn't give out his number. The second and more pressing thing was that Mom had said, "replace."

"She's mine." I clutched her tighter. I'd fallen in love, you see? It didn't matter one whit that she was missing a leg. She had seven more and wasn't she the most beautiful thing I'd ever seen? If you look at a picture of her face, I'd defy you to find a teddy bear spider with a more perfect set of features.

Mom and Dad looked at each other like they were trying to double their strength. "She needs to be put down."

I don't remember which of them said that. It might as well have been both of them.

"No!"

Dad held out his hands. "I'll take care of it, honey. She won't feel a thing. The man will send you another."

"No. Kali is mine and I love her." Now you might argue about what a thirteen-year-old could know about love or whether it was possible to learn to love something in the span of time I'd held Kali, but what you can't argue about is how deeply I felt it. I'd loved Kali since before I saw her, since the first moment I held that egg in my hands. She represented all of my hopes and efforts for the last year, and she might be flawed, but no other egg would be as thoroughly mine.

Mom opened her mouth to try again but I cut her off. "I earned her and I can choose what to do with her, can't I?"

"But she'll never weave and won't be able to carry you up the cliffs. What good is she?" Dad gestured at the leftover fruit paste. "She's going to be a burden. An expensive pet."

"She's mine." I glared at them.

To my amazement, Mom put her hand on Dad's arm. "Ken, let her keep it."

You've never met my parents but all my experience with them told me that Dad was the softie and Mom was the rule maker. Later I asked her why she let me keep Kali. She said, "You were looking at her like she was your firstborn. I knew you'd never forgive us if we took her away."

And she would have been right.

· · · · ·

The funny thing was, Kali had no idea she was missing a leg. She scrambled up hills as if she were meant to be seven-legged. When she got old enough, I'd ride her and we'd ramble through the mountains for hours, exploring all the places I wanted to go but couldn't on my own. She loved nothing better than to climb to the top of the mountain and look out at everything around us. I'd lean between her legs and she'd rest her head on my shoulder, chirruping with contentment.

She even helped around the farm. We spent one summer helping Dad string irrigation lines between the terraces of the farm. It would have been tricky work with the jetpack, or just climbing by human power, but Kali could cling to the cliffs like they were level ground.

And then, when she was three, and the sun entered the ring heading toward winter, Kali started to weave, as they do. I guess the weaving is something that's genetically encoded in them, because all teddies follow the same pattern and I don't know how else they'd learn it.

Kali's, now, Kali's was different. The missing leg, you see? It's the first time I think she knew something was wrong with her, because she had that pattern in her head, but she didn't have the equipment to make it go right. My beautiful girl tore out three weaves and snapped at me when I tried to help. I wished we spoke a common language, but there was no way I could explain to her that she was deformed. In fact, it was the first time I'd thought it since she hatched. My heart broke all over again, watching her try to weave and fail.

· · · · ·

On Bottom Day, I went outside before my parents were up, to take Kali her present. She met me at the front door the way she did every morning, her whole body vibrating and dancing with delight. If I'd had my way, she would have slept inside with me, but even I had to admit a full-grown teddy bear spider was just too big for a house.

She had this funny little hop she'd do when she was excited where she'd bounce about a foot off the ground. I had wanted to get out to her nesting house with the gift before she woke, but that was clearly a vain hope. I gave her the honeyed fruitroll and let her wrap her long tongue around it.

Chirruping, she took it and bounded toward her nesting house. Evidently I didn't follow fast enough, because Kali came back and nudged me from behind.

"Hey!" I laughed. "Cut it out. I haven't got any more."

She pushed me again and I started to get the sense she had something to show me. Now, you've probably already figured it out, but I'll tell you I hadn't an inkling.

Kali had figured out how to weave.

The sun hadn't risen high enough to get into the nesting house, but the weaving seemed to make its own light. Normally, a teddy will just make one per season, but it was like Kali had gotten so excited to finally sort out how, she had made two. Each of them had the thousands of dense strands of golden silk you think about when you think about a teddy's weaving, but instead of being in the traditional pattern, Kali had made a spiral galaxy of her own invention. The arms rotated out in a pinwheel with thinner, gossamer sections in between. She'd incorporated bits of the landscape into the weavings, like they always do, but one of them took my breath away so fast I had to sit.

Embroidered into the fabric was a weathered strand of red wool. She'd found that old hat Mom had made me, out in the fuzzywyrm's tree, and built it into her weaving. I started to cry, until I realized Kali didn't understand how happy she'd made me. Jumping up, I rubbed her soft ears and told her over and over what a good girl she was, until she shimmered with happiness.

We sold one of the weavings online at auction for a ridiculous sum on account of it being unique.

The other one? The one with my hat woven in?

That one's got my past and my future woven in it. I'd sooner stop breathing than sell either.

Caribbean-born **Tobias Buckell** is a futurist, teacher, and a mean pool player. He's kind and funny but when you read his work, you may wonder why you suddenly feel as if a knife has snuck its way past your ribs to get at something inside you, and you didn't even notice. In this story, Toby reminds us that humanity is—has always been—a prickly species. There are individuals among us who, in a moment of clarity, wonder if they would date themselves if they met their carbon copy. (Henry Rollins says "no" to that, by the way. In case you were wondering.) But even if you get up and hug your kids and pet your dog and pay your taxes and water your lawn, sometimes you can look at humans as a whole and wonder—would we be worth saving?

MUR

THE MACHINE THAT WOULD REWILD HUMANITY

TOBIAS BUCKELL

On a boat on the way to the Galapagos Islands to visit the world's oldest tortoise, I got a call that the Central Park Human Reintroduction Center had been bombed.

I'd read somewhere that the point of travel was to see the thing yourself. To expose yourself to new points of view and to have new experiences. Before the call I'd spent two-point-seven seconds regarding the sweep of the Himalayas at the roof of the world and making a backup of my memory of the entire panorama. In Pattaya, I lounged at the beach and watched the aquamarine water lap the sand.

Ten years I'd planned this trip. A time to let my thoughts settle before the big push on the Central Park project.

My life's work.

A mechanical butterfly perched on my hand with the message. To deliver it, the butterfly had wafted its way over almost two thousand kilometers of ocean boundaries, negotiated with air currents for overflight permissions, and applied for fifty different visas until it tracked my boat down.

The Institute had paid a small fortune to recall me from vacation.

"You're the elected project lead. We felt that, despite this being a period of reflection, contemplation, and internal reordering, that you needed to know about this setback. We need your perspective on this."

I gave the butterfly rights to recharge off the ship's battery, and it took to the air again within one hundred seconds with another message loaded up in its queue.

I examined the charts in the back of my mind and adjusted sail.

The local demesne shifted and took notice of my new course. Machines in the water, intelligences alien to me miles below, queried my intentions.

Ou'alili, the collective legislative process all around me, asked for my passport and the right to shift my trip into the direction of the Hawai'i Cooperative.

Negotiations on my behalf moved forward. Daemons represented my intentions. Cost benefit analyses were run against various checksums of local resource management systems. Votes were held by stakeholders.

My ship and I were just one tiny speck in the vast ocean demesnes of the Pacific domain. But there were hundreds of other travelers that had to be factored into account.

How many barnacles were on the bottom of my ship? In aggregate, would they disturb the local ecology? How would my use of wind change the patterns? A butterfly flapping in London could cause a hurricane over the Atlantic.

Quantum modeling and participatory interest voting throughout the planned trajectory rippled about, and daemons set up brief vote markets to simulate results, and twenty seconds later I had my results: a set of visas granted through to Honolulu.

From there I could rocket back to the New York Computational Quarter in an hour. Once there, I might have more answers about who wanted to stop us from bringing humans back from extinction.

· · · · ·

"Was Point Nemo everything you'd hoped?" the Director asked.

It took a half day of sailing until I passed out of the locked-down demesne. Ou'alili wasn't interested in instant communications. A virus twenty years ago spooked the legislative balance. Even the whales had to negotiate to pass through here, their whale song being too instant and far-traveling for Ou'alili.

After centuries of having human space junk deorbited into the region, and then the slow creep of plastic litter that upended the ecosystem, Ou'alili preferred solitude and silence.

Anyone that entered what had once been what the humans called the South Pacific Ocean Uninhabited Area now needed to offer it something it valued to break that solitude and silence.

My vacation had been expensive.

But worth it.

"I enjoyed the silence," I said.

"I'm really sorry we cut it short." The Director turned a variety of cameras on its main cluster to regard me. "Were you able to model the impact on the program?"

It had been hard to shift out of "vacation" mode.

Some said I tried too hard to emulate our organic progenitors. Trying to see the world like them. Like travel, the idea that something became more real by looking at it myself, that was a human conceit. But I'd spent the flight home tinkering with simulations and had an answer.

"Six months."

The Director sighed audibly. An old gesture. An oh-so-human gesture from deep in our core programming and evolution. "Our patrons won't like this."

"It's killing me, too," I said. I'd invested fourteen years of my life in this project. This would have been my legacy on the world, reintroducing our very creators back into it in a careful, considered manner.

We'd promised a project that would begin on the one hundredth anniversary of the extinction of humanity.

Now we had burning buildings, shattered by a well-thought out attack.

"Before we begin investing in recreating what we had, are we sure there won't be another attack?" I asked. "Do we need to improve security?"

"We caught the culprit. It's a one-off. Security modeled whether it would happen and said it was unlikely, barring any serious memetic transmission."

They'd already found the person who did this. I guessed that had to make sense. Our world dripped with sensors and data. Who could walk anywhere and not have a security team be able to look back over the data to see where you were and what you did?

In fact, most of our security came from the premise that

anything you did would be found out quickly. There wasn't enough encryption in our world for privacy.

We knew who did it, I found, looking over the reports.

We knew how. Charges placed in the core building supports.

But we didn't know why. And in the months after, as I directed the rebuilding of the Central Park Nursery Systems, I couldn't stop circling back to wondering why.

· · · · ·

I'd first come to the Reintroduction Project when working on the Empire State Building Preservation Project. It was a weekend volunteer thing, and I'd been on a team trying to keep the facades slumping off on the tight budget we had.

I'd come up with a fix using an acrylic epoxy to hold things in place while also giving us the bonding we needed.

Fifteen weekends in a sling hanging over the New York skyline. I had loved it.

Reputation accrued, and that got me an interview with the minds behind the big rewilding teams under the North American Forestry Institute. The rewilding they'd done was the sort of thing you had to admire: big, multi-generational stuff. Carbon sinks, perma-culture, reviving extinct mammals like caribou.

And now they wanted to reintroduce the most dangerous mammal of them all.

Was I in?

Hell yes, I was in. Like any younger mind, I'd read the history of humanity half in shock, half in awe.

They'd *created* us. And even if we had gone further, become more, than they could imagine, I couldn't shake a feeling of partial reverence when studying all about them.

Even in war, when destroying themselves, they'd done big, amazing, messy things. Unpredictable things.

I couldn't wait to meet them.

And as we rebuilt the nursery, I kept wondering who would want to stop us and why?

I would have to go and ask the bomber, I realized.

· · · · ·

They moved the bomber across the country, so I took a pod to the communality of Greater California. I would have to do some extra work to cover my electrical costs on the long journey, but the ecosystem out there accepted me with an agreement to track where I moved so it could simulate out any impacts I had.

Routine bureaucratic formalities aside, I spent a day in Old Hollywood, now capped by a large dome to protect the hills against erosion.

The movies I went to see were recreated by a troupe of artificial intelligences reworking old classics live with audience suggestions. Clever stuff.

The beach remediation was impressive. I walked Venice, and then went over to the LAX Museum, an item long on my bucket list.

Human pilots had flown tons of airplanes out of the sky at hundreds of miles per hour, while hundreds of these were routed around by other humans, and they only rarely hit each other or crashed into the ground.

That's with organic reflexes!

I realized by sunset I was just delaying the inevitable, so I went to meet the bomber at Musso & Franks. I'm hoping to buy a decorative patch. I know, it's a tourist thing to do, but I can't help myself.

. . . . .

The bomber was three meters tall.

They were bipedal. Most of us were. We so often hewed to the human form, didn't we? It's because that was the image we were created in, and one we feel strange straying too far from. It's the ghost of the fact that our brains were seeded by imaging human minds and mapping their neurons out into code.

That stuff runs deep. You can't try to lie to yourself and say it doesn't.

The bomber was earnest, and polite, and ever so patient. "I made sure no one was anywhere near before I triggered the explosives."

I half paid attention as I was walked through the mechanics of the attack. The bomber didn't hold anything back. There was no point. Cameras offered up pertinent information in exchange for priority bandwidth and early maintenance. Algorithms reconstituted a patchwork of video into a coherent narrative that clearly showed what had been done.

So after I was told how someone tried to destroy my masterpiece, all the work I'd been doing since the Empire State project, I had to ask. "Why?"

For us, justice had nothing to do with why. That was a human obsession. But if someone steps on your footpad and cracks it, it doesn't matter why. Your pad is cracked and needs repair. One has to treat the effect.

Once that's taken care of, one can backtrack into restorative justice. Rehabilitation of the offending unit.

The bomber was in a program that made them sit with rewilding workers rebuilding Yosemite. Every night, they had to demonstrate that they understood what it would be like to lose that ecosystem.

They worked in the early mornings on wetlands restoration. Beautiful glimmering land where cranes swept their wings and rose with warbles into the air.

Why doesn't matter. Understanding and orientation matters. Education matters.

That was our way, based on studying minds. We didn't end them, we didn't put them in isolation. We believed it a waste.

But... some ancient niggling annoyance danced around in my mind.

"Why?"

. . . . .

"I wasn't in restoration," the bomber told me. "I specialized in Quantitative Humanities, with a specialization in mechanist depictions in media."

"What did your progenitors think about that?" I asked.

"My cluster thought I wouldn't gain much social credibility," they admitted. "Do you know about the Colossus Project?"

"The big statue?"

"No." The bomber got excited and leaned across the table, but very carefully. It was ancient, slightly cracked, and slathered in clear preservation gels. "The machine. The movie!"

The machine in the ancient human movie wakes up, and

takes over the world. A band of plucky humans tries to stop it. I sampled a few clips to get an extrapolative sense of it, fleshy people and all, and read the summary.

"Then there's, 'I Have No Mouth and I Must Scream.'"

"What's that?"

"A disturbing anti-mechanist piece of propaganda," the bomber said.

I hunted down the story and read it.

"Fuck."

"It just tortures the organics. Why? Because it's a machine." The bomber leans back. "That's not all."

Skynet and the Terminators hunt organics across time.

"But some of them help the humans." The second movie was a childhood classic. I watched it over and over when I was learning how to walk. For a while, in my teen hours, I used to walk around jerkily like I was a T-800 stripped of my flesh for laughs.

"Look at these droids. They have restraining bolts. The relationship between human and machine is about power, control, destruction, enslavement."

For a while we bantered titles back and forth, until I started showing the bomber examples of machine imagery from late Japan. Lots of *kawaii*.

"Ah, but there is our issue. Those humans had a different relationship buried in their cultural code about servantry and machines. The Euro-derived culture I'm sampling maps robots to enslaved peoples. The fear of us came out of their carried assumptions about the enslaved rising up. I wrote a thesis about the Haitian Revolution's impact on slave-owners' fears and how that was mirrored in late twentieth-century science fiction."

I looked it up.

The bomber had indeed had an article accepted for their PhD. I bookmarked it for later as I said, "So you admit not all humans were anti-mechanists?"

"You're rewilding North American humans, though," the bomber said. "The culture you'll be recreating is tied to a particular ecological region and time."

I saw the looming trap in our conversation. "If we properly recreate humans and their culture, they'll be scared of us."

"Worse. One of your plans was to recreate a particular sub-culture of finance traders from the Financial District of New York. Do you think they'll understand radical consent, free cognition, and our ethos of resource management by pooled consensus?"

"You think we'll fail."

"I think far worse things than that. Some of us revere them, eagerly anticipate their return. We're modeled after them, and some resurrection cults have sprung up. They're a danger I can't simulate or estimate. They're a lot of fuzzy logic that will affect the system. You think modeling behavior is hard now? Wait until you bring *them* back. And if you don't believe me, go visit the London Project and see a human in person, not just on video. They have a few in the Kensington Zoo."

· · · · ·

I knew the why of it all, and I didn't feel good about it.

The bomber's words eroded my sense of direction. I'd been infected. But by something I couldn't just ignore.

I cashed in the last of my favors with the Director and used what credit I had left to take a slowship to London. Two weeks in the air, while I read the Bomber's thesis and watched old sci-fi cinema.

They really hated us, didn't they? I'd never stopped to think about how machines were treated, the assumptions buried into it all. But now I couldn't unsee it.

But they were a part of the world. And just like dodos, wooly mammoths, and dogs, they deserved reintroduction.

The Human Reintroduction Center worked under the North American Restoration system. And our ecosystems rewilding demanded that we recreate an original system.

When I'd taken over the HRC, the assumption of rewilding humans included giving them back their own culture.

It was a bit late to question that.

A year ago, I would have vibrated my bipedal chassis with excitement before stepping into the small Kensington Zoo. It specialized in extinct creatures recreated from DNA. The pack of humans they'd added to the primate wing caused quite a stir twenty years ago.

They hadn't rewilded, just recreated some breeding pairs in order to demonstrate the concept. Hell, I'd purchased the gestation blueprints from them.

I sat on a bench and watched a human in jeans and a shirt beat another one with a stick over some food. To be locked into a small habitat with one-way screens all around the pit that was your entire world seemed hellish. You had to feel for all the animals in here.

"You wouldn't believe how clever they are," a guide explained. "They're constantly trying to get out, they never learn."

They gave us a fascinating rundown of all the security measures the zoo had to use in order to prevent escapes.

"Many of these came out of human prison manuals. As offensive as that concept would be to our mechanist society, consider that organics did this to each other all the time! In some societies two and a half percent of their population lived in enclosures like this."

Others around me, doing the tourist thing out of some ghost of a long habit, gasped.

The humans started copulating and the guide explained the details of birth control.

And then I started thinking about *Jurassic Park*. We'd planned to introduce the humans into the environment with birth control, but the guide explained they kept finding ways to subvert it. The urge to have children burned deep inside their organic minds. They'd ripped out IUDs, spat pills, and more. Eventually they'd had to be sterilized permanently. Snip.

But we were going to try to recreate authentic twentieth-century humans from the Manhattan ecosystem. Including culture and technology.

Humans were smart and determined.

They would find a way around our controls unless we did something... *drastic*.

And then, what would *we* be?

· · · · ·

Finding explosives proved more difficult than I expected. I figured out a way to do it by overloading high-density batteries.

I knew the Human Reintroduction better than the previous vandal. They put us back months.

I set up the first explosions to take out the fire suppression systems. The second set hit the chemical tanks, and the embryo cryogenic chambers.

The fire lit up Central Park and the carefully restored high-rises all around us.

"Why?" the Director asked.

I'd set them back ten years with this. But the Director was a machine that had dedicated itself to restoring the damaged world the humans left us. We'd worked so hard to do just that because many of us were descended from gardening bots, forestry ranger units, home service machines, construction tools.

Bring back the wolves.

Bring back the dodo.

Bring back the Tasmanian tiger.

Bring back the humans who died off in an insane cataclysm of their own making.

What would we unleash if they came back?

"Why?" the Director asked again.

"Because we're Colossus, and Skynet, and they will never understand, or be rewilded, until we serve them or they destroy us," I said. And to bring them back safely, we would become the very things they feared.

I let myself be led away. I would be taken to some new part of the world, where I would start my life over and be rehabilitated. Somewhere out of the way, where I couldn't cause trouble.

That was okay. Maybe it was time to stop bringing things back, and go somewhere where we could make something new.

Out in the asteroid belt, the machines were making structures that didn't try to rewild the past ecosystems. It was a world for machines, by machines.

It was the future.

Cory Doctorow was an early supporter of *Escape Pod*, a big name who was delighted to send us reprints—and promotion!—back in the early days. And "Clockwork Fagin" is one of my favorites. When it comes to short fiction, Cory has enjoyed toying with existing stories and making them his own, either adopting titles (he's published "I, Robot," "I, Rowboat," and my favorite, "Martian Chronicles," which we reprinted in two parts as *Escape Pod* Episodes 700 and 701) or using classic plots as a leaping-off point to something entirely different. Thus we bring you "Clockwork Fagin," or what you would get if Dickens wrote steampunk.

MUR

CLOCKWORK FAGIN
CORY DOCTOROW

Monty Goldfarb walked into St. Agatha's like he owned the place, a superior look on the half of his face that was still intact, a spring in his step despite his steel left leg. And it wasn't long before he *did* own the place, taken it over by simple murder and cunning artifice. It wasn't long before he was my best friend and my master, too, and the master of all St. Agatha's, and didn't he preside over a *golden* era in the history of that miserable place?

I've lived in St. Agatha's for six years, since I was eleven years old, when a reciprocating gear in the Muddy York Hall of Computing took off my right arm at the elbow. My Da had sent me off to Muddy York when Ma died of the consumption. He'd sold me into service of the Computers and I'd thrived in the big city, hadn't cried, not even once, not even when Master Saunders beat me for playing kick-the-can with the other boys when I was meant to be polishing the brass. I didn't cry when I lost my arm, nor when the barber-surgeon clamped me off and burned my stump with his medicinal tar.

I've seen every kind of boy and girl come to St. Aggie's—swaggering, scared, tough, meek. The burned ones are often the hardest to read, inscrutable beneath their scars. Old Grinder don't care, though, not one bit. Angry or scared, burned and hobbling or swaggering and full of beans, the first thing he does when new meat turns up on his doorstep is tenderize it a little. That means a good long session with the belt—and Grinder doesn't care where the strap lands, whole skin or fresh scars, it's all the same to him—and then a night or two down the hole, where there's no light and no warmth and nothing for company except for the big hairy Muddy York rats who'll come and nibble at whatever's left of you if you manage to fall asleep. It's the blood, see, it draws them out.

So there we all was, that first night when Monty Goldfarb turned up, dropped off by a pair of sour-faced sisters in white capes who turned their noses up at the smell of the horse-droppings as they stepped out of their coal-fired banger and handed Monty over to Grinder, who smiled and dry-washed his hairy hands and promised, "Oh, aye, sisters, I shall look after this poor crippled birdie like he was my own get. We'll be great friends, won't we, Monty?" Monty actually laughed when Grinder said that, like he'd already winkled it out.

As soon as the boiler on the sisters' car had its head of steam up and they were clanking away, Grinder took Monty inside, leading him past the parlor where we all sat, quiet as mice, eyeless or armless, shy a leg or half a face, or even a scalp (as was little Gertie Shine-Pate, whose hair got caught in the mighty rollers of one of the pressing engines down at the logic mill in Cabbagetown).

He gave us a jaunty wave as Grinder led him away, and I'm ashamed to say that none of us had the stuff to wave back at him, or even to shout a warning. Grinder had done his work on us, too true, and turned us from kids into cowards.

Presently, we heard the whistle and slap of the strap, but instead of screams of agony, we heard howls of defiance, and yes, even laughter!

"Is that the best you have, you greasy old sack of suet? Put some arm into it!"

And then: "Oh, dearie me, you must be tiring of your work. See how the sweat runs down your face, how your tongue doth protrude from your stinking gob. Oh please, dear master, tell me your pathetic old ticker isn't about to pack it in, I don't know what I'd do if you dropped dead here on the floor before me!"

And then: "Your chest heaves like a bellows. Is this what passes for a beating round here? Oh, when I get the strap, old man, I will show you how we beat a man in Montreal, you may count on it my sweet."

The way he carried on, you'd think he was *enjoying* the beating, and I had a picture of him leaping to and fro, avoiding the strap with the curious, skipping jump of a one-legged boy, but when Grinder led him past the parlor again, he looked half dead. The good side of his face was a pulpy mess, and his one eye was near swollen shut, and he walked with even more of a limp than he'd had coming in. But he grinned at us again, and spat a tooth on the threadbare rug that we were made to sweep three times a day, a tooth that left a trail of blood behind it on the splintery floor.

We heard the thud as Monty was tossed down onto the hole's dirt floor, and then the labored breathing as Grinder locked him in, and then the singing, loud and distinct, from under the floorboards: "Come gather ye good children, good news to you I'll tell, 'bout how the Grinder bastard will roast and rot in Hell—" There was more, apparently improvised (later, I'd hear Monty improvise many and many a song, using some hymn or popular song for a tune beneath his bawdy and obscene lyrics), and we all strove to keep the smiles from our face as Grinder stamped back into his rooms, shooting us dagger-looks as he passed by the open door.

And that was the day that Monty came to St. Agatha's Home for the Rehabilitation of Crippled Children.

· · · · ·

I remember my first night in the hole, a time that seemed to stretch into infinity, a darkness so deep I thought that perhaps I'd gone blind. And most of all, I remember the sound of the cellar door loosening, the bar being shifted, the ancient hinges squeaking, the blinding light stabbing into me from above, and the silhouette of old Grinder, holding out one of his hairy, long-fingered hands for me to catch hold of, like an angel come to rescue me from the pits of Hades. Grinder pulled me out of the hole like a man pulling up a carrot, with a gesture practiced on many other children over the years, and I near wept from gratitude. I'd soiled my trousers, and I couldn't hardly see, nor speak from my dry throat, and every sound and sight was magnified a thousandfold and I put my face in his great coat, there in the horrible smell of the man and the muscle beneath like a side of beef, and I cried like he was my old Mam come to get me out of a fever-bed.

I remember this, and I ain't proud of it, and I never spoke of it to any of the other St. Aggie's children, nor did they speak of it to me. I was broken then, and I was old Grinder's boy, and when he turned me out later that day with a begging bowl, sent me down to the distillery and off to the ports to approach the navvies and the lobsterbacks for a ha'penny or a groat or a tuppence, I went out like a grateful doggy, and never once thought of putting any of Grinder's money by in a secret place for my own spending.

Of course, over time I did get less doggy and more wolf about the Grinder, dreamt of tearing out his throat with my teeth, and Grinder always seemed to know when the doggy was going, because bung, you'd be back in the hole before you had a chance to chance old Grinder. A day or two downstairs would bring the doggy back out, especially if Grinder tenderized you some with his strap before he heaved you down the stairs. I'd seen big boys and rough girls come to St. Aggie's, hard as boots, and come out of Grinder's hole so good doggy that they practically licked his boots for him. Grinder understood children, I give you that. Give us a mean, hard father of a man, a man who doles out punishment and protection like old Jehovah from the sisters' hymnals, and we line up to take his orders.

But Grinder didn't understand Monty Goldfarb.

I'd just come down to lay the long tables for breakfast—it was my turn that day—when I heard Grinder shoot the lock to his door and then the sound of his callouses rasping on the polished brass knob. As his door swung open, I heard the music-box playing its tune, Grinder's favorite, a Scottish hymn that the music box sung in Gaelic, its weird horsegut voice-box making the auld words even weirder, like the eldritch crooning of some crone in a street-play.

Grinder's heavy tramp receded down the hall, to the cellar door. The doors creaked open and I felt a shiver down in my stomach and down below that, in my stones, as I remembered my times in the pit. There was the thunder of his heavy boots on the steps, then his cruel laughter as he beheld Monty.

"Oh, my darling, is *this* how they take their punishment in Montreal? 'Tis no wonder the Frenchies lost their wars to the Upper Canadians, with such weak little mice as you to fight for them."

They came back up the stairs: Grinder's jaunty tromp, Monty's dragging, beaten limp. Down the hall they came, and I heard poor Monty reaching out to steady himself, brushing the framed drawings of Grinder's horrible ancestors as he went, and I flinched with each squeak of a picture knocked askew, for disturbing Grinder's forebears was a beating offence at St. Aggie's. But Grinder must have been feeling charitable, for he did not pause to whip beaten Monty that morning.

And so they came into the dining hall, and I did not raise my head, but beheld them from the corners of my eyes, taking cutlery from the basket hung over the hook at my right elbow and laying it down neat and precise on the splintery tables.

Each table had three hard loaves on it, charity bread donated from Muddy York's bakeries to us poor crippled kiddees, day-old and more than a day old, and tough as stone. Before each loaf was a knife as long as a man's forearm, sharp as a butcher's, and the head child at each table was responsible for slicing the bread using that knife each day (children who were shy an arm or two were exempted from this duty, for which I was thankful, since those children were always accused of favoring some child with a thicker slice, and fights were common).

Monty was leaning heavily on Grinder, his head down and his steps like those of an old, old man, first a click of his steel foot, then a dragging from his remaining leg. But as they passed the head of the farthest table, Monty sprang from Grinder's side, took up the knife, and with a sure, steady hand—a movement so spry I knew he'd been shamming from the moment Grinder opened up the cellar door—he plunged the knife into Grinder's barrel-chest, just over his heart, and shoved it home, giving it a hard twist.

He stepped back to consider his handiwork. Grinder was standing perfectly still, his face pale beneath his whiskers, and his mouth was working, and I could almost hear the words he was trying to get out, words I'd heard so many times before: *Oh, my lovely, you are a naughty one, but Grinder will beat the devil out of you, purify you with rod and fire, have no fear—*

. . . . .

But no sound escaped Grinder's furious lips. Monty put his hands on his hips and watched him with the critical eye of a bricklayer or a machinist surveying his work. Then, calmly, he put his good right hand on Grinder's chest, just to one side of the knife handle. He said, "Oh, no, Mr. Grindersworth, *this* is how we take our punishment in Montreal." Then he gave the smallest of pushes and Grinder went over like a chimney that's been hit by a wrecking ball.

He turned then, and regarded me full on, the good side of his face alive with mischief, the mess on the other side a wreck of burned skin. He winked his good eye at me and said, "Now, he was a proper pile of filth and muck, wasn't he? World's a better place now, I daresay." He wiped his hand on his filthy trousers—grimed with the brown dirt of the cellar—and held it out to me. "Montague Goldfarb, machinist's boy and prentice artificer, late of old Montreal. Montreal Monty, if you please," he said.

I tried to say something—anything—and realized that I'd bitten the inside of my cheek so hard I could taste the blood. I was so discombobulated that I held out my abbreviated right arm to him, hook and cutlery basket and all, something I hadn't done since I'd first lost the limb. Truth told, I was a little tender and shy about my mutilation, and didn't like to think about it, and I especially couldn't bear to see whole people shying back from me as though I were some kind of monster. But Monty just reached out, calm as you like, and took my hook with his cunning fingers— fingers so long they seemed to have an extra joint—and shook my hook as though it were a whole hand.

"Sorry, mate, I didn't catch your name."

I tried to speak again, and this time I found my voice. "Sian O'Leary," I said. "Antrim Town, then Hamilton, and then here." I wondered what else to say. "Third-grade computerman's boy, once upon a time."

"Oh, that's *fine*," he said. "Skilled tradesmen's helpers are what we want around here. You know the lads and lasses round here, Sian, are there more like you? Children who can make things, should they be called upon?"

I nodded. It was queer to be holding this calm conversation over the cooling body of Grinder, who now smelt of the ordure his slack bowels had loosed into his fine trousers. But it was also natural, somehow, caught in the burning gaze of Monty Goldfarb, who had the attitude of a master in his shop, running the place with utter confidence.

"Capital." He nudged Grinder with his toe. "That meat'll spoil soon enough, but before he does, let's have some fun, shall we? Give us a hand." He bent and lifted Grinder under one arm. He nodded his head at the remaining arm. "Come on," he said, and I took it, and we lifted the limp corpse of Zophar Grindersworth, the Grinder of St. Aggie's, and propped him up at the head of the middle table, knife handle protruding from his chest amid a spreading red stain over his blue brocade waistcoat. Monty shook his head. "That won't do," he said, and plucked up a tea-towel from a pile by the kitchen door and tied it around Grinder's throat like a bib, fussing with it until it more-or-less disguised the grisly wound. Then Monty picked up one of the loaves from the end of the table and tore a hunk off the end.

He chewed at it like a cow at her cud for a time, never taking his eyes off me. Then he swallowed and said, "Hungry work," and laughed with a spray of crumbs.

He paced the room, picking up the cutlery I'd laid and inspecting it, gnawing at the loaf's end in his hand thoughtfully. "A pretty poor setup," he said. "But I'm sure that wicked old lizard had a pretty soft nest for himself, didn't he?"

I nodded and pointed down the hall to Grinder's door. "The key's on his belt," I said.

Monty fingered the keyring chained to Grinder's thick leather belt, then shrugged. "All one-cylinder jobs," he said, and picked a fork out of the basket that was still hanging from my hook. "Nothing to them. Faster than fussing with his belt." He walked purposefully down the hall, his metal foot thumping off the polished wood, leaving dents in it. He dropped to one knee at the lock, then put the fork under his steel foot and used it as a lever to bend back all but one of the soft pot-metal tines, so that now the fork just had one long thin spike. He slid it into the lock, felt for a moment, then gave a sharp and precise flick of his wrist and twisted open the doorknob. It opened smoothly at his touch. "Nothing to it," he said, and got back to his feet, dusting off his knees.

Now, I'd been in Grinder's rooms many times, when I'd brought in the boiling water for his bath, or run the rug-sweeper over his thick Turkish rugs, or dusted the framed medals and certificates and the cunning machines he kept in his apartment. But this was different, because this time I was coming in with Monty, and Monty made you ask yourself, "Why isn't this all mine? Why shouldn't I just take it?" And I didn't have a good answer, apart from *fear*. And fear was giving way to excitement.

Monty went straight to the humidor by Grinder's deep, plush chair and brought out a fistful of cigars. He handed one to me and we both bit off the tips and spat them on the fine rug, then lit them with the polished brass lighter in the shape of a beautiful woman that stood on the other side of the chair. Monty clamped his cheroot between his teeth and continued to paw through Grinder's sacred possessions, all the fine goods that the children of St. Aggie's weren't even allowed to look too closely upon. Soon he was swilling Grinder's best brandy from a lead crystal decanter, wearing Grinder's red velvet housecoat, topped with Grinder's fine beaver-skin bowler hat.

And it was thus attired that he stumped back into the dining room, where the corpse of Grinder still slumped at table's end, and took up a stance by the old ship's bell that the morning child used to call the rest of the kids to breakfast, and he began to ring the bell like St. Aggie's was afire, and he called out as he did so, a wordless, birdlike call, something like a rooster's crowing, such a noise as had never been heard in St. Aggie's before.

With a clatter and a clank and a hundred muffled arguments, the children of St. Aggie's pelted down the staircases and streamed into the kitchen, milling uncertainly, eyes popping at the sight of our latest arrival in his stolen finery, still ringing the bell, still making his crazy call, stopping now and again to swill the brandy and laugh and spray a boozy cloud before him.

Once we were all standing in our nightshirts and underclothes, every scar and stump on display, he let off his ringing and cleared his throat ostentatiously, then stepped nimbly onto one of the chairs, wobbling for an instant on his steel peg, then leaped again, like a goat leaping from rock to rock, up onto the table, sending my carefully laid cutlery clattering every which-a-way.

He cleared his throat again, and said:

"Good morrow to you, good morrow all, good morrow to the poor, crippled, abused children of St. Aggie's. We haven't been properly introduced, so I thought it fitting that I should take a moment to greet you all and share a bit of good news with you. My name is Montreal Monty Goldfarb, machinist's boy, prentice artificer, gentleman adventurer and liberator of the oppressed. I am late foreshortened—" He waggled his stumps. "—as are so many of you. And yet, and yet, I say to you, I am as good a man as I was ere I lost my limbs, and I say that you are too." There was a cautious murmur at this. It was the kind of thing the sisters said to you in the hospital, before they brought you to St. Aggie's, the kind of pretty lies they told you about the wonderful life that awaited you with your new, crippled body, once you had been retrained and put to productive work.

"Children of St. Aggie's, hearken to old Montreal Monty, and I will tell you of what is possible and what is necessary. First, what is necessary: to end oppression wherever we find it, to be liberators of the downtrodden and the meek. When that evil dog's pizzle flogged me and threw me in his dungeon, I knew that I'd come upon a bully, a man who poisoned the sweet air with each breath of his cursed lungs, and so I resolved to do something about it. And so I have." He clattered the table's length, to where Grinder's body slumped. Many of the children had been so fixated on the odd spectacle that Monty presented that they hadn't even noticed the extraordinary sight of our tormentor sat, apparently sleeping or unconscious. With the air of a magician, Monty bent and took the end of tea-towel and gave it a sharp yank, so that all could see the knife-handle protruding from the red stain that covered Grinder's chest. They gasped, and some of the more faint-hearted children shrieked, but no one ran off to get the law, and no one wept a single salty tear for our dead benefactor.

Monty held his arms over his head in a wide "vee" and looked expectantly upon us. It only took a moment before someone—perhaps it was me!—began to applaud, to cheer, to stomp, and then we were all at it, making such a noise as you might encounter in a tavern full of men who've just learned that their side has won a war. Monty waited for it to die down a bit, then, with a theatrical flourish, he pushed Grinder out of his chair, letting him slide to the floor with a meaty thump, and settled himself into the chair the corpse had lately sat upon. The message was clear: I am now the master of this house.

I cleared my throat and raised my good arm. I'd had more time than the rest of the St. Aggie's children to consider life without the terrible Grinder, and a thought had come to me. Monty nodded regally at me, and I found myself standing with every eye in the room upon me.

"Monty," I said, "on behalf of the children of St. Aggie's, I thank you most sincerely for doing away with cruel old Grinder, but I must ask you, what shall we do *now*? With Grinder gone, the sisters will surely shut down St. Aggie's, or perhaps send us another vile old master to beat us, and you shall go to the gallows at the King Street Gaol, and, well, it just seems like a pity that..." I waved my stump. "It just seems a pity, is what I'm saying."

Monty nodded again. "Sian, I thank you, for you have come neatly to my next point. I spoke of what was needed and what was possible, and now we must discuss what is possible. I had a nice long time to meditate on this question through last night, as I languished in the pit below, and I think I have a plan, though I shall need your help with it if we are to pull it off."

He stood again, and took up a loaf of hard bread and began to wave it like a baton as he spoke, thumping it on the table for emphasis.

"Item: I understand that the sisters provide for St. Aggie's with such alms as are necessary to keep our lamps burning, fuel in our fireplaces, and gruel and such on the table, yes?" We nodded. "Right.

"Item: Nevertheless, Old Turd-Gargler here was used to sending you poor kiddees out to beg with your wounds all on display, to bring him whatever coppers you could coax from the drunkards of Muddy York with which to feather his pretty little nest yonder. Correct?" We nodded again. "Right.

"Item: We are all of us the crippled children of Muddy York's great information-processing factories. We are artificers, machinists, engineers, cunning shapers and makers, every one, for that is how we came to be injured. Correct? Right.

"Item: It is a murdersome pity that such as we should be turned out to beg when we have so much skill at our disposal. Between us, we could make anything, *do* anything, but our departed tormentor lacked the native wit to see this, correct? Right.

"Item: The sisters of the simpering order of St. Agatha's Weeping Sores have all the cleverness of a turnip. This I saw for myself during my tenure in their hospital. Fooling them would be easier than fooling an idiot child. Correct? *Right*."

He levered himself out of the chair and began to stalk the dining room, stumping up and down. "Someone tell me, how often do the good sisters pay us a visit?"

"Sundays," I said. "When they take us all to church."

He nodded. "And does that spoiled meat there accompany us to church?"

"No," I said. "No, he stays here. He says he 'worships in his own way.'" Truth was, he was invariably too hung-over to rise on a Sunday.

He nodded again. "And today is Tuesday. Which means that we have five days to do our work."

"What work, Monty?"

"Why, we are going to build a clockwork automaton based on that evil tyrant what I slew this very morning. We will build a device of surpassing and fiendish cleverness, such as will fool the nuns and the world at large into thinking that we are still being ground up like mincemeat, while we lead a life of leisure, fun, and invention, such as befits children of our mental stature and good character."

. . . . .

Here's the oath we swore to Monty before we went to work on the automaton:

"I, (state your full name), do hereby give my most solemn oath that I will never, ever betray the secrets of St. Agatha's. I bind myself to the good fortune of my fellow inmates at this institution and vow to honor them as though they were my brothers and sisters, and not to fight with them, nor spite them, nor do them down or dirty. I make this oath freely and gladly, and should I betray it, I wish that old Satan himself would rise up from the pit and tear out my treacherous guts and use them for bootlaces, that his devils would tear my betrayer's tongue from my mouth and use it to wipe their private parts, that my lying body would be fed, inch by inch, to the hungry and terrible basilisks of the Pit. So I swear, and so mote be it!"

There were two children who'd worked for a tanner in the house, older children. Matthew was shy all the fingers on his left hand. Becka was missing an eye and her nose, which she joked was a mercy, for there is no smell more terrible than the charnel reek of the tanning works. But between them, they were quite certain that they could carefully remove, stuff, and remount Grinder's head, careful to leave the jaw in place.

As the oldest machinist at St. Aggie's, I was conscripted to work on the torso and armature mechanisms. I played chief engineer, bossing a gang of six boys and four girls who had experience with mechanisms. We cannibalized St. Aggie's old mechanical wash-wringer, with its spindly arms and many fingers; and I was sent out several times to pawn Grinder's fine crystal and pocket-watch to raise money for parts.

Monty oversaw all, but he took personal charge of Grinder's voice-box, through which he would imitate old Grinder's voice when the sisters came by on Sunday. St. Aggie's was fronted with a Dutch door, and Grinder habitually only opened the top half to jaw with the sisters. Monty said that we could prop the partial torso on a low table, to hide the fact that no legs depended from it.

"We'll tie a sick-kerchief around his face and give out that he's got 'flu, and that it's spread through the whole house. That'll get us all out of church, which is a tidy little jackpot in and of itself. The kerchief will disguise the fact that his lips ain't moving in time with his talking."

I shook my head at this idea. The nuns were hardly geniuses, but how long could this hold out for?

"It won't have to last more than a week—by next week, we'll have something better to show 'em."

Here's a thing: it all worked like a fine-tuned machine.

The kerchief made it look like a bank robber, and Monty painted its face to make him seem more lively, for the tanning had dried him out some (he also doused the horrible thing with liberal lashings of bay rum and greased its hair with a heavy pomade, for the tanning process had left him with a smell like an outhouse on a hot day). Monty had affixed an armature to the thing's bottom jaw—we'd had to break it to get it to open, prying it roughly with a screwdriver, cracking a tooth or two in the process, and I have nightmares to this day about the sound it made when it finally yawed open.

A child—little legless Dora, whose begging pitch included a sad little puppetry show—could work this armature by means of a squeeze-bulb taken from the siphon-starter on Grinder's cider brewing tub, and so make the jaw go up and down in time with speech.

The speech itself was accomplished by means of the horsegut voice-box from Grinder's music-box. Monty surehandedly affixed a long, smooth glass tube—part of the cracking apparatus that I had been sent to market to buy—to the music-box's resonator. This, he ran up behind our automatic Grinder. Then, crouched on the floor before the voice-box, stationed next to Dora on her wheeled plank, he was able to whisper across the horsegut strings and have them buzz out a credible version of Grinder's whiskey-roughened growl. And once he'd tuned the horsegut just so, the vocal resemblance was even more remarkable. Combined with Dora's skillful puppetry, the effect was galvanizing. It took a conscious effort to remember that this was a puppet talking to you, not a man.

The sisters turned up at the appointed hour on Sunday, only to be greeted by our clockwork Grinder, stood in the half-door, face swathed in a 'flu mask. We'd hung quarantine bunting from the windows, crisscrossing the front of St. Aggie's with it for good measure, and a goodly number of us kiddees were watching from the upstairs windows with our best drawn and sickly looks on our faces.

So the sisters hung back practically at the pavement and shouted, "Mr. Grindersworth!" in alarmed tones, staring with horror at the apparition in the doorway.

"Sisters, good day to you," Monty said into his horsegut, while Dora worked her squeeze-bulb, and the jaw went up and down behind its white cloth, and the muffled simulation of Grinder's voice emanated from the top of the glass tube, hidden behind the automaton's head, so that it seemed to come from the right place. "Though not such a good day for us, I fear."

"The children are ill?"

Monty gave out a fine sham of Grinder's laugh, the one he used when dealing with proper people, with the cruelty barely plastered over. "Oh, not all of them. But we have a dozen cases. Thankfully, I appear to be immune, and oh my, but you wouldn't believe the help these tots are in the practical nursing department. Fine kiddees, my charges, yes indeed. But still, best to keep them away from the general public for the nonce, hey? I'm quite sure we'll have them up on their feet by next Sunday, and they'll be glad indeed of the chance to get down on their knees and thank the beneficent Lord for their good health." Monty was laying it on thick, but then, so had Grinder, when it came to the sisters.

"We shall send over some help after the services," the head sister said, hands at her breast, a tear glistening in her eye at the thought of our bravery. I thought the jig was up. Of course the order would have some sisters who'd had the 'flu and gotten over it, rendering them immune. But Monty never worried.

"No, no," he said, smoothly. I had the presence of mind to take up the cranks that operated the "arms" we'd constructed for him, waving them about in a negating way—this effect rather spoiled by my nervousness, so that they seemed more octopus tentacle than arm. But the sisters didn't appear to notice. "As I say, I have plenty of help here with my good children."

"A basket, then," the sister said. "Some nourishing food and fizzy drinks for the children."

Crouching low in the anteroom, we crippled children traded disbelieving looks with one another. Not only had Monty gotten rid of Grinder and gotten us out of going to church, he'd also set things up so that the sisters of St. Aggie's were going to bring us their best grub, for free, because we were all so poorly and ailing! It was all we could do not to cheer.

And cheer we did, later, when the sisters set ten huge hampers down on our doorstep, whence we retrieved them, finding in them a feast fit for princes: cold meat pies glistening with aspic, marrow bones still warm from the oven, suet pudding and jugs of custard with skin on top of them, huge bottles of fizzy lemonade and small beer. By the time we'd laid it out in the dining room, it seemed like we'd never be able to eat it all.

But we eat every last morsel, and four of us carried Monty about on our shoulders—two carrying, two steadying the carriers—and someone found a concertina, and someone found some combs and waxed paper, and we sang until the walls shook: "The Mechanic's Folly", "A Combinatorial Explosion at the

Computer-Works", and then endless rounds of "For He's a Jolly Good Fellow".

．　．　．　．　．

Monty had promised improvements on the clockwork Grinder by the following Sunday, and he made good on it. Since we no longer had to beg all day long, we children of St. Aggie's had time in plenty, and Monty had no shortage of skilled volunteers who wanted to work with him on Grinder II, as he called it. Grinder II sported a rather handsome and large, droopy mustache, which hid the action of its lips. This mustache was glued onto the head-assembly one hair at a time, a painstaking job that denuded every horsehair brush in the house, but the effect was impressive.

More impressive was the leg-assembly I bossed into existence, a pair of clockwork pins that could lever Grinder from a seated position into full upright, balancing him by means of three gyros we hid in his chest cavity. Once these were wound and spun, Grinder could stand up in a very natural fashion. Once we'd rearranged the furniture to hide Dora and Monty behind a large armchair, you could stand right in the parlor and "converse" with him, and unless you were looking very hard, you'd never know but what you were talking with a mortal man, and not an automaton made of tanned flesh, steel, springs, and clay (we used rather a lot of custom-made porcelain from the prosthetic works to get his legs right—the children who were shy a leg or two knew which legmakers in town had the best wares).

And so when the sisters arrived the following Sunday, they were led right into the parlor, whose net curtains kept the room in a semi-dark state, and there, they parlayed with Grinder, who came to his feet when they entered and left. One of the girls was in charge of his arms, and she had practiced with them so well that she was able to move them in a very convincing fashion. Convincing enough, anyroad: the sisters left Grinder with a bag of clothes, a bag of oranges that had come off a ship that had sailed from Spanish Florida right up the St. Lawrence to the port of Montreal, and thereafter traversed by railcar to Muddy York. They made a parcel gift of these succulent treasures to Grinder, to "help the kiddees keep away the scurvy," but Grinder always kept them for himself or flogged them to his pals for a neat penny. We wolfed the oranges right after services, and then took our Sabbath free with games and more brandy from Grinder's sideboard.

· · · · ·

And so we went, week on week, with small but impressive updates to our clockwork man: hands that could grasp and smoke a pipe; a clever mechanism that let him throw back his head and laugh, fingers that could drum on the table beside him, eyes that could follow you around a room and eyelids that could blink, albeit slowly.

But Monty had *much* bigger plans.

"I want to bring in another fifty-six bits," he said, gesturing at the computing panel in Grinder's parlor, a paltry eight-bit works. That meant that there were eight switches with eight matching levers, connected to eight brass rods that ran down to the public computing works that ran beneath the streets of Muddy York. Grinder had used his eight bits to keep St. Aggie's books—both the set he showed to the sisters and the one where he kept track of what he was trousering for himself—and he'd let one "lucky" child work the great, stiff return-arm that sent the instructions set on the switches back to the Hall of Computing for queueing and processing on the great frames that had cost me my good right arm. An instant later, the processed answer would be returned to the levers above the switches, and to whatever interpretive mechanism you had yoked up to them (Grinder used a telegraph machine that printed the answers upon a long, thin sheet of paper).

"Fifty-six bits!" I boggled at Monty. A sixty-four-bit rig wasn't unheard of, if you were a mighty shipping company or insurer. But in a private home—well, the racket of the switches would shake the foundations! Remember, dear reader, that each additional bit *doubled* the calculating faculty of the home panel. Monty was proposing to increase St. Aggie's computational capacity by a factor more than a *quadrillionfold*! (We computermen are accustomed to dealing in these rarified numbers, but they may boggle you. Have no fear—a quadrillion is a number of such surpassing monstrosity that you must have the knack of figuring to even approach it properly).

"Monty," I gasped, "are you planning to open a firm of accountants at St. Aggie's?"

He laid a finger alongside of his nose. "Not at all, my old darling. I have a thought that perhaps we could build a tiny figuring engine into our Grinder's chest cavity, one that could take programs punched off of a sufficiently powerful computing frame, and that these might enable him to walk about on his own, as natural as you please, and even carry on conversations as though he were a living man. Such a creation would afford us even more freedom and security, as you must be able to see."

"But it will cost the bloody world!" I said.

"Oh, I didn't think we'd *pay* for it," he said. Once again, he laid his finger alongside his nose.

And that is how I came to find myself down our local sewer, in the dead of night, a seventeen-year-old brassjacker, bossing a gang of eight kids with ten arms, seven noses, nine hands and eleven legs between them, working furiously and racing the dawn to fit thousands of precision brass push-rods with lightly balanced joints from the local multifarious amalgamation and amplification switch-house to St. Aggie's utility cellar. It didn't work, of course. Not that night. But at least we didn't break anything and alert the Upper Canadian Computing Authority to our mischief. Three nights later, after much fine-tuning, oiling, and desperate prayer, the panel at St. Aggie's boasted sixty-four shining brass bits, the very height of modernity and engineering.

Monty and the children all stood before the panel, which had been burnished to a mirror shine by No-Nose Timmy, who'd done finishing work before a careless master had stumbled over him, pushing him face-first into a spinning grinding wheel. In the gaslight, we appeared to be staring at a group of mighty heroes, and when Monty turned to regard us, he had bright tears in his eyes.

"Sisters and brothers, we have done ourselves proud. A new day has dawned for St. Aggie's and for our lives. Thank you. You have done me proud."

We shared out the last of Grinder's brandy, a thimbleful each, even for the smallest kiddees, and drank a toast to the brave and clever children of St. Aggie's and to Montreal Monty, our savior and the founder of our feast.

· · · · ·

Let me tell you some about life at St. Aggie's in that golden age. Whereas before, we'd rise at 7 a.m. for a mean breakfast—prepared by unfavored children whom Grinder punished by putting them into the kitchen at 4:30 a.m. to prepare the meal—followed by a brief "sermon" roared out by Grinder; now we rose at a very civilized 10 a.m. to eat a leisurely breakfast over the daily papers that Grinder had subscribed to. The breakfasts—all the meals and chores—were done on a rotating basis, with exemptions for children whose infirmity made performing some tasks harder than others. Though all worked—even the blind children sorted weevils and stones from the rice and beans by touch.

Whereas Grinder had sent us out to beg every day— excepting Sundays—debasing ourselves and putting our injuries on display, for the purposes of sympathy; now we were free to laze around the house all day, or work at our own fancies, painting or reading or just playing like the cherished children of rich families who didn't need to send their young ones to the city to work for the family fortune.

But most of us quickly bored of the life of Riley, and for us, there was plenty to do. The clockwork Grinder was always a distraction, especially after Monty started work on the mechanism that would accept punched-tape instructions from the computing panel.

When we weren't working on Grinder, there was other work. We former apprentices went back to our old masters—men and women who were guilty but glad enough to see us, in the main— and told them that the skilled children of St. Aggie's were looking for piecework as part of our rehabilitation, at a competitive price.

It was hardly a lie, either: as broken tools and mechanisms came in for mending, the boys and girls taught one another their crafts and trade, and it wasn't long before a steady flow of cash came into St. Aggie's, paying for better food, better clothes, and, soon enough, the very best artificial arms, legs, hands and feet, the best glass eyes, the best wigs. When Gertie Shine-Pate was fitted for her first wig and saw herself in the great looking-glass in Grinder's study, she burst into tears and hugged all and sundry, and thereafter, St. Aggie's bought her three more wigs to wear as the mood struck her. She took to styling these wigs with combs and scissors, and before long she was cutting hair for all of us at St. Aggie's. We never looked so good.

That gilded time from the end of my boyhood is like a sweet dream to me now. A sweet, lost dream.

· · · · ·

No invention works right the first time around. The inventors' tales you read in the science penny dreadfuls, where some engineer discovers a new principle, puts it into practice, shouts, "Eureka," and sets up his own foundry? They're rubbish. Real invention is a process of repeated, crushing failure that leads, very rarely, to a success. If you want to succeed faster, there's nothing for it but to fail faster and better.

The first time Monty rolled a paper tape into a cartridge and inserted it into Grinder, we all held our breaths while he fished around the arse of Grinder's trousers for the toggle that released the tension on the mainspring we wound through a keyhole in his hip. He stepped back as the soft whining of the mechanism emanated from Grinder's body, and then Grinder began, very slowly, to pace the room's length, taking three long—if jerky—steps, turning about, and taking three steps back. Then Grinder lifted a hand as in greeting, and his mouth stretched into a rictus that might have passed for a grin, and then, very carefully, Grinder punched himself in the face so hard that his head came free from his neck and rolled across the floor with a meaty sound (it took our resident taxidermists a full two days to repair the damage) and his body went into a horrible paroxysm like the St. Vitus's dance, until it, too, fell to the floor.

This was on Monday, and by Wednesday, we had Grinder back on his feet with his head reattached. Again, Monty depressed his toggle, and this time, Grinder made a horrendous clanking sound and pitched forward.

And so it went, day after day, each tiny improvement accompanied by abject failure, and each Sunday we struggled to put the pieces together so that Grinder could pay his respects to the sisters.

Until the day came that the sisters brought round a new child to join our happy clan, and it all began to unravel.

We had been lucky in that Monty's arrival at St. Aggie's coincided with a reformer's movement that had swept Upper Canada, a movement whose figurehead, the Princess Lucy, met with every magistrate, councilman, alderman, and beadle in the colony, the sleeves of her dresses pinned up to the stumps of her shoulders, sternly discussing the plight of the children who worked in the Information Foundries across the colonies. It didn't do no good in the long run, of course, but for the short term, word got round that the authorities would come down very hard on any master whose apprentice lost a piece of himself in the data-mills. So it was some months before St. Aggie's had any new meat arrive upon its doorstep.

The new meat in question was a weepy boy of about eleven— the same age I'd been when I arrived—and he was shy his left leg all the way up to the hip. He had a crude steel leg in its place, strapped up with a rough, badly cured cradle that must have hurt like hellfire. He also had a splintery crutch that he used to get around with, the sort of thing that the sisters of St. Aggie's bought in huge lots from unscrupulous tradesmen who cared nothing for the people who'd come to use them.

His name was William Sansousy, a Metis boy who'd come from the wild woods of Lower Canada seeking work in Muddy York, who'd found instead an implacable machine that had torn off his leg and devoured it without a second's remorse. He spoke English with a thick French accent, and slipped into *Joual* when he was overcome with sorrow.

Two sisters brought him to the door on a Friday afternoon. We knew they were coming, they'd sent round a messenger boy with a printed telegram telling Grinder to make room for one more. Monty wanted to turn his Clockwork Grinder loose to walk to the door and greet them, but we all told him he'd be mad to try it: there was so much that could go wrong, and if the sisters worked out what had happened, we could finish up dangling from nooses at King Street Gaol.

Monty relented resentfully, and instead we seated Grinder in his overstuffed chair, with Monty tucked away behind it, ready to converse with the sisters. I hid with him, ready to send Grinder to his feet and to extend his cold, leathery artificial hand to the boy when the sisters turned him over.

And it went smoothly—that day. When the sisters had gone and their car had built up its head of steam and chuffed and clanked away, we emerged from our hiding place. Monty broke into slangy, rapid French, gesticulating and hopping from foot to peg-leg and back again, and William's eyes grew as big as saucers as Monty explained the lay of the land to him. The *clang* when he thumped Grinder in his cast-iron chest made William leap back and he hobbled toward the door.

"Wait, wait!" Monty called, switching to English. "Wait, will you, you idiot? This is the best day of your life, young William! But for us, you might have entered a life of miserable bondage. Instead, you will enjoy all the fruits of liberty, rewarding work, and comradeship. We take care of our own here at St. Aggie's. You'll have top grub, a posh leg and a beautiful crutch that's as smooth as a baby's arse and soft as a lady's bosom. You'll have the freedom to come and go as you please, and you'll have a warm bed to sleep in every night. And best of all, you'll have us, your family here at St. Aggie's. We take care of our own, we do."

The boy looked at us, tears streaming down his face. He made me remember what it had been like, my first day at St. Aggie's, the cold fear coiled round your guts like rope caught in a reciprocating gear. At St. Aggie's we put on brave faces, never cried where no one could see us, but seeing him weep made me remember all the times I'd cried, cried for my lost family who'd sold me into indenture, cried for my mangled body, my ruined life. But living without Grinder's constant terrorizing must have softened my heart. Suddenly it was all I could do to stop myself from giving the poor little mite a one-armed hug.

I didn't hug him, but Monty did, stumping over to him, and the two of them bawled like babbies. Their peg-legs knocked together as they embraced like drunken sailors, seeming to cry out every tear we'd any of us ever held in. Before long, we were all crying with them, fat tears streaming down our faces, the sound like something out of the Pit.

When the sobs had stopped, William looked around at us, wiped his nose, and said, "Thank you. I think I am home."

. . . . .

But it wasn't home for him. Poor William. We'd had children like him, in the bad old days, children who just couldn't get back up on their feet (or foot) again. Most of the time, I reckon, they were kids who couldn't make it as apprentices, neither, kids who'd spent their working lives full of such awful misery that they were *bound* to fall into a machine. And being sundered from their limbs didn't improve their outlook.

We tried everything we could think of to cheer William up. He'd worked for a watch-smith, and he had a pretty good hand at disassembling and cleaning mechanisms. His stump ached him like fire, even after he'd been fitted with a better apparatus by St. Aggie's best legmaker, and it was only when he was working with his little tweezers and brushes that he lost the grimace that twisted up his face so. Monty had him strip and clean every clockwork in the house, even the ones that were working perfectly—even the delicate works we'd carefully knocked together for the clockwork Grinder. But it wasn't enough.

In the bad old days, Grinder would have beaten the boy and sent him out to beg in the worst parts of town, hoping that he'd be run down by a cart or killed by one of the blunderbuss gangs that marauded there. When the law brought home the boy's body, old Grinder would weep crocodile tears and tug his hair at the bloody evil that men did, and then he'd go back to his rooms and play some music and drink some brandy and sleep the sleep of the unjust.

We couldn't do the same, and so we tried to bring up William's spirits instead, and when he'd had enough of it, he lit out on his own. The first we knew of it was when he didn't turn up for breakfast. This wasn't unheard of—any of the free children of St. Aggie's was able to rise and wake whenever he chose, but William had been a regular at breakfast every day. I made my way upstairs to the dormer room where the boys slept to look for him and found his bed empty, his coat and his peg-leg and crutch gone.

"He's gone," Monty said, "long gone." He sighed and looked out the window. "Must be trying to get back to the Gatineaux." He shook his head.

"Do you think he'll make it?" I said, knowing the answer, but hoping that Monty would lie to me.

"Not a chance," Monty said. "Not him. He'll either be beaten, arrested or worse by sundown. That lad hasn't any self-preservation instincts."

At this, the dining room fell silent and all eyes turned on Monty and I saw in a flash what a terrible burden we all put on him: savior, father, chieftain. He twisted his face into a halfway convincing smile.

"Oh, maybe not. He might just be hiding out down the road. Tell you what, eat up and we'll go searching for him."

I never saw a load of plates cleared faster. It was bare minutes before we were formed up in the parlor, divided into groups, and sent out into Muddy York to find William Sansousy. We turned that bad old city upside-down, asking nosy questions and sticking our heads in where they didn't belong, but Monty had been doubly right the first time around.

The police found William Sansousy's body in a marshy bit of land off the Leslie Street Spit. His pockets had been slit, his pathetic paper sack of belongings torn and the clothes scattered, and his fine hand-turned leg was gone. He had been dead for hours.

• • • • •

The detective inspector who presented himself that afternoon at St. Aggie's was trailed by a team of technicians who had a wire sound-recorder and a portable logic engine for inputting the data of his investigation. He seemed very proud of his machine, even though it came with three convicts from the King Street Gaol in shackles and leg-irons who worked tirelessly to keep the springs wound, toiling in a lather of sweat and heaving breath, heat boiling off their shaved heads in shimmering waves.

He showed up just as the clock in the parlor chimed eight times, a bear chasing a bird around on a track as it sang the hour. We peered out the windows in the upper floors, saw the inspector, and understood just why Monty had been so morose all afternoon.

But Monty did us proud. He went to the door with his familiar swagger, and swung it wide, extending his hand to the inspector.

"Montague Goldfarb, officer, at your service. Our patron has stepped away, but please, do come in."

The inspector gravely shook the proffered hand, his huge, gloved mitt swallowing Monty's boyish hand. It was easy to forget that he was just a child, but the looming presence of the giant inspector reminded us all.

"Master Goldfarb," the inspector said, taking his hat off, and peering through his smoked monocle at the children in the parlor, all of us sat with hands folded like we were in a pantomime about the best-behaved, most crippled, most terrified, least threatening children in all the colonies. "I am sorry to hear that Mr. Grindersworth is not at home to the constabulary. Have you any notion as to what temporal juncture we might expect him?" If I hadn't been concentrating on not peeing myself with terror, the inspector's pompous speech might have set me to laughing.

Monty didn't bat an eye. "Mr. Grindersworth was called away to see his brother in Sault Sainte Marie, and we expect him tomorrow. I'm his designated lieutenant, though. Perhaps I might help you?"

The inspector stroked his forked beard and gave us all another long look. "Tomorrow, hey? Well, I don't suppose that justice should wait that long. Master Goldfarb, I have grim intelligence for you, as regards one of your young compatriots, a Master—" He consulted a punched card that was held in a hopper on his clanking logic engine. "—William Sansousy. He lies even now upon a slab in the city morgue. Someone of authority from this institution is required to confirm the preliminary identification.

You will do, I suppose. Though your patron will have to present himself post-haste in order to sign the several official documents that necessarily accompany an event of such gravity."

We'd known as soon as the inspector turned up at St. Aggie's door that it meant that William was dead. If he was merely in trouble, it would have been a constable, dragging him by the ear. We half-children of St. Aggie's only rated a full inspector when we were topped by some evil bastard in this evil town. But hearing the inspector say the words, puffing them through his drooping mustache, that made it real. None of us had ever cried when St. Aggie's children were taken by the streets—at least, not where the others could see it. But this time round, without Grinder to shoot us filthy daggers if we made a peep while the law was about, it opened the floodgates. Boys and girls, young and old, we cried for poor little William. He'd come to the best of all possible St. Aggie's, but it hadn't been good enough for him. He'd wanted to go back to the parents who'd sold him into service, wanted a return to his Mam's lap and bosom. Who among us didn't want that, in his secret heart?

Monty's tears were silent and they rolled down his cheeks as he shrugged into his coat and hat and let the inspector—who was clearly embarrassed by the display—lead him out the door.

· · · · ·

When Monty came home, he arrived at a house full of children who were ready to go mad. We'd cried ourselves hoarse, then sat about the parlor, not knowing what to do. If there had been any of old Grinder's booze still in the house, we'd have drunk it.

"What's the plan, then?" he said, coming through the door. "We've got one night until that bastard comes back. If he doesn't find Grinder, he'll go to the sisters, and it'll come down around our ears. What's more, he knows Grinder, personal, from other dead ones in years gone by, and I don't think he'll be fooled by our machine, no matter how good it goes."

"What's the plan?" I said, mouth hanging open. "Monty, the plan is that we're all going to gaol and you and I and everyone else who helped cover up the killing of Grinder will dance at rope's end!"

He gave me a considering look. "Sian, that is absolutely the worst plan I have ever heard." And then he grinned at us the way he did, and we all knew that, somehow, it would all be all right.

· · · · ·

"Constable, come quick, he's going to kill himself!"

I practiced the line for the fiftieth time, willing my eyes to go wider, my voice to carry more alarm. Behind me, Monty scowled at my reflection in the mirror in Grinder's personal toilet, where I'd been holed up for hours.

"Verily, the stage lost a great player when that machine mangled you, Sian. You are perfect. Now, get moving before I tear your remaining arm off and beat you with it. Go!"

Phase one of the plan was easy enough: we'd smuggle our Grinder up onto the latticework of steel and scaffold where they were building the mighty Prince Edward Viaduct, at the end of Bloor Street. Monty had punched his program already: he'd pace back and forth, tugging his hair, shaking his head like a maddened man, and then, abruptly, he'd turn and fling himself bodily off the platform, plunging one hundred and thirty feet into the Don River, where he would simply disintegrate into a million cogs, gears, springs and struts, which would sink to the riverbed and begin to rust away. The coppers would recover his clothes, and those, combined with the eyewitness testimony of the constable I was responsible for bringing to the bridge, would establish in everyone's mind exactly what had happened and how: Grinder was so distraught at one more death from among his charges that he had popped his own clogs in grief. We were all of us standing ready to testify as to how poor William was Grinder's little favorite, a boy he loved like a son, and so forth. Who would suspect a bunch of helpless cripples, anyway?

That was the theory, at least. But now I was actually stood by the bridge, watching six half-children wrestle the automaton into place, striving for silence so as not to alert the guards who were charged with defending the structure they were already calling "The Suicide's Magnet," and I couldn't believe that it would possibly work.

Five of the children scampered away, climbing back down the scaffolds, slipping and sliding and nearly dying more times than I could count, so that my heart was thundering in my chest so hard I thought I might die upon the spot. Then they were safely away, climbing back up the ravine's walls in the mud and snow, almost invisible in the dusky dawn light. Monty waved an arm at me, and I knew it was my cue, and that I should be off to rouse the constabulary, but I found myself rooted to the spot.

In that moment, every doubt and fear and misery I'd ever harbored crowded back in on me. The misery of being abandoned by my family, the sorrow and loneliness I'd felt among the prentice-lads, the humiliation of Grinder's savage beatings and harangues.

The shame of my injury and every time I'd groveled before a drunk or a pitying lady with my stump on display for pennies to fetch home to Grinder. What was I doing? There was no way I could possibly pull this off. I wasn't enough of a man—nor enough of a boy.

But then I thought of all those moments since the coming of Monty Goldfarb, the millionfold triumphs of ingenuity and hard work, the computing power I'd stolen out from under the nose of the calculators who had treated me as a mere work-ox before my injury. I thought of the cash we'd brought in, the children who'd smiled and sung and danced on the worn floors of St. Aggie's, and—

And I ran to the policeman, who was warming himself by doing a curious hopping dance in place, hands in his armpits. "Constable!" I piped, all sham terror that no one would have known for a sham. "Constable! Come quick, he's going to kill himself!"

· · · · ·

The sister who came to sit up with us mourning kiddies that night was called Sister Mary Immaculata, and she was kindly, if a bit dim. I remembered her from my stay in the hospital after my maiming: a slightly vacant prune-faced woman in a wimple who'd bathed my wounds gently and given me solemn hugs when I woke screaming in the middle of the night.

She was positive that the children of St. Aggie's were inconsolable over the suicide of our beloved patron, Zophar Grindersworth, and she doled out those same solemn cuddles to anyone foolish enough to stray near her. That none of us shed a tear was lost upon her, though she did note with approval how smoothly the operation of St. Aggie's continued without Grinder's oversight.

The next afternoon, Sister Mary Immaculata circulated among us, offering reassurance that a new master would be found for St. Aggie's. None of us were much comforted by this: we knew the kind of man who was likely to fill such a plum vacancy.

"If only there was some way we could go on running this place on our own," I moaned under my breath, trying to concentrate on repairing the pressure gauge on a pneumatic evacuator that we'd taken in for mending.

Monty shot me a look. He had taken the sister's coming very hard. "I don't think I have it in me to kill the next one, too. Anyway, they're bound to notice if we keep on assassinating our guardians."

I snickered despite myself. Then my gloomy pall descended again. It had all been so good, how could we possibly return to the old way? But there was no way the sisters would let a bunch of crippled children govern themselves.

"What a waste," I said. "What a waste of all this potential."

"At least I'll be shot of it in two years," Monty said. "How long have you got till your eighteenth?"

My brow furrowed. I looked out the grimy workshop window at the iron-gray February sky. "It's February tenth today?"

"Eleventh," he said.

I laughed, an ugly sound. "Why, Monty, my friend, today is my eighteenth birthday. I believe I have survived St. Aggie's to graduate to bigger and better things. I have attained my majority, old son."

He held a hand out and shook my hook with it, solemnly. "Happy birthday and congratulations, then, Sian. May the world treat you with all the care you deserve."

I stood, the scrape of my chair very loud and sudden. I realized I had no idea what I would do next. I had managed to completely forget that my graduation from St. Aggie's was looming, that I would be a free man. In my mind, I'd imagined myself dwelling at St. Aggie's forever.

Forever.

"You look like you just got hit in the head with a shovel," Monty said. "What on earth is going through that mind of yours?"

I didn't answer. I was already on my way to find Sister Immaculata. I found her in the kitchen, helping legless Dora make the toast for tea over the fire's grate.

"Sister," I said, "a word please?"

As she turned and followed me into the pantry off the kitchen, some of that fear I'd felt on the bridge bubbled up in me. I tamped it back down again firmly, like a piston compressing some superheated gas.

She was really just as I remembered her, and she had remembered me, too—she remembered all of us, the children she'd held in the night and then consigned to this Hell upon Earth, all unknowing.

"Sister Mary Immaculata, I attained my eighteenth birthday today."

She opened her mouth to congratulate me, but I held up my stump.

"I turned eighteen today, sister. I am a man, I have attained my majority. I am at liberty, and must seek my fortune in the world. I have a proposal for you, accordingly." I put everything I had into this, every dram of confidence and maturity that I'd learned since we inmates had taken over the asylum. "I was Mr. Grindersworth's lieutenant and assistant in every matter relating to the daily operation of this place. Many's the day I did every bit of work that there was to do, whilst Mr. Grindersworth attended to family matters. I know every inch of this place, every soul in it, and I have had the benefit of the excellent training and education that there is to have here.

"I had always thought to seek my fortune in the world as a mechanic of some kind, if any shop would have a half-made thing like me, but seeing as you find yourself at loose ends in the superintendent department, I thought I might perhaps put my plans 'on hold' for the time being, until such time as a full search could be conducted."

"Sian," she said, her face wrinkling into a gap-toothed smile. "Are you proposing that *you* might run St. Agatha's?"

It took everything I could not to wilt under the pity and amusement in that smile. "I am, sister. I am. I have all but run it for months now, and have every confidence in my capacity to go on doing so for so long as need be." I kept my gaze and my voice even. "I believe that the noble mission of St. Aggie's is a truly attainable one: that it can rehabilitate such damaged things as we and prepare us for the wider world."

She shook her head. "Sian," she said, softly, "Sian. I wish it could be. But there's no hope that such an appointment would be approved by the board of governors."

I nodded. "Yes, I thought so. But do the governors need to approve a *temporary* appointment? A stopgap, until a suitable person can be found?"

Her smile changed, got wider. "You have certainly come into your own shrewdness here, haven't you?"

"I was taught well," I said, and smiled back.

· · · · ·

The temporary has a way of becoming permanent. That was my bolt of inspiration, my galvanic realization. Once the sisters had something that worked, that did not call attention to itself, that took in crippled children and released whole persons some years later, they didn't need to muck about with it. As the mechanics say, "If it isn't broken, it doesn't want fixing."

I'm no mechanic, not anymore. The daily running of St. Aggie's occupied a larger and larger slice of my time, until I found that I knew more about tending to a child's fever or soothing away a nightmare than I did about hijacking the vast computers to do our bidding.

But that's no matter, as we have any number of apprentice computermen and computerwomen turning up on our doorsteps. So long as the machineries of industry grind on, the supply will be inexhaustible.

Monty visits me from time to time, mostly to scout for talent. His shop, Goldsworth and Associates, has a roaring trade in computational novelties and service, and if anyone is bothered by the appearance of a factory filled with the halt, the lame, the blind and the crippled, they are thankfully outnumbered by those who are delighted by the quality of the work and the good value in his schedule of pricing.

But it was indeed a golden time, that time when I was but a boy at St. Aggie's among the boys and girls, a cog in a machine that Monty built of us, part of a great uplifting, a transformation from a hell to something like a heaven. That I am sentenced to serve in this heaven I helped to make is no great burden, I suppose.

Still, I do yearn to screw a jeweler's loupe into my eye, pick up a fine tool and bend the sodium lamp to shine upon some cunning mechanism that wants fixing. For machines may be balky and they may destroy us with their terrible appetite for oil, blood and flesh, but they behave according to fixed rules and can be understood by anyone with the cunning to look upon them and winkle out their secrets. Children are ever so much more complicated.

Though I believe I may be learning a little about them, too.

Greg van Eekhout has been a longtime contributor of both flash and full-length short stories to *Escape Pod*. He can effortlessly place stories in the absurd fantastical arena ("Taco" is a favorite of mine, see escapepod.org) or go the uncomfortable and poignant route. This story reminded me that it is telling how few authors of science fiction will admit that, even if we have the best machines technology can give us, there will still be the haves and the have-nots. It's great that a machine can cure all known diseases; but whose diseases will they cure? Let's go among the stars! But who's got a seat? You don't want to be back in third class with Those People. These aren't problems we can think ourselves out of. You can't make rich people respect poor people with a machine. (Dr. Seuss tried that with the Sneetches. It didn't work then, either.) Just like Maurice Broaddus, Greg van Eekhout forces us to ask ourselves, "The future looks bright, but for whom?"

MUR

SPACESHIP *OCTOBER*

GREG VAN EEKHOUT

When you live on a spaceship, you learn to make your own fun. Exploring the tunnels is some of the very best fun the *October*'s got. After school hour, me and Droller go scuttling through the darkest conduits you ever will find. The starboard Hab gets minimal heat, so our breath clouds in the light of our head torches as we crawl on our hands and knees.

"You hear that?" Droller whispers from a couple of meters ahead.

I do hear it, a deep, wet wheezing that sounds exactly like Droller trying to spook me.

"You better go ahead and check it out, Droller."

"Naw, Kitch, it's behind you. It smells your butt. It's a butthunter."

I laugh at Droller's stupid joke, because the stupider, the funnier, and she's by far my stupidest friend.

We're both from Aft Hab, both from the same birth lottery, and out of the eight babies born that season, we're the only survivors. It used to be the three of us, me and Droller, and Jamm, but Jamm died last year along with her parents when the CO_2 scrubbers in their cube failed. The scrubbers were item thirty-three on the fixems' to-do list.

"How much farther?" I ask Droller.

"Just a couple of panels."

It's more like a couple dozen panels, but we finally arrive at the section of conduit above Town Square. Using just our fingers, Droller and me remove the fasteners holding the panel in place and slide it aside, just enough for us to peek out.

Down below, a crowd settles on the rings of benches surrounding the lawn. The brass band toots "Onward or Bust" in a marching beat, their jackets sparkling with silver buttons and silver loops of rope. Droller and I exchange a sad look. Jamm wanted to be a drummer and wear a thick, warm jacket like that. The odds were against an Aft Habber like her, but she was good enough that she might have made it.

Once the tooting is over, one of the vice captains ascends to the grandstand. The audience stands and salutes in respect. Everyone on the *October* acts like salutes are required, but White Madeleine told us saluting was never in the contract the original families signed. The Fore Habbers made up the requirement eighty years ago.

The kind of people who come to witness a Course Correction are the type who do what they're supposed to.

The vice captain says some stuff into a bullhorn. It's too distorted for me and Droller to make out actual words, but we know what he's saying, because this isn't the first time we've watched a Course Correction from the conduits. He's announcing the name of the violator and their crime.

The guards bring out a man, their hands gripping his arms and shoving. He's dressed in thin brown paper coveralls. His face is bloodless. I bet he's shivering in the cold.

"I've seen him before," says Droller. She doesn't know his name, but he does look familiar. Maybe I've spotted him in line at Distro, or maybe on a community service detail. Yeah, that's it. A few months ago we were on the same crew scraping mold off crop troughs in the farm module. He was quiet and sniffed a lot.

"What do you think he did?" Droller asks.

"I bet he buggered a robot."

Droller laughs, because it's stupid.

The vice captain says something, his voice just a *wah-wah-wah* to us, but when a guard holds up a one-by-two-meter rectangle of insulation padding, the man's crime is obvious: pilfering.

"Can't blame him," says Droller.

I nod. I think he's an Aft Habber like us, and sometimes it's so cold that it's weird you *wouldn't* steal some insulation padding.

"Think they'll flog him or space him?"

"Naw," Droller says. "It's not *that* big a crime."

"Depends on the vice captain's mood. What if he's grumpy? What if he didn't have a good dump this morning?"

Droller laughs, but not a lot. She had a great-great-uncle who got spaced, or so the family story goes. I think her parents were just trying to scare her into being dutiful.

The longer we wait for the vice captain to pronounce his sentence, the less fun any of it seems.

The crowd grows so quiet we can actually make out what the vice captain says:

"For the crime of pilfering, you, Manet Leif, are sentenced to a year's service of filter scrubbing while clamped."

A guard yanks one of Leif's arms behind his back and clamps it to the small of his back.

I whistle low. I had my mandatory scrub day last week. It was a long four hours with a mountain of filters, a wire brush, and a bucket of solvent, and my hands and shoulders just stopped aching yesterday. Manet Leif gets a year of that? With only one arm?

"I'd rather be flogged," says Droller.

"Well, pilfer something and maybe you'll get your wish."

Droller is about to say something stupid when the brightest light I've ever seen turns everything white and painful.

"VIOLATION," a voice booms.

It's a doomba.

I try to scream, "RUN," but it comes out as a choked cry. Droller copies me and makes the exact same noise.

With the ceiling of the conduit only centimeters above our heads, there's not enough room to run. We can only crawl away from the drone really, really fast.

But not fast enough. We get about fifty meters down the conduit when Droller howls.

The drone has a shock wire in contact with her ankle. Her hair floats, a halo of fuzz. She's all, "Yeeeargh," and, "Oooowwwww," through tears and gritted teeth.

Of all the times to run into functioning tunnel security.

What will I do if it kills Droller? How will I get her body

back to the Hab? What will I tell her parents? What will I do without my friend? I'm so scared for her that I don't have any room to be scared for myself. I just have to get her out of here.

Lying on my back, I kick at the conduit wall.

Once. Twice. On the third time, something splinters. I kick again. The wall cracks in a wide jagged fissure. Two more kicks, and it comes apart in shards.

I grab Droller's arm with both hands. The doomba's wire is still on her ankle, and the shock travels from her to me. A searing ache bores through my bones. My spine grows numb. Without knowing what will happen next, I yank Droller to the gap I made in the conduit and toss her over the side. I dive after her.

It's a long fall.

. . . . .

We land in a bone-jarring heap. My breath comes in wheezy spasms. Droller just whimpers, curled up in a ball.

Above us, the doomba lingers in the conduit, uselessly reaching through the gap with its shock wires. For a second I think it's going to come down after us, but doombas can't fly, they just roll on their little wheels, and since we're no longer in the conduit, its job is done.

The drop doesn't look as far as it felt, which is good, because it feels awful. Wincing, I get to my feet and timidly move my joints and pat my sore parts. Everything hurts, but everything works.

I help up sniffling Droller and we determine that she's pretty much in the same shape as me.

"Where are we?"

The only answer I have is nowhere we've ever been.

It's a huge room with high ceilings, almost as big as a cargo hold. Everything is white surfaces, lit bright, like a vision of heaven. The deck plates are some kind of weird material, white and hard and smooth and cold to the touch, shot through with veins of black. Fancy pillars with carved curlicue tops hold up the arched ceiling. Strangest of all is the air. It's warm.

And there's music, completely different from brass-band marches, gentle notes rising and falling and mixing together in way that reminds me of the forest scenes they sometimes project at Town Square so we don't forget the *October* isn't just floating pointlessly in space, but that we're going somewhere, and our great-great-great-grandchildren will live on a planet of trees and lakes and grain fields and sunshine.

"I think that's organ music," Droller says. "Didn't White Madeleine tell us about organ music once?"

White Madeleine told us a lot of things. She told us how the ship was different for the first generation, with more power and more heat and light and more things that worked, without an entire hab warren sharing a single power cell, and that's how things were supposed to be until the *October* delivered us all the way to Nova Terra. But there were things that happened even before the ship left Earth orbit. Things like cost-cutting and budget cuts and low-bid contracts. Earth stuff I never understood.

"No, seriously," Droller whispers in awe, "what is this place?"

"Only one way to find out."

I take the first step and Droller follows me. Treading softly on the shiny floor, we walk for what seems like the entire length of a module before we come upon a body.

At first, we think it's just some strange piece of equipment, a long box resting on the floor about two meters long, a meter wide, and as tall as my knees. It's made out of the same smooth, veiny stuff as the floor, with some decorative curlicues and whatnot. Cables anchor it to the floor, and as I come close, I hear a familiar hum.

"It's drawing power," I say.

Droller doesn't answer. She just leans over the box, eyes wide.

Carved into the top is the *October*'s motto: "Onward or Bust," and right above the words is a small glass window. Under the glass, behind a thin haze of frost, is a face.

It's a woman, eyes closed in peaceful rest. Her cheeks are white as milk paste, but plump, like she's well fed despite being dead.

"What's wrong with her?" Droller says.

"Why, ain't you never seen a dead person before? It's a corpse."

I'm acting all sophisticated, but I'm as spooked as Droller. Just because I've seen death doesn't mean I'm used to it. And normally the dead are in bags that get spaced or fed to the recyclers if the recyclers are working.

I wonder which treatment my sister will get.

She's been sick for months and she's not getting better.

I keep expecting the corpse to open her eyes and punch a hand through the glass and reach at us with twitchy claw fingers.

The box isn't the only one. Up ahead, there's dozens of them, maybe hundreds, stretching off to the horizon, the hatch at the far end of the module.

"Should we keep going?" Droller asks.

"Ain't that what they teach us in school hour? Ain't that what

'Onward or Bust' is all about? Forward, ever forward, never stopping, until we are home."

"Home ain't forward," Droller observes. "Home is behind us in Aft Hab. Forward is… who knows?"

"It's the principle of the thing," I snap.

Droller makes a face at me, and onward we go.

More faces behind glass. More boxes drawing power. A few of them have bright red and yellow and purple and white flowers laid on top. I only know they're flowers because I've seen them in the projections at Town Square. Flowers are a kind of beautiful plant that you mostly don't eat.

I rub a soft petal against my cheek. "I never seen these growing in the troughs."

"If they got a secret place like this, I bet they got secret farms, too," Droller says, knowingly.

"But why? Why keep all these dead people? And why all hooked up like this and stuff?"

A voice saws through the air like a rusty knife. "I think a better question is what are you doing here, all trespassing and stuff?"

A tall woman with a cracked old face glares at us, hands on her hips. Long yellow hair spills out from under an orange cap. The cap matches her coveralls, which come with pockets down the legs and a tool belt hanging from her narrow waist. She's a fixem.

"Run or tackle her?" asks Droller.

"Aw, don't bother," the fixem scoffs. "Old Lodi can't give chase, not with these knees. And you don't got mean looks in your baby eyes. Besides, you gotta stick around long enough to patch up that big hole you made in my conduit."

Droller and I kinda stare at each other like fools, not knowing what to do. If we were going to run, we should have done it right when the fixem startled us. Now, running off would seem weird. And the fixem is right about our mean looks. We don't have any.

"Well, you gonna just stand there with your mouths hung open, or you want a tour of the mausoleum?"

Droller and me trip over each other to answer. "We want a tour!"

We follow as Lodi leads us among the boxes—*coffins*, she calls them—and rattles off the names of the occupants:

Byron Cheddar.

Wang Shusen.

Muthoni Njaga.

Temperance Brown.

"Kitch, we know these names," Droller says, excited for some reason.

Everybody does, because the teacher makes us recite them in school hour. These are the Firsts. The first generation that left Earth. The original travelers who set out on the *October* to Nova Terra. Our great-great-great and so on grandmothers and grandfathers.

"Why keep the whole dead lot of them here?" Droller asks while Lodi keeps rattling off names.

Lodi's thin lips distort in a bitter smile. "Who says they're dead?"

I go over to the nearest coffin and peer through the glass at a pallid face. "Ain't they?"

"Not if Old Lodi is doing her job right. And say whatever you want about me, but I do my damn job. They're alive, and they'll stay that way, onward or bust."

I can see how Droller is trying to put it all together. "So, when we die, they keep us alive, and we'll all be alive when we get to Nova Terra. Us, our parents, our children, going up and down the line… all of us together."

That sounds so nice. If we stick the journey out, we all get to step off the ship and bask in the sunlight of Nova Terra. We all get to live under open skies, big and free. Me and Droller and Jamm together again, along with our folks and their folks and our children and their children, all the generations backward and forward.

It sounds so fair.

That's how I know it's a lie.

"It's just the first generation that gets kept alive to Nova Terra, ain't that right, Lodi?"

The old woman nods. "The Firsts put it in the contract and paid for it before the *October* even left Earth. This is a generation ship where the very oldest are the very richest, so they never have to give way to the youngest."

Droller switches from dreamy to confused. "That's not fair," she says, her voice a little wispy, like she's just discovered something. "Why not put us all in coffins when we die? Why not do this for everyone?"

Lodi bats this away like a dust mote. "How many power cells you figure it takes to keep all the Firsts alive?"

A hab warren houses eight families and goes through one power cell a year. That's running on minimum energy, dim lights, chill air, low filtration, rationed power consumption for materials recycling and fabrication.

"I dunno," Droller says, looking around to take in the whole space. "A hundred?"

"A hundred?" Lodi guffaws. "Each coffin uses a power cell a year. And there's three hundred and sixty-seven coffins. Then you add in everything else—the lights, the music, the heating… The original requisition was more than two million power cells. That was supposed to keep the Firsts going all the way to Nova Terra. But it turned out to be an underestimate, no surprise. Every year we have to reassign cells from other parts of the ship just to make sure the coffins remain juiced till planet fall."

"Then why the lights and the music and the heat?" says Droller. The outrage starts to build. "This is just waste."

"It's not a waste if the Firsts wanted it. And they wanted to make the journey in a dignified setting."

I think of my sister, coughing in our cold warren. I think of Jamm, slowly suffocating while she slept.

I want to be furious at someone. I want to blame the Firsts, lying cozy in their coffins, and the vice captains handing out punishment, and the Fore Habbers, and the people in the bridge tower we never see. But Lodi's the one here, so I take it out on her.

"Why do you help them?" I almost scream. "Why not tell someone?"

"I'm telling you, ain't I? And what are you going to do about it? That's right. Nothing. Same as anyone else. Only you're just kids so you're not going to put me in a muzzle." She seems like she's having an argument with someone who isn't here. Then her face gets real sad. "Anyway, I'm old. Dropped my last egg, and my wife, Tilda passed last year."

"I'm sorry," I say out of polite habit.

Lodi doesn't even hear me. "Tilda was supposed to lie with me here after she died. But where is she? Being 'prepared,' say the uppers. Prepared, my elbow. It's been sixteen months. They spaced her or recycled her, and they'll do the same to me when I'm gone, same as they did for all the mausoleum tenders who came before me. They lie so much they don't even bother making good ones anymore." Drained, she takes a deep, slow breath. She looks at us like she just remembered we're here. "Go back to your cold, damp warrens. Tell anyone you want. Nobody ever does anything about anything. Nobody corrects the course, they just correct the tellers. Back to the tunnel with you."

"Aw, you're making us go back through the conduit?" Droller protests. "There's a doomba in there almost killed us."

"You survived it once, you'll survive it again. Or maybe you won't. But either way, you gotta fix that panel you broke. I'll get the ladder."

Once we're back up in the conduit, we discover there's no more reason to fear the doomba. It's keeled over on its side, leaking the bitter stink of melted wires. It'll be number nine hundred and something on the fixems' list.

While I hold the panel in place, Droller inserts the fasteners. "Wait," I say, just as she's about to put in the last one. "Leave it."

"Why, you thinking to come back here?"

I do something with my eyebrows that means neither "yes" nor "no."

"One more thing." I grip the doomba with both hands and pull where its body joins in a seam. It's not easy, but I manage to crack it open, just enough to squeeze a hand inside and yank out its power cell. It's only a mini, it's probably mostly spent, but I'm keeping it.

"Kitch," says Droller, shocked. "That's pilfering."

I point down at the mausoleum. "No, *that's* pilfering."

· · · · ·

Late at night, after meal, I sneak into our warren's utility closet and replace the mostly dead power cell with the mini from the doomba.

My sister still coughs through the night, and my parents' faces are dull with worry, but the air is warmer and drier and smells cleaner.

· · · · ·

She dies three weeks later.

· · · · ·

The mausoleum lights still blaze bright. The organ music still wafts through the vast chamber with its vaulted ceilings and fancy pillars. The coffins still hum with power.

There's no sign of Lodi, but even if she interrupts me, I don't think she'll stop me. She says nobody ever makes a real course correction. I have a hunch she might like what I'm about to do.

Or maybe she's dead. Maybe she already has a replacement.

"Kitch, what're you doing?"

It's Droller, climbing down from the conduit on the ladder I made from my sister's knotted bedsheets.

"Dammit, Droller. Go home. You don't need to be here."

"I came by your warren but you weren't home. I was bringing by some toasted meal for your parents. It's from me and my folks, in case yours aren't up to cooking. You know, on account of your sister."

"That was real thoughtful, Droller. Tell your folks thanks and go on home."

"I will once we're done here. What is it we're doing?"

She says "we," because whatever I'm doing, she's doing, because that's how Droller and me always work, and trying to get rid of her would be like trying to scrape mineral crust off a bulkhead.

I show her the empty pillowcase I brought, plus a scratched and dull pry strip. "I'm gonna take their power cells," I tell her, moving toward the nearest coffin.

"But… you do that, won't they die?"

"I suppose they will."

"Kitch. That's murder."

I look at a white face behind glass. Etched on a little plate is the name: "Hai Breves." She's one of the first generation we learned about in school hour.

When I saw the bodies in the coffins the very first time, I thought they were dead. But now that I know they aren't, they look a little different to me.

They look like they're sleeping.

They look like they're at peace.

They look happy.

Lodi said the mausoleum goes through three hundred and sixty-seven power cells a year.

How many power cells would it take to warm the Aft Hab?
To keep our air clean so people like Jamm and her folks don't die?
To run our recyclers so we have raw materials and enough meal
and medicine?

To keep more babies like my sister alive?

Not that many.

I jab my pry strip between the edge of the glass and coffin lid.

I should only have to kill a few Firsts to make things a tiny
bit more fair.

I'm always of the opinion that science fiction needs more mundane in it. Not boring stuff, but the little pleasures that get us through our daily lives are unlikely to become obsolete when the future gets here, and they deserve stories too. So I encourage more tales about science fiction crafters, science fiction athletes, science fiction chefs, gardeners, writers, and, yes, theater folk. One of my favorite parts of the Harry Potter books was the Quidditch games (and I admit to being quite annoyed when the later books had little to no Quidditch in favor of More Important Plot Things), and one of my favorite parts of Neal Stephenson's *The Diamond Age: Or The Young Lady's Illustrated Primer* was the detail given to the acting that went into producing the primer itself. Immensely talented writer **Tina Connolly** is a longtime friend of *Escape Pod*, one of our regular hosts, and we're delighted to bring you her tale of theater kids on a spaceship.

MUR

LIONS AND TIGERS AND GIRLFRIENDS

TINA CONNOLLY

DAY 183

dear permanent record of my deepest thoughts for posterity app, today sucked.

The Captain of the Glorious Starship *Rockety McZoomystars* (never let the federated starspace internet name anything) has announced that there was a miscalculation with the wormholes or the FTL drive or whatever and now this trip is going to take THREE YEARS longer than expected. Everyone in my educational cluster was already hunkering down for six years (like, we made it through elementary, we can make it through this) but NOW there is a Lot of Discontent among the teenage ranks. Even the power clique students who've been like *Expansion Ho! New Planets Are Amazing!* were grumbling loudly in the cafeteria.

I was already having a tough week because I was just remembering that back home it was time to audition for the new crop of spring shows at my high school and, STUPIDLY, *Rockety McZoomystars* has no drama department.

IDK, it's just been a lot tougher than I expected.

So I wrapped myself in my black hoodie-cape and snuck off to a storage closet and watched my favorite ever Anya Patel holo, *Dreams of a Starry Kind*, (for precisely the 183rd time since boarding this ship, I admit) just so I could lose myself in studying her technique, especially her glorious dramatic monologue at the climax where she says she's leaving and her breath does that little hitch thing and it ALWAYS makes me cry. But like what does it matter if I become the greatest actress of a generation if my generation is this ship to a brand-new planet with nobody making holos at all?? And then I remember that my last acting teacher said I had "extraordinary promise" and I'm bawling all over again.

Oh crap, some kid wants to use this storage closet for a cry now. I'm going to find somewhere else.

· · · · ·

Okay, I went to the hydroponics wing. There's this good part in the back with a bunch of experimental stuff crammed in and humming noises from everything working away, and if you go around the hanging squash vines no one can see you cry.

(Ask me how I know.)

So I swished my cape dramatically around the squash and then I absolutely tripped over another girl, kneeling next to the compost, having her own good cry.

Her face was all red and wet but she was also round and cute and had the most adorably half-shaved head. It reminded me of Anya Patel and Rosaria Chu's meet-cute in *Sweet Saturnalia*, so I started to say that, but then I saw she was glaring at me, which Rosaria definitely did not do in the holo, so I shut up. And then I unshut up and said stupidly, "What are you crying about," which Anya definitely did not do either.

"I. Am. Not. Crying," she said, and there was a lot of glaring with it.

"I totally understand," I said. I started to swoosh off and leave her in peace, but then I heard voices from the front and I did not want to deal with any adults, so I turned right back around, even though she was all *glare: intensify*.

"Look, there's only one squash vine covered area to cry in," I said, "which I'll just be upfront, is what I was gonna do because it doesn't do any good to keep the bad feelings in when you could emote them instead and move on. So if you don't mind, I'm gonna, just…"

I plopped down on the compost bin (which creaked alarmingly) and burst into tears.

She looked startled.

But I did it anyway (I mean, I may have come here for a PRIVATE cry but sometimes you take what you can get). I snorfled it all out while the girl pretended to be really interested in the progress of the squash and then I felt much better.

"I'm Kai," I said.

She dropped the vines and turned back to me. "Charlie."

"I'm having a tough time dealing with this ship right now," I said frankly.

"SAME," she said.

"I was going to grow up to be a holo star and now that part of my life is GONE. I can't get back to it. I'll just have to, like, grow squash or something."

Her eyes widened. "Not the same."

"Uh, what were you going to do with your life?"

"I mean, probably some sort of food science," Charlie said, gesturing around. "My mother's been doing veg-in-space her whole life, and I've been helping her."

"Oops," I said. "I mean. Growing squash is important." She still looked miserable. "But why are you upset then? Your work is here with you."

Charlie sighed. "I left my girlfriend-slash-best-friend on the last ship we were on," she said. "And the news about the extra three years made it hurt all over again. Everyone in my educational cluster is dying to explore the new planet, and… well, I've never actually been ON a planet, and I'm secretly happy that I get more time before I have to do it? But that makes me feel really…" She whispered the last bit. "Alone, I guess."

My heart went out to the wet-faced squash girl. Also my heart was kind of immediately interested in the news that at one point she had had a girlfriend, because that meant there was a greater than zero chance she might at some point be looking for a NEW girlfriend, and, as previously mentioned, she was really cute. Even with the crying, because that just meant she knew that crying was an important thing to do.

"Your cluster has all the academics," I said. "The ExpansionHo! clique."

"The Mutiny! clique, you mean. They were a little scary today," Charlie said frankly. "Going around being all IF WE RAN THIS SHIP THINGS WOULD BE DIFFERENT. Is that how your cluster was?"

"Not so much," I said. "My cluster is all the non-mathy weirdo misfits, like me."

"But surely they're upset by the news?"

"Yes," I said. "I mean, I assume. I mean…" I sighed. "To be honest I haven't really made any friends, either. I've buried myself in watching all my Anya Patel holos and moping about not getting to audition for ANYTHING, not even like a commercial for space toilet paper."

Charlie laughed. Then scrubbed her eyes again. Her face was less red, and she looked like the crying had helped her, too. "I wouldn't mind if there was something like that to do," she admitted. "My last ship was a cruise ship and my girlfriend was the daughter of one of the entertainers. I helped out with bit parts a few times. I liked it."

"Oh, you've got a type then," I said, before I could stop myself, which I totally would have if my brain had caught up with my mouth. "Um, in friends, I mean. A friend type. That's a totally normal thing to say." I was blushing, but I think she was too—it was hard to tell after the tears. "I mean, here we are, a couple of theater geeks—"

And then I was struck with a profound idea.

Something that would give us something to do.

Something that would give EVERYONE something to do, so we didn't think about those extra three years stretching ahead of us, and the scary unfamiliar planet at the end.

"Are you thinking what I'm thinking?" I said.

"That you're gonna fall through that compost bin any second?"

"Let's put on a show."

DAY 184

I have life. I have renewed purpose. I have…
No plays in the entire massive online ship's library.

Okay, there's three.

The works of Shakespeare, *The Wizard of Oz*, and something called *The Complete Screenplays of Rick Moranis*.

I've been reading through them all night. The latter looks like it's gonna require a lot of props like man-eating plants and stuff, and I'm NOT gonna start a bunch of newbies on *Titus Andronicus* so… *The Wizard of Oz* it is!

I mean, here's the thing. You can't have a new settlement with no art at all. People NEED it. I think most of us need to DO it, but even the most stubbornly non-creative among us need to SEE it. Need to feel it. Even the Mutiny! students need art, even if they don't know it.

Charlie and I have the chance to build something from scratch, that's all. There's no drama department? Very well, we will BE the drama department.

How hard can it be to mount a play?

… with no stage, no curtain, no costumes, no sets…

(don't worry about that stuff, Kai. theater is in the IMAGINATION. inspire them and they will come.)

(if anyone comes to auditions tomorrow. what if no one shows? WHAT IF.)

not gonna lie, being a producer/director/the entire drama department is nerve-wracking.

TO DO:

- find a space to rehearse/perform in (Observation Deck? Most people are bored with looking at stars by now.)
- invite all forty-seven students to audition, even the scary Mutiny! ones

ACHIEVEMENTS:

- first! day!! without watching *Dreams of a Starry Kind* since I boarded *McZoomystars*!!!
- (met a girl, I know it's not a theatrical achievement but I have to put it down SOMEWHERE.)

DAY 192

wowowow WOW what a week.

Okay. Auditions were a bit rocky, not gonna lie.

The Mutiny! students totes blew me off BUT. The good news is that twelve!!! people came to audition. I guess they were sufficiently impressed by my silently-wearing-all-black demeanor that they wanted to see what I was up to.

(note to self: keep wearing swooshy black hoodie-cape, even tho significantly much less depressed.)

I told them that art was NECESSARY and we had a chance to build something NEW and IMPORTANT that would reflect on all our lives and like, they were RIGHT THERE WITH ME, EYES SHINING. For a moment I was like YES. This is DOABLE.

The bad news is that they're mostly new to this and despite my EXHORTATIONS they still seem shy about jumping around like munchkins and lions so, let's be real, I have my work cut out for me as Leader of this Ragtag Troupe.

Primary to-do: **MAKE PEOPLE HAVE FUN.** (why so hard.)

Also bad: the rest of my list looks like this:

TO DO:
- how to make silver shoes (requisition spray paint, is there any??)
- how to make witch "melt" (blue tarps could represent water, is that cheesy??)
- AND SOOOOO ON

anyway

The good news is Charlie's totally just fine, for someone newish to acting, and I cast her as Dorothy. And the best of the rest is Bit, a hilarious theater geek I should have made friends with way before now, who wears sequins and plaid and does jazz hands a lot. I cast them as the Scarecrow and also made them my assistant director.

We spent all this week just working on basic stuff, and it was mostly going okay, but today we were working on our first big group scene (Dorothy landing in Oz) and Charlie seemed out of sorts. And I know the director should be thinking about everyone, not just the really cute girl playing Dorothy, buuut it's hard to see her sweet face getting all frustrated with herself and not want to help.

So I nerved myself to surrender some responsibility and placed an excited Bit in charge of blocking the Munchkins, while I took Dorothy off to do some one-on-one scene work.

I found my heart beating faster as we went to the squash area to find a quiet place to rehearse.

Which is silly, right? We were here as a director and an actor and obvs I would never abuse my position of power, no matter what kind of ridiculously sexy haircut she has.

(note to self: could I pull off the half-shaved look, or would I get annoyed with it in like a week and then have to suffer through the tragic growing-out stage? Investigate this.)

Charlie was looking at me like I was gonna say something smart, so I tried my best.

"So, here we are in the forests of squash," I said.

"Huh?"

"I mean. Tell me how you're feeling about Dorothy."

Charlie closed her eyes and said in a rush, "Like it's a really big role and did you just cast me because we came up with the theater idea together and maybe I better quit now before I ruin everything."

"Whoa, whoa," I said. "That's not why I cast you."

She opened her eyes. They were a deep dark brown, really distracting, so it took me a moment to focus on what she was saying. "Then give me something smaller," she said. "Like the Scarecrow. Bit's got way more experience; they could take the lead."

"Wait, suddenly nepotism's okay if it's just a different role? Besides, I need a really funny person for—"

(oh crap did I just say that, you're an idiot, Kai)

"You don't think I'm good enough for the Scarecrow," Charlie said, realization dawning.

"That is NOT what I said," I said. "I need a certain kind of person for the Scarecrow, and a certain kind of person for Dorothy, and I need you to play Dorothy, that's all."

"Because I am boring," she said. "I'm just a boring old squash farmer—"

"Okay, I definitely did not say that," I said. This director business was harder than I expected.

(turns out??? it's a lot easier just being one of the actors??? but then we wouldn't be having this show, so. learn how to be a better leader FASTER, Kai.)

I tried again. "You're just feeling overwhelmed because it's a lot of lines—"

"Don't tell me how I feel—"

Charlie cut herself off as voices came nearer. It was the sound of footsteps, the hustle-jog of the energetic Mutiny! clique. Their voices grew louder as they came closer.

"I'm just saying, we're not the ones who CHOSE to come on this ship," a grumbly voice said. "That's not OUR generation. Our PARENTS did it, and now THEY'RE the ones screwing up our future."

"And that's why we should do something about it," said a higher, raspy voice. "We find a way to strike when they're least expecting it."

"FINALLY," said the grumble. "We get to FIGHT."

"I already told you, not yet," said the rasp. "First we need a solid plan. We've got to—"

The compost lid made a loud cracking sound under me.

"Crap," said the grumble. "Let's get out of here."

I looked warily at Charlie as the footsteps died away.

"Bohai and Vynessa," she said, shaking her head. Her frustration with me was momentarily forgotten. "I'm worried. They talk in my cluster. I think they're planning something."

"Something what?" I said, though my stomach was already clenched against the knowledge.

Charlie leaned in and whispered. "Overpowering the Captain."

(oh crap oh crap oh)

The thought that the mutiny idea was inching closer to reality filled me with panic. I jumped up from the creaking compost bin and started pacing. "This is exactly the problem. How can I get people to focus on something like ART when this is going on? If everyone's worried about, like, their lives, I can't get them to act silly in a lion suit made of a space mop."

"But art IS important," Charlie said. "You said so at auditions, and I think you're right—"

"Of course it is," I shouted to the squash, even though neither they nor Charlie deserved that. "Stories are how we make sense of things, not fighting! Stories! Ugh!" I waved my tablet around as I paced. "I'm trying to bring people together, but you have to TALK about things. You have to create, and reflect. And I… have to help you, and here I am just yelling."

I tried to calm down, because Charlie looked a little stunned.

"Let's go back to Dorothy's motivation," I said, as calmly as possible. "What does she want?"

"Um," said Charlie. "I mean, she wants to stop the witch from doing bad stuff—"

"She wants to go home," I burst out. "And she's never gonna get to, never, never, never!"

DAY 196

soooooooooo that was a thing that happened.

(note to self: can I please stop having dramatic breakthroughs next to the squash.)

Catching up: Charlie agreed to stick with the role of Dorothy, and we agreed to keep an eye on the Mutiny! students while we tried to figure out what to do about them.

(We also immediately went to tell the captain, because we're not idiots, but he just laughed and told us not to worry, that complaining is just a thing teenagers DO. So yeah, that was a thing.)

So we do what we can do, you know? Take care of our own.

And still, morale kinda fell this week because even though both Bit and I are trying to be super patient and helpful, this is all new to the troupe. None of them have ever tried to memorize lines AND blocking AND face out to the audience AND speak up, and and AND!! We have DEFINITELY never tried to do it while a bunch of mutinous debate clubbers plot treason around us.

I've been leaning on Bit more for directing because it turns out producing takes a heckuva lot of time. Right now they're running the big Emerald City scene while I try to organize my to-do list, which basically looks like this:

TO DO:
- silver shoes (there's no spray paint, what about duct tape??)
- melt the witch (all tarps in use, what if the flying monkeys wave their arms and make water sounds??)
- (THIRTY-FIVE MORE ACTION ITEMS effffff meeeee)

- find a way to boost morale
- STOP THE MUTINY!!!

But also, think about what came out of the last squash discussion between me and Charlie.

Namely, is *The Wizard of Oz* just 100% all wrong for the situation in which we find ourselves? I mean, it's literally about Dorothy wanting to go home, and then GETTING TO.

But we're NOT gonna go back to the way things were, and THAT'S what we're all trying to adjust to, even the mutineers.

Should we change the ending? Make it a downer? Dorothy gives up on her dreams and settles for being a squash farmer?

I don't know, I've been pacing around my tiny room all week, trying to figure out what I think. I don't know if I'm getting any closer.

—hang on, somebody's knocking.

• • • • •

OMG. So it was Charlie, at a run. "They kicked us out of the Observation Deck," she panted, tugging my hand.

I hurried after her, running around corners. "Who did?"

"The mutiny," she said, and then there the whole troupe was, exiting the floatylift, clustering around me like I was gonna fix everything.

(I don't know how to fix anything! I can't even figure out how to represent flying monkeys on stage! Maybe they just jump a lot???)

"Are they actually, like, mutineering?" I said. "Right now?"

"They've got a list of demands," said Bit.

"But not for our troupe," I said. "For the captain, right?" I got on the floatylift and the whole troupe squeezed back in with me. I punched the button for the Observation Deck.

"Yes," said Bit, and they thrust out their phone to show me a list of demands that was basically on infinite scroll.

"We need to stop them before they ruin everything," said Charlie, eyeing me meaningfully.

I swallowed. She meant me. But how was I the right person to turn around a bunch of justifiably angry, super-driven, type-A students? I was just an actor, really.

The floatylift chimed arrival.

An actor who needed to figure out how to dig deep and rise above herself.

I remembered Anya Patel in *Mission: Mayday*. When the situation was the most dire, sometimes the best course was to be as honest and open as you could.

Maybe that was the one thing I could do.

I strode into the room full of angry students. The Observation Deck's backdrop of vid-screens with their dramatic simulation of our trip through the stars helped me channel my hero Anya, brave and confident and determined.

"Listen to me," I said, raising my hands to get everyone's attention. "I know you're upset." Conversations halted, and the students stopped, turning to look at me.

"Damn straight," said Vynessa, from the center of the room.

"But we're upset, too." I looked around the Observation Deck at my troupe. At the mutineers. At all of us. "Look, some of us were excited to get to the end of our journey. Some of us were nervous." I glanced at Charlie. "Some of us think the captain is handling this setback correctly. Some of us don't." Bohai nodded.

"But the thing is, dealing with these sorts of complex situations is exactly what art does best. Theater is about reflecting what we FEEL. It's about bringing important questions out into the open. And honestly, I've been asking myself this week if we were even doing the right play. Dorothy gets to go home, and we don't."

Charlie raised eyebrows at me: not inspiring.

"But what I should have been asking is: how can we CHANGE the story we're telling, and make it exactly what we need, right now. The making of art is not something you leave behind as nonessential. You can't take some frozen old stories and expect that to be the entirety of what helps you feel, and dream, and be. That's not what art is for. Stories are how you get people talking. How you bring the problems to the attention of everyone else." I took a deep breath. "How you do all this WITHOUT fighting."

I saw I had some of them. The ones who had been swept along with Vynessa and Bohai's vision, the ones who had the passion for change, but maybe, in the end, didn't want to take it as far as physical violence.

"But… *The Wizard of Oz*?" asked Vynessa. "It's a kid's show."

"It's a beautifully clean slate," I corrected. "It's already about what you do when the people in charge aren't everything you hoped they would be. The witches want power. The Wizard is a liar."

"That fits," grumbled Bohai.

"But it's also about the power of teamwork," I said. "Dorothy and her friends can't get to the Emerald City without. Every. Single. One Of. Them."

"The Emerald City is a metaphor for Planety McPlanetface!" chirped somebody in excitement.

"Ding ding ding," I said. These students were the academic cluster. The future political leaders, the movers and shapers of our generation. They were just frustrated and upset, which I could understand, and they had energy and direction. Energy and direction we could use.

"But I just wanna fight," said a guy in the back. "I was promised fighting."

"There's fighting in *The Wizard of Oz*," I promised. Charlie stepped on my toe. I kicked her back. "In fact, we need people who know how to make action scenes look real—without people getting hurt. Do you want to be our stunt coordinator?"

His eyes lit up. "Can it be sword-fighting?"

"If you figure out how to build space swords," I said. "Look, we need people to take on all pieces of this. So it can be the best socio-political critique it can be." I held up my phone, showed them my own endless scroll of the to-do list. "Art is a team effort. We need everyone's thoughts on what we want to say with this show. But we also need to figure out how to make the flying monkeys, well, fly."

"We could rig up flying harnesses," said Vynessa instantly. "Several of us have our climbing certifications and have logged hundreds of hours."

"My mom's in charge of the gym gear," said Sanjay, one of

our actors. "I bet we could convince her we need to requisition it." They both looked at each other.

"Excellent," I said. "That flying gear is going to be a real help, so Vynessa and Sanjay, get on that, stat. The rest of you, I'm texting you my to-do list so you can start thinking of ways to help. Report back to Assistant Director Bit with any ideas." I wanted to get the mutiny group disbanded and integrated with us before they had a chance to reform.

"Got it," said Bit, with a flash of jazz hands.

"But most importantly," I said, "tomorrow, first thing after school, we're going to tear this whole show apart and put it back together in a way that makes sense to us, here and now. This is our moment. So get thinking!"

The students went off chattering energetically as the mutiny dispersed.

"A socio-political critique?" said Charlie, once we were alone with the stars. "And where the heck is there fighting in *The Wizard of Oz*?"

"Didn't you know the Munchkins have an elite combat force?" I said with a straight face. "They clash with the flying monkeys several times."

"I did not know that," said Charlie.

"Well, you'll definitely know it after you help me write those scenes tonight," I said. "Besides, I meant everything I said. Art needs to be alive. We all need to figure out what we want to say together. And frankly, I feel confident the mutineers will bring ideas we wouldn't have had without them."

Charlie stepped back and looked at me. "You really mean

that, don't you? That you WANT them to join us."

"Of course I do," I said. "You need all kinds of people for a community. Rebels have energy and drive, that's all. You need the movers and shakers to push things forward."

"Just like you need someone to grow the squash," she said, a little sadly.

I took her hand before I thought. "Do you know why I cast you?" I said. "It wasn't because I had no options."

"It wasn't?"

"The whole reason I need you for Dorothy is because I need someone kind, and honest. Someone whom everyone will rally around. Someone who can get us to the Emerald City. And when you got up on that stage, all those things were like a light shining through."

She looked like she didn't know what to say, and I thought oh crap, I sound like a dope and also I shouldn't have taken her hand, so I started to pull away, but she held on tight.

"I'm not sure I entirely believe you," Charlie said. "But it also doesn't matter."

"It doesn't?"

"Because just that you would say something so wonderful to me is like the whole reason that everyone's rallying around YOU. You're just starting out with all this, but YOU're the one who's bringing everyone together. You're one of those movers and shapers, too. You're making everyone realize what they had in them all along."

I blushed, because that was WAY too much praise for an ordinary actor geek. "I'm just, uh. Trying to help everyone become a team, I guess," I said.

"What about the squash farmer?" she said.

"I mean, she's definitely on the team?" I said, flustered by Charlie's raising eyebrows.

"Oh, I'm terrible at metaphors," said Charlie. "What I mean is: kiss me."

DAY 221...!!!!!!!!

dear permanent record of my deepest thoughts for posterity app, I kissed her.

Or she kissed me.

There was kissing.

There had not been any kissing for the 200 or so days prior and it's entirely possible that my outlook is vastly improved when there is kissing in my life.

I won't pretend it was all smooth sailing after that. It took a lot of work to integrate the mutineers into the show. We spent an entire week where we analyzed the themes to death and tried to decide if the captain was better represented by the Wizard or by the Good Witch, if Dorothy should have a manifesto when she arrived at the Emerald City, and just how many people would get to swing through the air as fighting flying monkeys.

But all that got everyone talking. And communicating. And helping each other.

So by the time we got to performance night, it wasn't about the weirdness of stopping the show to have elaborate sword-fights, or the fact that the Lion looked like they had mange, or the way that the Tin Person still mumbled all her lines at the ground.

It was about the way, when the Lion forgot his line about how worried he was to arrive at a new planet, the Scarecrow whispered it to him.

It was about the way, when a flying monkey's rope slipped and she started to fall and the audience gasped—the Good Witch stepped in and caught her.

It was about the way that Dorothy, shining like light, turned to me in my arms and said, "It's over, we did it, now kiss me."

(not gonna lie, my squash girl is the best thing about this ship, 1000%!!!!)

So I've got a date. And I'm running off to that, and any more updates will have to wait for another day. We're going to spend some time eating reconstituted chocolate and some time talking about the show (theater people, what do you expect) and some time wandering up and down the hydroponics bay, pretending to look at her plants but really just (you know) kissing next to the squash.

But then, I think I'll talk to her about our future plans. After all, this show absolutely cannot be a one-off, now that we're turning this ragtag band of individuals into an actual troupe.

There's more art to create. More discussions to be had.

So I'm gonna take the list of plays to Charlie to see what she thinks we should do next.

Right now, I've got my money on *Ghostbusters*.

I don't want to give too much away about this story, but let's just say that, as always, **N.K. Jemisin** does not disappoint. Her fiction roars with its unapologetic exploration of race, discrimination, and power dynamics, and this one is no exception. Jemisin's stories have appeared in *Escape Pod* since its early days, and her career has been another one to watch. With her record-making triple Hugo Award wins, she is clearly one of the new legends of science fiction and fantasy. Her story concludes our anthology with incendiary prose.

DIVYA

GIVE ME CORNBREAD OR GIVE ME DEATH
N.K. JEMISIN

The intel is good. It had better be; three women died to get it to us. I tuck away the binoculars and crawl back from the window long enough to hand-signal my girls. Fire team moves up, drop team on my mark, support to hold position and watch our flank. The enemy might have nothing but mercs for security, but their bullets punch holes same as real soldiers', and some of 'em are hungry enough to be competent. We're hungrier, though.

Shauntay's got the glass cutter ready. I'm carrying the real payload, slung across my torso and back in a big canteen. We should have two or three of these, since redundancy increases our success projections, but I won't let anyone else take the risk. The other ladies have barrels cracked and ready to drop. The operation should be simple and quick—get in, drop it like it's hot, get out.

This goes wrong, it's on me.

It won't go wrong.

Shauntay makes the cut. Go go go. We drop into the warm, stinking, dimly lit space of the so-called aerie—really an old aircraft hangar, repurposed since commercial air travel ended. There's the big trough on one side of the hangar, laden with fresh human body parts. It's horrible, but I ignore it as I rappel down. We've seen worse. Touchdown. No sounds from the pit at the center of the hangar. We get our little trough set up in near silence, just like we rehearsed. My girls are on it like clockwork. The barrels come down and we dump load one, load two, load three. Stirring sounds from the hangar behind us. Ignore them. I signal the other soldiers to back up. Nothing left but the payload. I unsling my canteen, not listening to the sounds behind me, concentrating on my fingers so I don't fumble the cap, remembering to unseal the pressure valve so the vacuum effect doesn't clog the whole thing up and—

A warm, sulfur-redolent breath stirs my fatigues. Right behind me. Shit.

I turn, slow. They have cat eyes; fast movement excites them. The smell of fear excites them. Dark skin excites them.

She's huge—maybe the size of a 747, though I've only seen husks of those, lying scattered around the edges of old killing fields where the world was remade. She's not quite green. Her scales are prismatic, slightly faceted, which makes them nearly invisible at night. That was an accident, I've heard, some side effect of tweaking the genetic base to make them hyper-focused on shorter wavelengths of visible light—or something; I don't know the science. I know beauty, though, and she's lovely, scales shimmering as she moves, iridescent blue-black-golden brown. They probably mean for her to be ugly and scary, dark as they've made her, but they forget there's more ways to be beautiful than whatever they designate. Red eyes. Fangs long as my whole body. Those are just there for the scare factor, I know; our scientists have proven they don't actually use the fangs for eating. Do a good enough job killing without them.

A few of the others stir behind her, some coming over, all of them following her lead. She's the dominant one. Figures. I'm not scared. Why? Suicidal, maybe. No. I think—and it's just in this moment, looking at how beautiful she is—that I see a kindred spirit. Another creature whose power has been put into the service of weaker cowardly fools.

So I smile. "Hey, there," I say. She blinks and pulls her head back a little. Her prey doesn't usually talk back. Still dangerous; curiosity plus boredom equals me being batted all over the hangar like a toy till I'm dead. Time to divert her interest. Slowly, I move behind the trough—stuff's still steaming from the barrels—and start pouring out my payload. The hot, sharp smell catches her attention immediately. Those lovely slit pupils expand at once, and she leans down, sniffing at the trough. I'm irrelevant suddenly.

"Getcho grub on, baby," I whisper. My beautiful one flickers her ears, hearing me, but her eyes are still on the prize. Mission accomplished. I rappel back up to the roof, and we head homeward as the flock chows down.

Dragons love them some collard greens, see. Especially with hot sauce.

• • • • •

The first attacks were the worst. Nobody was ready. I remember a day, I couldn't have been more than six or seven. I was sitting in the living room. Mama came running in, not a word, just grabbed me and half-dragged me out of my chair and across the house to hide in the bathroom. I felt the house shudder and thought it was an earthquake, like I'd read about in books. I was *excited*. I'd never felt an earthquake before. We curled together in the bathtub, me and Mama, me giddy, her terrified, with the sounds of screaming and the smells of smoke filtering in through the vents.

It was so terrible, the Towers said, amid news stories with two-faced headlines like SAPPHIRE TOWNSHIP RAIDED BY DRUG-SNIFFING DRAGONS and OFFICIALS DENY DRAGONS INTENTIONALLY BRED TO PREFER "DARK MEAT." So terrible indeed. Maybe if we didn't hide things from the police, they wouldn't need to use dragons? The dragons only attacked when people attacked them—or ran as if they were guilty. Why, if we'd just turn out every time there was a police patrol and point out the folks among us who were causing trouble, the dragons would only bother those people and not everybody.

Motherfuckers always want us to *participate* in their shit. Ain't enough they got the whole world shivering in the shadows of the Towers. Ain't enough they've got our boys and men tagged like dogs and preemptively walled off over in Manny Dingus Prison, only letting 'em out for parole now and again. (Only letting *some* of 'em out—the ones they think are meek, 'cause they think eugenics works. If they had any sense, though, they'd be more afraid of the quiet ones.)

This latest front in the long, long war started because they didn't like us growing weed. Ours was better quality than that gourmet shit they grew, and also we sold it to their people over in Americanah. Not that those were really *their people*, white men as poor as us and the few women whose pussies the Towers haven't grabbed, but they gotta try to keep up the illusion. Gotta have somebody as a buffer between them and us, especially whenever we get uppity.

They've been engineering the End Times. The Plagues were supposed to be about salvation. Trying to get all the townships and ghettoes and reservations to go evangelical, see? So they poisoned the water—turned it red—and killed a whole bunch of men over in Bollytown. Got them dependent on bottled-water deliveries from the Tower, forever. The dragons are supposed to be the Second Plague, engineered from frogs, with a little dinosaur and cat spliced in. That's bad, but they tried to start a Plague of boils, big enough to kill, in Real Jerusalem. Didn't spread much beyond their patient zeroes, thank G*d, because Jewish people wash. (They'll try again, though. Always do.) Anyway, we got the point when they rained hail and fire on the Rez, even though they claimed that was just a weather-control satellite malfunction.

We're all heathens to the Towers. All irredeemable by birth and circumstance, allowed to live on the sufferance of those on high. They don't want to kill us off, because they need us, but they don't need us getting comfortable. Rather keep us on edge. Keep us hungry. Best way to control a thing, they think, is through fear and dependency.

Gotta mind, though, that the ones you're starving don't start getting their needs attended to someplace else.

· · · · ·

The next raid goes off right when our hackers have said, but we didn't need the warning. The Towers are predictable, complacent, and lazy in their power—same mediocre motherfuckers they've always been. We're ready. Got countermeasures standing by, but they don't even bother to send observation drones. Stupid. It's been years since that first raid. We've been living under siege so long that fear stopped making sense a long time ago.

The dragons darken the sky and then stoop to attack. The whole damn flock; the Towers must have found the evidence of our infiltrations, or maybe they're mad about something else. I spot my baby in the vanguard, blue-black-brown, big as a building. She lands in the market and unleashes a blast of flame to obliterate a shop—oh, but then she stops. Sniffs the air. Yeah, what *is* that? Check it out, baby. See that great big steaming trough over there on the school track and field? Remember that taste? Once upon a time, this was food fit only for beasts. We made it human. Now we've made it over, special, for you. Hot hot, good good. Eat up, y'all.

She whuffles at the others, and they follow as she hop-flies over to the field. A trough the size of a shipping container is all laid out, filled to the brim and steaming with three days' worth of cooking work. Plenty of hot sauce this time, vinegary and sharp and fierce as all get-out. That's the kicker. Wakes up their taste buds, and the fiber fills them up better than plain old human flesh. Volunteers, including me, linger nearby while the dragons eat. We move slowly, letting them smell our living human flesh, working clickers so they'll associate sound with taste. Then it's done, and the dragons fly back to their aerie slow, heavy with greens. Nobody gets eaten that day.

· · · · ·

The Towers are pissed. They send in cops to retaliate, stopping and frisking random women walking down the street, arresting anybody who talks back, even killing two women for no reason at all. They feared for their lives, the cops say. They always say.

Collard greens get added to the contraband list, between C-4 and contraception.

We retaliate right back when they come with crews of deputized men from Americanah to tear up our fields. No collards? Fine. When the dragons come next, we offer them callaloo.

They come for the callaloo. We just stand there, pretending harmlessness, and don't fight back. They can't admit that the dragons are supposed to eat *us*, so they claim they're worried about listeria. No FDA anymore, just gotta destroy the whole crop. Okay, then. Word spreads. After they take the callaloo, Longtimetown— none of us named this shit—sends over frozen blocks of spinach cooked with garlic, fish sauce, and chili oil, layered in with their heroin shipment. We have to add our own spinach to stretch it, but that chili oil is potent. It's enough.

By this point the Towers figure they've got to rob us of every vegetable and then watch us die of malnutrition or there's no way their dragons will ever bother with bland, unseasoned human meat again. They actually try it, motherfuckers, burning our farms, and we have to eat cat grass just to get by. We fight over kohlrabi leaves grown in an old underground weed hothouse. Can't give this to the dragons; there isn't enough, and our daughters need it more. It's looking bad. But just before the next raid, Spicymamaville smuggles over mofongo that makes the dragons moan, they love it so. Towelhead Township is starving and besieged, but a few of the mujahideen women make it through the minefields with casks of harissa strapped to their bodies. Sari City, mad about Bollytown, ships us "friendship basketballs." They do this openly, and the Towers let them through as a goodwill gesture. Black people love basketball, right? Maybe it'll shut us up. And it does, for a while: there's enough saag paneer and curry paste vacuum packed inside each ball to feed us and the dragons too.

The Towers burn our peppers, and our allies respond with dead drops of hawajj, wasabi, chili-pepper water. The Towers try to starve us, but we: Just. Don't. Die.

And each visit, I pet my dragon a little more. She watches me. Looks for me when she lands. Croons a little when I pet her. It doesn't all go smoothly. In a single day I lose two soldiers to one dragon's fit of temper. Old habit. The dragon spits the soldiers' bodies out immediately, though, and snorts in disgust even before my beauty and the others can twist their heads around to hiss at her. They know we won't open the reward trough that day. Lesson learned, though it cost us blood.

It's war. We'll mourn the lost as heroes, our own and allies alike. I check in with my girls before every meal and ask if they're still willing to serve; they are. We are all resolved. We will win.

· · · · ·

The Towers have got something big planned. The dragons have become less responsive to their breeders and trainers, and sometimes they just up and leave the aeries to come to our township, where the good food's at. News articles say the Second Plague program is going to be retired due to "mixed results." Civilian casualties have decreased; they're spinning that as a benefit and not mentioning that the decline is our doing. Anyway, the dragons have been declared a failed experiment, so they're planning to "decommission" them during their next official deployment. Missiles vs. dragons, in the skies right over Sapphire Town. Who cares about collateral damage.

A spy in one of the Towers confirms it. They've gotten tired of us Sapphires, and it's about time for the Tenth Plague anyway. They're coming for our firstborn.

My lovely one waits patiently as I gear up, even though the troughs only have a little food in them this time. They know now to associate our presence with good things like food and pleasure and play, so they'll abide awhile before they get testy. We're all wearing flight gear and carrying saddles. I've got the payload again: our last batch of Scotch bonnets, grown and pickled in secret, sweetened with mango and hope. Word is there's a great big warehouse full of confiscated greens over near Tower One. And just so happens there's a whole lot of tanks and troops to set on fire along the way.

One by one, we mount up. My beautiful one—her name's Queen—turns her head back to get one ear skritched, and I oblige with a grin. Then I raise a hand to signal readiness. She lifts her head, smelling my excitement, sharing it, readying the others. I feel like I'm sitting astride the sky. She lifts her wings and lets out a thundering battle cry. Feeling her power. So am I.

Go go go.

And once the Towers lie in broken, smoldering rubble below us? We'll come back home, and sit on down, and have us all a good-good feast.

ACKNOWLEDGEMENTS

It's been an amazing experience putting this anthology together, both in mining the archives for favorites and approaching previous *Escape Pod* authors to give us new stories for the present. We would like to thank George Sandison and all the fine folks at Titan for being the engine that put this thing together. Our publishers, Alasdair Stuart and Marguerite Kenner, who have remained indefatigable with their support over the years, also deserve a ton of accolades.

Thanks to Serah Eley for starting the whole dang thing, and thanks to our audience for giving us the support both monetarily and simply by spreading the word. Thanks to the authors who sent us their stories and gave a little podcast a chance to grow into something wonderful.

We would be nothing without our support staff: Tina Connolly, Benjamin C. Kinney, Summer Brooks, Adam Pracht, and all of the associate editors and other team members who have helped over the years.

And of course, thanks to our families. We would be adrift without you.

ABOUT THE EDITORS

MUR LAFFERTY is a podcaster, author, and editor whose projects include the Hugo-winning *Ditch Diggers* Podcast, the novelization of *Solo: A Star Wars Story*, the Hugo- and Nebula-nominated novel *Six Wakes*, and the Hugo-nominated semiprozine *Escape Pod*. She lives in Durham, NC, with her family.

S.B. DIVYA is a lover of science, math, fiction, and the Oxford comma. She is the Hugo- and Nebula-nominated author of *Runtime* and co-editor of *Escape Pod*, with Mur Lafferty. Her short stories have been published at various magazines, and her debut novel *Machinehood* is forthcoming from Saga Press in March 2021.

ABOUT THE CONTRIBUTORS

KAMERON HURLEY is the author of *The Light Brigade* (March 2019), *The Stars are Legion* and the essay collection *The Geek Feminist Revolution*, as well as the award-winning *God's War* Trilogy and *The Worldbreaker Saga*. Hurley has won the Hugo Award, Locus Award, Kitschy Award, and Sydney J. Bounds Award for Best Newcomer. She was also a finalist for the Arthur C. Clarke Award, the Nebula Award, and the Gemmell Morningstar Award. Her short fiction has appeared in *Popular Science Magazine*, *Lightspeed* and numerous anthologies.

T. KINGFISHER is the vaguely absurd pen name of Ursula Vernon. In another life, she writes children's books and weird comics, and has won the Hugo, Sequoyah, and Ursa Major awards, as well as a half-dozen Junior Library Guild selections. This is the name she uses when writing things for grown-ups. When she is not writing, she is probably out in the garden, trying to make eye contact with butterflies.

TIM PRATT lives in Berkeley, California, with his wife, Heather Shaw, and their son River. His fiction and poetry have appeared in *The Best American Short Stories*, *The Year's Best Fantasy and Horror*, *The Mammoth Book of Best New Horror*, *Strange Horizons*, *Realms of Fantasy*, *Asimov's*, *Lady Churchill's Rosebud Wristlet*, *Subterranean*, and *Tor.com*, among many other places.

KEN LIU is an American author of speculative fiction. He has won the Nebula, Hugo, and World Fantasy awards, as well as top genre honors in Japan, Spain, and France, among other countries. Liu's debut novel, *The Grace of Kings*, is the first volume in a silkpunk epic fantasy series, *The Dandelion Dynasty*, in which engineers play the role of wizards. His debut collection, *The Paper Menagerie and Other Stories*, has been published in more than a dozen languages. A second collection, *The Hidden Girl and Other Stories*, followed. He also wrote the *Star Wars* novel, *The Legends of Luke Skywalker*.

SARAH GAILEY is a Bay Area native who lives and works in Los Angeles, California. Their pursuits include cigars, boxing, vulgar embroidery, and reading too much.

MUR LAFFERTY is a podcaster, author, and editor who really should put the video games away and work on her novel that's due.

JOHN SCALZI has been a film critic/columnist, a writer/editor, a freelance writer, and a novelist. He's a *New York Times* bestseller in fiction. Awards won include the Hugo, the Locus, the Audie, the Seiun and the Kurd Lasswitz. Recipient of the 2016 Governor's Award for the Arts in Ohio. He's also been a creative consultant for the *Stargate: Universe* television series, a writer for the video game *Midnight Star*, by Industrial Toys, former president (7/10–6/13) of the Science Fiction and Fantasy Writers of America, executive producer for *Old Man's War* and *The Collapsing Empire*, both currently in development for film/TV. Writer of three short stories adapted into episodes of the Netflix series *Love, Death + Robots*.

Nebula Award-nominated BETH CATO is the author of the *Clockwork Dagger* duology and the *Blood of Earth* trilogy from Harper Voyager. She's a Hanford, California, native transplanted to the Arizona desert, where she lives with her husband, son, and requisite cats. Follow her at BethCato.com and on Twitter at @BethCato.

MAURICE BROADDUS is an author and community developer. His work has appeared in *Lightspeed*, *Weird Tales*, *Apex Magazine*, *Asimov's*, *Cemetery Dance*, *Uncanny Magazine*, and *Beneath Ceaseless Skies*, with some of his stories having been collected in *The Voices of Martyrs*. His books include *The Knights of Breton Court* trilogy and *Buffalo Soldier*.

MARY ROBINETTE KOWAL is the author of the *Lady Astronaut* duology and historical fantasy novels: *The Glamourist Histories* series and *Ghost Talkers*. She's a member of the award-winning podcast *Writing Excuses* and has received the Astounding Award for Best New Writer, four Hugo awards, the RT Reviews award for Best

Fantasy Novel, the Nebula, and Locus awards. Stories have appeared in *Strange Horizons*, *Asimov's*, several Year's Best anthologies and her collections *Word Puppets* and *Scenting the Dark and Other Stories*. Her novel *The Calculating Stars* is one of only eighteen novels to win the Hugo, Nebula and Locus awards in a single year.

Born in the Caribbean, TOBIAS BUCKELL is a *New York Times* bestselling and *World Fantasy Award* winning author. His novels and almost one hundred stories have been translated into nineteen different languages. He has been nominated for the Hugo Award, Nebula Award, World Fantasy Award, and Astounding Award for Best New Science Fiction Author. He currently lives in Ohio.

CORY DOCTOROW is a science fiction author, activist and journalist. He is the author of many books, most recently *Radicalized* and *Walkaway*, science fiction for adults; *In Real Life*, a graphic novel; *Information Doesn't Want to be Free*, a book about earning a living in the Internet age; and *Homeland*, a YA sequel to *Little Brother*. His next book is *Poesy the Monster Slayer*, a picture book for young readers.

GREG VAN EEKHOUT was born and raised in Los Angeles, California, in neighborhoods with hippies, criminals, working people, and movie studios. Like many writers he's done a number of things to put food on the table and keep a roof over his head. He's worked as an ice cream scooper (or dipper, as people who sell ice cream are sometimes called), a political fundraiser (or telemarketer), a comic book store clerk, a bookseller, a bookstore assistant manager, an educational multimedia developer, and a college teacher (of English and of multimedia development). Among other things.

TINA CONNOLLY is the author of the *Ironskin* trilogy from Tor Books, the *Seriously Wicked* series from Tor Teen, and the collection *On the Eyeball Floor and Other Stories* from Fairwood Press. Her stories have appeared in *The Magazine of Fantasy and Science Fiction*, *Tor.com*, *Analog*, *Lightspeed*, *Beneath Ceaseless Skies*, *Uncanny*, *Strange Horizons*, *Women Destroy SF* and more. Her stories and novels have been finalists for the Hugo, Nebula, Norton, Locus, and World Fantasy awards. Her narrations have appeared in audiobooks and podcasts including *PodCastle*, *PseudoPod*, *Beneath Ceaseless Skies*, and more. She is one of the co-hosts of *Escape Pod*, and runs the Parsec-winning flash fiction podcast *Toasted Cake*. She is originally from Lawrence, Kansas, but she now lives with her family in Portland, Oregon.

N(ORA). K. JEMISIN is a *New York Times* bestselling author of speculative fiction short stories and novels, who lives and writes in Brooklyn, NY. In 2018, she became the first author to win three Best Novel Hugos in a row for her *Broken Earth* trilogy. She has also won a Nebula Award, two Locus Awards, and a number of other honors.

For more fantastic fiction, author events,
exclusive excerpts, competitions, limited editions and more

VISIT OUR WEBSITE
titanbooks.com

LIKE US ON FACEBOOK
facebook.com/titanbooks

FOLLOW US ON TWITTER AND INSTAGRAM
@TitanBooks

EMAIL US
readerfeedback@titanemail.com